THE DARK SWALLOWS (HISTORIC) HONOURS AND PRAISE

Helen Griffiths was elected the honorary title of '*A Daughter of Mark Twain*' by Cyril Clemens, Editor of *The Mark Twain Journal,* on 10 May 1967 for *The Dark Swallows.* Cyril Clemens was a cousin of Samuel Clemens, also known as Mark Twain. This honorary title was also awarded to Helen Keller in 1956.

THE DARK SWALLOWS
(RECENT) HONOURS AND PRAISE

The Dark Swallows is as historically significant today as it was when it was written over half a century ago. This section is for honours and praise from those whom, until now, this important work of historical fiction was unavailable or out of print.

Concordis Publishing intends to garner reviews, honours, and commentary from the next generation of readers worldwide and in many different languages. We believe that this novel will also resonate with those who are of ages slightly younger than those for whom *The Dark Swallows* was originally intended in 1967 and will thus present this title to those of secondary school age (12-18) for commentary.

This novel will be presented as an Advance Reader Copy (ARC) to readers of all socioeconomic statuses. Reading and knowledge are not reserved for the elite class as it was many centuries ago. Today, more than ever, enrichment through the literary arts is an essential gateway toward self-empowerment and fulfilment.

'I should have expected it, but I'm amazed at how well this author writes people—the delicate and unspoken connections in relationships . . . I connected with these characters easily, so perceptive and adroit is the description of their thoughts, feelings and intentions . . . Such a touchingly deep, bitterly heartfelt story. So alive and nuanced.'

– Jeane Nevarez, *Dogear Diary*

THE DARK SWALLOWS (CELEBRATED) HONOURS AND PRAISE

'Immensely impressive' – *The Daily Telegraph*

'Anyone who imagines that tragic themes can no longer be tackled head-on (if at all) and that 'traditional' modes of expression are inadequate for this day and age (1966) should look to the work of this greatly gifted, self-effacing young writer and think again.'

– Iain Hamilton, The Daily Telegraph, 1966

'It is a poignant and tragic story, told in an impersonal manner. The author's style is limpid and poetic, with many passages of great beauty. Her understanding of Spanish village life is first-rate. All in all, it is a fine piece of workmanship and should prove absorbing reading for adults.'

– Bestsellers New York, 1966

'There have been few more poignant books about a revolution and a brave people's suffering.'

– The Miami Herald

'Griffiths' evocation of the Spanish background is masterly.'

– The Malay Mail

'Miss Griffiths, who now [1966] lives in Spain, has written for children since she was fifteen. There is nothing childlike, however, about this quietly authoritative first novel which takes place during the Spanish Civil War and deals with the love of Bernardo, a gentle carpenter, for Elvira, from another village. It is a *Romeo and Juliet* situation since intermarriage between the natives of these villages is prohibited until the war sweeps such private barriers away while creating new hopeless circumstances. Bernardo is shot on false charges, and Elvira and some of her relatives pull through as best they can. Since this is a novel about survival, its understatement is most impressive in the closing sections.'

– Kirkus Reviews, February 1966

BY THE SAME AUTHOR

HORSE IN THE CLOUDS *(1957)*

MOONLIGHT *(1959)*

AFRICANO *(1961)*

THE WILD HEART *(1963)*

THE GREYHOUND *(1964)*

THE WILD HORSE OF SANTANDER *(1966)*
Highly Commended by the Carnegie and Kate Greenaway Medal Awards

STALLION OF THE SANDS *(1968)*

MOSHIE CAT *(1969)*

PATCH *(1970)*

FEDERICO *(1971)*

LEON *(1972)*

RUSSIAN BLUE *(1973)*

JUST A DOG *(1974)*

THE MYSTERIOUS APPEARANCE OF AGNES (WITCH FEAR) *(1975)*
Winner of the Dutch Silver Pencil Award for Best Children's Book

RUNNING WILD (PABLO) *(1977)*

THE KERSHAW DOGS (GRIP: A DOG STORY) *(1978)*

THE LAST SUMMER: SPAIN 1936 *(1979)*

BLACKFACE STALLION *(1980)*

DANCING HORSES *(1981)*

HARI'S PIGEON *(1982)*

RAFA'S DOG *(1983)*

THE DOG AT THE WINDOW *(1984)*

THE DARK SWALLOWS

A NOVEL OF THE SPANISH CIVIL WAR

HELEN GRIFFITHS

Concordis
Publishing

FOURTH EDITION

*Volverán las oscuras golondrinas
En tu balcón sus nidos a colgar,
Y otra vez con el ala a sus cristales
Jugando llamarán;*

*Pero aquellas que el vuelo refrenaban
Tu hermosura y mi dicha al contemplar,
Aquellas que aprendieron nuestros nombres,
Esas…¡no volverán!*

*The dark swallows will return
To hang their nests on your balcony,
And their wings playing against your window-panes,
Again will call;*

*But the ones that interrupted their flight
To contemplate your beauty and my happiness,
That learned our names,
They . . . will not return!*

INTRODUCTION

This is the story of two villages, two lovers, two brothers and two Spains.

The dark swallows of the title are those that witness the doomed passion of Bernardo, carpenter and dreamer whose older brother is a lawyer in Madrid, and Elvira, self-willed daughter of the despotic leader of local affairs, who live in neighbouring villages on the austere Castilian plain. At first, it is the clash of opposing villages and hostile parents that threatens their happiness, but in the end, it is the far greater conflict of the Spanish Civil War that destroys it.

The two themes of this impressive novel are the annihilation of love by outside forces and the age-old question, 'Am I my brother's keeper?'

With the skill of a Greek dramatist, the author builds the inevitable tragedy. Her writing evokes the pettiness of life in a Spanish village and the harrowing bitterness of the war. Her characters are simple people whose lives are controlled by events too oppressive and powerful for them to escape. The evocations of the Spanish background are masterly, and it is against these majestic settings that the drama of Bernardo and Elvira is played out.

The Dark Swallows is written with a directness that brings the story to a moving conclusion and reveals with rare understanding the emotions and background of Spain's brutal war.

Helen Griffiths is an international author of remarkable sensitivity whose children's books have all received high praise. This adult novel—drawn from the background of her Spanish husband's family's direct involvement on both sides in the conflict—confirms that her talents are by no means restricted, for *The Dark Swallows*, in this new revised edition, is a powerful and convincing work by any standards.

CONTENTS

THE DARK SWALLOWS

SETTING THE STAGE

In this section, we shall provide a brief history of the Spanish Civil War. The setting plays an important part as to the context of the storylines and is a character in itself. There are many storylines that will appeal to a wide variety of sensibilities, and we shall provide the reader with important context which will enhance further the reader's understanding of this important story. The following is a brief history of the Spanish Civil War as written by *History.com*.

Spanish Civil War (1936-1939)

On July 18, 1936, the Spanish Civil War began as a revolt by right-wing Spanish military officers in Spanish Morocco and spread to mainland Spain. From the Canary Islands, General Francisco Franco broadcast a message calling for all army officers to join the uprising and overthrow Spain's leftist Republican government. Within three days, the rebels captured Morocco, much of northern Spain, and several key cities in the south. The Republicans succeeded in putting down the uprising in other areas, including Madrid, Spain's capital. The Republicans and the Nationalists, as the rebels were called, then proceeded to secure their respective territories by executing thousands of suspected political opponents. Meanwhile, Franco flew to Morocco and prepared to bring the Army of Africa over to the mainland.

In 1931, Spanish King Alfonso XIII authorized elections to decide the government of Spain, and voters overwhelmingly chose to abolish the monarchy in favour of a liberal republic. Alfonso went into exile, and the Second Republic, initially dominated by middle-class liberals and moderate socialists, was proclaimed. During the first two years of the Republic, organized labour and leftist radicals forced widespread liberal reforms, and the independence-minded region of Catalonia and the Basque provinces achieved virtual autonomy.

The landed aristocracy, the church and a large military clique opposed the Republic, and in November 1933, conservative forces regained control of the government in elections. In response, socialists launched a revolution in the mining districts of Asturias, and Catalan nationalists rebelled in Barcelona. General Franco crushed the so-called October Revolution on behalf of the conservative government, and in 1935 he was appointed army chief of staff. In February 1936, new elections brought the Popular Front, a leftist coalition, to power, and Franco, a strict monarchist, was sent to an obscure command in the Canary Islands off Africa.

Fearing that the liberal government would give way to Marxist revolution, army officers conspired to seize power. After a period of hesitation, Franco agreed to join the military conspiracy, which was scheduled to begin in Morocco at 5 a.m. on July 18 and then in Spain 24 hours later. The difference in time was to allow the Army of Africa time to secure Morocco before being transported to Spain's Andalusian coast by the navy.

On the afternoon of July 17, the plan for the next morning was discovered in the Moroccan town of Melilla, and the rebels were forced into premature action. Melilla, Ceuta, and Tetuan were soon in the hands of the Nationalists, who were aided by conservative Moroccan troops that also opposed the leftist government in Madrid. The Republican government learned of the revolt soon after it broke out but took few actions to prevent its spread to the mainland.

On July 18, Spanish garrisons rose up in revolt all across Spain. Workers and peasants fought the uprising, but in many cities, the Republican government denied them weapons, and the Nationalists soon gained control. In conservative regions, such as Old Castile and Navarre, the Nationalists seized control with little bloodshed, but in other regions, such as the fiercely independent city of Bilbao, they didn't dare leave their garrisons. The Nationalist revolt in the Spanish navy largely failed, and warships run by committees of sailors were instrumental in securing a number of coastal cities for the Republic. Nevertheless, Franco managed to ferry his Army of Africa over from Morocco, and during the next few months, Nationalist forces rapidly overran much of the Republican-controlled areas in central and northern Spain. Madrid was put under siege in November.

During 1937, Franco unified the Nationalist forces under the command of the Falange, Spain's fascist party, while the Republicans fell under the sway of the communists. Germany and Italy aided Franco with an abundance of planes, tanks, and arms, while the Soviet Union aided the Republican side. In addition, thousands of communists and other radicals from France, the USSR, America, and elsewhere formed the International Brigades to aid the Republican cause. The most significant contribution of these foreign units was the successful defence of Madrid until the end of the war.

In June 1938, the Nationalists drove to the Mediterranean Sea and cut Republican territory in two. Later in the year, Franco mounted a major offensive against Catalonia. In January 1939, its capital, Barcelona, was captured, and soon after, the rest of Catalonia fell. With the Republican cause all but lost, its leaders attempted to negotiate a peace, but Franco refused. On March 28, 1939, the Republicans finally surrendered Madrid, bringing the Spanish Civil War to an end. Up to a million lives were lost in the conflict, the most devastating in Spanish history. Franco subsequently served as dictator of Spain until his death in 1975.

Article Title
Spanish Civil War breaks out

Author
History.com Editors

Website Name
HISTORY

Publisher
A&E Television Networks

URL
https://www.history.com/this-day-in-history/spanish-civil-war-breaks-out

Last Updated
July 16, 2020

Original Published Date
February 9, 2010

THE DARK SWALLOWS

PROLOGUE

Castilla la Vieja is an arid land, parched by the summer's heat and frozen by the winter's coldness. It is mostly flat, occasionally hilly, and in the distance, there is the hint of a mountain range in the purple-grey haze that divides the ochre of the earth from the blue of the endless sky. There are clusters of pine trees, dark, umbrella-like shade givers, junipers, and evergreen oaks, but there are vast expanses of emptiness, for the trees generally surround the little villages or follow a watercourse, and these are few and far between.

In springtime, the monotony of the clay-coloured countryside is broken by wide stretches of growing wheat and barley, brilliantly green, and as the greenness fades, hordes of poppies spread their riotous scarlet everywhere. But even the volatile poppies cannot defy the insistent sun indefinitely, and by July, there is nothing but ochre dust and yellow corn, glaring like the sun beneath which it lies naked and unprotected. The only shadows are those made by a tractor or a plodding mule and its human companion, and the mule shuts its eyes and does not see them. Neither the man nor the mule can reap the benefit of the shadows, but both are accustomed to the heat and can work in spite of it. The skin of the man's face is as dry and furrowed as the earth, faithfully reflecting the acidity of the land, and his clear-coloured eyes often scan the skies, anxiously looking for the rain which would assure a good harvest.

To a stranger, this farmer may seem a surly individual, as barren of conversation as is the countryside of colour, but among family and friends, he is a kindly man, his character formed by his work, that of struggling to produce crops from a challenging land.

In Castilla la Vieja, there appears to be more sky than land. The earth is always still, suspended from action by the weight of the heat which pours down upon it, but the sky is an intense arc of endless movement. Huge white clouds race before the swiftness of a wind whose coolness never touches the earth in summer until dusk has fallen and whose cold fingers never cease to clutch in winter; and little puffy clouds scud along in its wake. The dry, quiet earth produces an austere man, and perhaps it is this great expanse of intensely coloured sky, with its extremes of temperature and movement, forever an arc over the farmer's head that makes him religious too, believing with sincerity but little show in a severe but understanding creator.

II

In the province of Burgos, there is a village called Los Pinos and a village called Quintera. Between them stretch five miles of arable land, four of which belong to the people of Quintera. The people of Los Pinos are poorer than their neighbours, for the land there is rough and scrubby, with a scattering of southerly inclined pines to which it owes its name. Its fields produce better wine than corn and are generally divided into vegetable-producing strips, providing the basics for their owners who depend more on the sheep that wander far and wide, doing well on the wild-growing shrubs and wiry herbs and grasses that need no tending beyond what the good God sends in rain.

Los Pinos is a village of shepherds and craftsmen. It is smaller than Quintera, though equal in appearance, the houses the colour of the surrounding countryside. The red-tiled roofs look dusty and faded as if they were ashamed to be red and longed to be yellow like everything else. There is a shabby, almost forlorn look about Los Pinos, bordered by the bent pines. The streets are narrow, uneven, and the walls of the houses are greasy where mules, sheep and oxen have eternally rubbed against them. There is a small tavern, but its customers are all past middle age. The youngsters prefer the big tavern in Quintera with its billiard table and its juke-box and its talk of installing a television. There is a weekly cinema, too, in Quintera, and Los Pinos has nothing to compete against that.

Los Pinos has always been Quintera's poor neighbour, long before the installation of the cinema, the billiard table, and the jukebox. Its grocery store is a branch of the grocer's in the other village, and vendors of fish come once a week from Quintera too. No one, either in Quintera or Los Pinos, can remember which village was in existence first, but from time immemorial, the latter has been dependent upon the former.

In two things, however, the people of Los Pinos think themselves the superior. They are more literate, for a shepherd has time to read while guarding his flocks, whereas an arable farmer must work with his hands and stay on his feet all day. They have better craftsmen, also. Quintera has always been a pushing village, anxious to keep up with the changing world. It has tractors, and a combine harvester and the smith there has for so long been a mechanic that his hand no longer turns easily to shoeing an animal or shaping iron in the forge. The farmers prefer the smith in Los Pinos when they have a mule to be shod, and the mechanic can't deal with a broken plough.

Thus, in one way and another, Los Pinos manages to hold its own, struggling but proud, and even the inhabitants of Quintera have to admit that when preparing for a wedding feast or some other special occasion, there is nothing more likely to please than a Los Pinos lamb.

Quintera, for all its go-ahead enthusiasm, remains a village by its size alone. Set in the middle of a deserted plain, there is no one not already born there who would choose to live in such a place, and many are anxious to escape, bored with the eternal sameness of their existence, restless for a new-found prosperity which their fathers never had. Those who own land sell it recklessly for a high price, and they arrive in Madrid or some other city innocent, unsuspecting, easy prey to many temptations. Pride won't allow them to return and they dream and talk of their village as if it were paradise lost, uncomfortable in their modern flats, crushed in the crowded streets.

Only the old of both villages prefer to stay where they are. They remember past feuds and resentments in which the young have no interest and regard with amusement or scorn, and below the necessary facade of friendly commerce, there is an antipathy between the two places which resists even the disinterest of the younger generation. There used to be only three things capable of dragging the unwilling older generation from Los Pinos to mingle with the inhabitants of Quintera—the annual pilgrimage, the bull caping and the market.

Quintera is a hub for the surrounding smaller villages. It has an inexhaustible supply of fresh, clear water on its outskirts, and from custom, farmers brought their thirsty oxen, mules and sheep to this place when all other local sources failed during the hottest months of summer. They began to exchange gossip and, later, animals, so from being once a watering place with shade-giving oaks, it developed into a market. A leading citizen of Quintera, who owned the tavern and the casino, the store, the pledges, debts and title deeds of the poorer inhabitants, quickly saw the advantage of establishing a regular market. Now local produce is sold, chickens and hares, sheep and mules, pots and pans, even old wireless sets and tarnished mirrors, and dealers from further afield pay for the privilege of selling clothes and trinkets.

By tradition, the mayor, who had jurisdiction over both villages, arranged the bull caping, supplying most of the funds for it out of his own pocket, probably to guard his favour among the oft-time fickle inhabitants. It was held on the day of Corpus Christi. The plaza was barricaded with farm carts to form an arena, and a couple of thin-faced, half-starved youngsters would come from God knew where to risk their lives for a pittance, just because they loved the bulls and dreamt of becoming toreros. Now, instead of the bull caping, there's a travelling fair, its blaring noise keeping the older folk away.

They still make the annual pilgrimage to the ancient and long deserted monastery a few miles beyond Quintera. Twice during the past century, strangers stumbled into the shelter of the half-ruined building when bitter winds and swirling snow had threatened to destroy them, and on both occasions, they swore that a brilliant light had suddenly appeared before them above the ruins, guiding them to the place where before they could see nothing in the snowy darkness, and their lives had been saved. A worm-eaten wooden figure of the Virgin had been found there, supposed by experts to be of the twelfth century, and she was called the Virgin of the Light.

The priest at the time declared it to be a holy place where special intercessions might be answered and where the Virgin might again put in an appearance and from what had begun as a humble gathering has grown into a great event with a mass and procession, and everyone wearing their Sunday best. The monastery is all of ten miles from Los Pinos but, as it is always an eagerly anticipated event, even the oldest members of the village have to attend, some still arriving at the place in a rickety, ox-drawn cart, looking none the worse for the rough journey beneath the blazing sun. Now, those who can afford them come in cars.

Los Pinos, like every other village in Spain, however small, has its own church, built by the people a long time ago, and its walls are of solid, uneven stone, worn smooth with the passing of the years. It is the same colour as the houses huddled against it, the same colour as the earth. Only its bell tower, stretching above every other roof, distinguishes it from the jumble of buildings that cluster around the main square. The church in Quintera is almost its twin.

But although each village has its individual church, one priest has to be shared between them. Special masses are held in Quintera only, to which church the villagers of Los Pinos must come, much to their chagrin, as their neighbours give themselves airs about this and consider themselves to be superior. This situation has been in existence for a long time, and the inhabitants of Los Pinos have never enjoyed using Quintera's church, even occasionally. Still less do they like to think of their dead being buried among strangers, for at one time, there was only one burial ground between the two villages.

In 1920, a certain shepherd who aspired to become mayor let it be known that he would contribute a piece of his own land to make good this lack which galled the populace, and when he was elected, he fulfilled his promise. This graveyard, set on the western side of the village, away from Quintera, which lies to the east, is sparsely populated in comparison with the other. From time immemorial, Quintera's cemetery has served both villages, and there are communal graves for some of the families of Los Pinos who have no choice but to be buried there when they die, regardless of the fact that they now have a place of their own. Therefore the Los Pinos cemetery has a deserted, neglected air. It is set among boulders and wiry grass, walled off from wandering sheep, planted with cypresses to give it a formal appearance, but, except for the occasion of a burial, it has few visitors. Habit is an ingrained thing among the villagers, and when the novelty of its inauguration had worn off, most people continued to be buried in Quintera.

Father Montero has been the priest of the two villages since 1937, and from the beginning, he felt the antagonism that exists between them. He had been a young man then, recently ordained, inspired by his superiors at the seminary whose words still rang in his ears and stirred in his heart, especially at that time of persecution and sudden death. He was used to country people, for he had come from the land himself, the youngest of a family which included five sisters. His parents, longing desperately for a son, promised to give him to the Church were their prayers heeded, and thus it came about that Ignacio Montero, son of a village blacksmith, was faced with the problem of uniting two opposing villages, both under his jurisdiction.

He had spoken with the leading men of both places, listened to the prejudiced views of the ordinary people and came to the conclusion that, on the whole, the dislike and mistrust were based only on long-standing tradition and one or two isolated incidents which fanned this latent feeling into flame perhaps only once in a decade.

'Martínez is a swindler,' complained the housewives of Los Pinos, forced to use his store. 'He charges more here for his goods than he does in Quintera.'

Father Montero found that this was true, but Martínez defended himself when questioned by talking of transport costs and overheads and refused to change his policy.

'If the women don't like it, they can come to Quintera to buy what they need. They'll soon start singing a different tune.'

Martínez was definitely the most unpopular man in the eyes of the other village, just as in Quintera, most people sang his praises. He was a money-lender as well as a shopkeeper, and it was wise not to offend him. Father Montero soon learned, as had his predecessor, that Martínez was the church's greatest supporter and that it would be foolish to ruffle his feathers unnecessarily. He had hopes of repairing the damage with time—the scandal of the grocer's daughter and the doctor's son from Los Pinos would be forgotten—and, indeed, the naked hatred which glowed between the two villages when he arrived there has healed over into a scab at which it is wiser not to pick.

But, like all scabs, it itches from time to time, and Father Montero is not satisfied. It is 1964. He has been in this post for twenty-seven years. Most of his illusion has been lost in petty detail, but the delivery of a roll of posters to the mayor one morning early in the year begins again the itch which has so often irritated him. The posters, now decorating the village walls, are simple in the extreme - small white houses at the bottom surrounded by the blue Spanish sky. In big letters, they proclaim '25 Years of Peace.'

Their simplicity stirs something in the priest's somewhat atrophied soul. The little houses represent his own two villages—for he looks upon Los Pinos and Quintera as his own—which have been staunchly Nationalist from the beginning, courageously routing out their anarchists and priest-haters in the year of his advent. He decides that it would be a good thing to base his future sermons on the slogan—it is an inspiring one, twenty-five years of peace. It is more than the rest of Europe can claim, but . . . and there begins the itch. In his own particular parishes, there has been anything but twenty-five years of peaceful co-existence.

Old Martínez is dead. No one can hate him now, but these traditionally-minded people who have nothing to do but till their land, watch their sheep and remember scandals, keep alive the bitterness and injustices of those times, especially the older ones. The young ones can't be bothered, thank God, with ancient scandals. They are twisting and jiving and escaping to the cities. The grocer's only surviving son Fidel is determined to keep up with the times - hence the cinema and the jukebox and his newly built house, which he shares with his elderly mother – so the young people of both places have no complaints. It's easy to convince them of the value of twenty-five years of peace. But how to convince the old people, especially those like Dionisia Zabaco, that if the whole of Spain can overcome its grievances, a truce should be declared between the two villages?

That accursed grave she visits so often! This is the biggest itch of all to the middle-aged priest. It seems so much in defiance of all that the poster stands for. The scab can never heal while that grave with its inscription exists, but the old mother will not have it changed.

Was it not the fault of Martínez that her only grandchild—for the others are surely lost to her—should be scorned as a bastard in Quintera and disowned by those of her relations who live there? Was it not the fault of Martínez that her younger son is dead?

He is buried in the new graveyard, where lie some fifteen people, mostly children and young folk. She is its only regular visitor, an old woman, her once cheery features hardened by bitterness, summer and winter her head shrouded by a black shawl. Whenever Father Montero sees her on her way there, he curses (then hastily crosses himself and begs forgiveness of the One above), and every time he looks at one of the posters, he remembers the purposeful figure in black and her lonely steadfastness. The one contradicts the other, and he is tired of contradiction. She must be all of eighty, this old woman, and yet still she will not forgive. So near to death she is, but she holds this feud with God and with the Martínez family.

She stands and stares at the stark wooden cross which marks the ground beneath which lies her most loved child, a cross erected at her command when his body was brought here from its prison grave. The words on the notice nailed to its centre are not only engraved upon her memory so that she can see them even when her eyes are closed but upon Father Montero's also, words dictated from a heart incapable of forgiveness or acceptance:

Bernardo de Rosas Zabaco
Age 27
Murdered

III

In the summertime, Bernardo's mother sits on a chair outside the door like all the old women of Los Pinos. They are mostly silent. The young think they are asleep and compare them with the toddlers that are often plumped down beside them, incapable of thought, hardly aware that life exists, hardly anything more than worn-out mules. They think that the old have forgotten how to feel and are impatient with them. They are so used all their lives to seeing old women in black sitting in doorways that they pass them by without even noticing.

But they are not mules that don't reason or feel, and they are not babies who haven't yet learned what joy and sorrow are, and they are not shadows without substance. They are all mothers of sons who have made them proud or caused them to weep, and while they sit silent in the sun, they think about them, and it doesn't seem long ago at all that they themselves were young and their children babies.

THE DARK SWALLOWS

PART ONE

Bernardo was a lovely baby, blond and chubby and always gurgling with contentment. He had a smile for everyone from babyhood onwards, not like Arturo, who withdrew from friends and strangers alike, nor Adriana, who liked some and not others. Bernardo was like a puppy before it has felt a boot, offering itself unselfconsciously, and he never really changed.

When he was five, he went with his family to Burgos for a holiday. His mother had always wanted to see the famous cathedral, and her husband took them there for a few days. They stayed in a boarding-house near the cathedral so that she could go there every day if she wanted to, and they had their photograph taken before they returned home. It is the only photograph that Dionisia Zabaco has of her sons, a bit faded now, turning brown round the edges, but it is all she has to cling to of days long gone, proving that she once had two boys who were her life. She has no photo of little Adriana.

Arturo looks very serious, thin as he always was, already forming features which, had his face not been marred by the pitted scars of the smallpox which had killed Adriana two years earlier, could have been called handsome. He was ten then and had begun a passion for the Church which lasted so long that his father, in spite of strong reservations, considered sending him to a seminary in training for priesthood. He and his mother spent time in the cathedral every day, while Bernardo and his father meandered round the ancient city, doing nothing in particular.

Bernardo's face in the photograph reminds his mother of how he looked when she last saw him. His usual cheery expression is gone, for he was rather scared of the photographer's big camera with its black cloth, and his eyes are full of anxiety. In the photo, he is no longer blond. His hair was beginning to darken to the black that it later became. He was a sturdy boy, neither quick nor handsome like his brother, and took after his paternal grandfather in looks and character, a man who had been appreciated by many both for his integrity and his mischievous sense of humour.

This man had been a great storyteller and, before settling down to raise the merinos whose fine and much sought-after fleece added to his fortune, had had such an adventurous life that few thought to question the truth of his tales. Bernardo loved being in his rough and ready company and was grief-stricken when he died, whereas Arturo instinctively withdrew from what was for him his grandfather's too physical heartiness and showed no sorrow at all.

Sometimes it was difficult for Dionisia to believe that Arturo and Bernardo were brothers, the same flesh, so different were they in both appearance and personality. Arturo grew tall and bony, and there was a constant aura of intensity about him, a gleam of passion in his eyes. He always seemed to be in a hurry and with such a lot to do; he had so many books and papers.

Stocky Bernardo was something of a dreamer. Contentment was in his nature; he rarely bothered to assert himself and never hurried. He would have made a good shepherd, for he was gentle and patient, and his father once hoped that he would like to be a doctor because he had the right character for it. But gentleness on its own isn't enough, and Bernardo never showed any willingness to study hard. He was more often out of the classroom than in it, and no amount of punishment would force him to go to school when he didn't feel like it. He would endure the pain and then please himself, holding no grudge against the teacher who was obliged to uphold the rules.

The only thing that the brothers had in common was their love of reading, but in this, too, their tastes diverged. Arturo's books were all serious in nature, and he used to date them as he got them. In 1915, when he was ten, he started his mania for religious books, and there was quite a collection of them. Whether he understood them or not, he read them all, especially biographies of the saints, Ignacio de Loyola being his favourite, perhaps because he was a valiant soldier before he formed the Society of Jesus. He also had a lot of historical books and some Russian novels.

Bernardo had no factual books at all, except for a couple of medical manuals, which his father once hopefully handed to him. He only liked romances and poetry, and of the score or so books that he possessed, there was Cervantes, Lope de Vega, San Juan de la Cruz, and Becquer. There were only two books that they both liked to read. One was the life of El Cid Campeador and the other Don Quijote, but doubtless, they read them for different purposes, Bernardo because they were romances and Arturo because they demonstrated the conditions and injustices of the age.

When faced with educating his sons, the doctor had been torn between sending them away, as he had been sent, or trying to educate them himself. For a time, he resisted the temptation to surrender Arturo to the Jesuits, afraid of how deeply they might influence him, but on recognizing the keenness of his mind, the burgeoning academic ability which had to be harnessed, not frustrated, he finally let him go, much to his son's satisfaction. He was twelve then and had outgrown his religious zeal, so his father was less anxious about him becoming a priest.

Bernardo, he left to himself, seeing him so much like his mother in his attitude to life, undemanding, accepting whatever came his way, with no aspiration beyond reading as many classics as he could and indulging himself with words. He could hardly be persuaded to sit in the classroom for any length of time. It was as if the world around him was his teacher, offering him all he wanted to know, and he taking his time to ponder and absorb it, as was his wont. He learned about sheep, the stars and something about the mystery of turning grapes into wine from his maternal uncles, an exotic geography, history and culture of the Americas from his grandfather, and the wonderful inconsistencies, follies and passions of human nature from the tattered classics on the shelf in the kitchen. When he was about ten, and the doctor once rebuked him, after having to apologise to the schoolmaster for his son's many absences, his guileless explanation was, 'Arturo's clever enough for the two of us. I'm not like him, Papa. I can only be me.' What he said was so true that his father could not but agree with him and suggest that he make more effort to please the teacher from time to time. 'It's not kind to make him angry, and it's not good for his health.'

The neighbours used to make fun of all the reading the doctor's boys did, some genuinely surprised and unable to understand that they should prefer books to the rough behaviour that most of the lads indulged in. And if sometimes their mother repeated to a neighbour something that she had learned from her sons, they would think she was trying to prove herself superior to them, and a jealous one would exclaim, 'Oh, listen to the Señora de Rosas. How clever she is!'

But Dionisia wasn't clever, nor had she any pretensions about herself, as artless as a child in many ways. It was only that she liked her sons to read to her when they were in the kitchen together on a winter's night. Bernardo would sit as close to the fireplace as he could, a shabby book devouring all his attention. He was always in his mother's way when she had cooking to do, but she didn't like to disturb him. Then suddenly, he would exclaim, 'Listen to this verse. It's beautiful!' or he would start laughing and have to read out the adventures of a picaroon who was getting himself into all kinds of mischief.

And then Arturo, who preferred to sit at the table with several books and an old encyclopaedia piled in front of him, with a few sheets of paper and a pen to jot down important notes, would say, 'Don't you think this is a funny custom?' or, many a time, 'Did you know that such-and-such a thing is true?' which, of course, she didn't. When he was going through his religious phase, he lectured them all on the differences between venial and mortal sins, on the observance of saints' days and other such things, but only she listened, deeply impressed. Sometimes she would accidentally splash soup over a page of Arturo's writing or pick up one of Bernardo's books with floury hands. Arturo would be furious and insist on writing out the whole page again, even if the little blot hardly discoloured the paper, but Bernardo only laughed if his mother left one of his books sticky.

'If I get hungry, I can eat the covers,' he said, and, even though he valued the contents of his books, he didn't much care what state they were in.

He was an untidy lad who always came home from school with more ink on his fingers than he could have possibly put in his exercise books, but his was a carefree nature, and he was never aware of his appearance. Still, he was a good boy, even though he could be as stubborn as any when it suited him. He'd run errands for her; he'd bring her a bunch of wildflowers from the fields, already wilting from what they'd had to endure in his hot and careless hands; he would help in lots of little ways that his brother would never think of. He was demonstrative too and always had to show his love for his mother rather than let her take it for granted. He never ran off with his friends or went to bed without first giving her a kiss, whereas she had no memory of any kisses from Arturo.

He had a fondness for animals and couldn't be kept away from the pig and the chickens in the corral, much to his mother's annoyance and concern. He was only about three at the time, and she was afraid the pig might crush him. Then came the day of the pig-sticking, always a long day which kept family, friends and neighbours fully occupied until every part of the animal had been processed, and only the bladder remained, which became a ball for the children to kick about, getting under everyone's feet.

Halfway through the day, Dionisia suddenly realized that Bernardo wasn't among them. When none of them could find him, she anxiously began searching herself, eventually discovering him curled up under the blankets of the big bed he shared with his brother. There he had cried himself to sleep, traumatised by the squeals, the shouts, the ropes, the struggles of men and beast before it was overcome, tied to the table, silenced by the knife that slit its throat and slowly began to pant out its life-blood into a large bowl.

He kept away from pigs after that and took to going out with his shepherd uncle, watching over the sheep and goats with him, learning their names and their characters, walking miles with him to different grazings and often being carried home half asleep on his shoulders.

'Perhaps he'll be a shepherd like his grandfather,' the doctor said.

But then he returned home one day with such a troubled expression on his usually cheerful face that Dionisia knew something had deeply upset him. When she asked him why he was sad, he burst into tears and hid his face in her skirt, clinging to her with both hands, brokenly explaining that his uncle had cut one of the kids' throats and then skinned it. While she tried to make him understand what had happened, Arturo, with the sadistic delight of an eleven-year-old, reminded him of the horrors of the annual pig-sticking and couldn't be silenced.

'And pigs really scream,' he relished. 'They start squealing even before they're stretched out for killing. Killing kids is tame after killing pigs. Don't you remember?' and he didn't stop tormenting his brother until she boxed his ears.

Another time Bernardo had a dog which someone gave him as a puppy. They went around everywhere together, and while Bernardo was in school, the dog used to hang about the door waiting for him to come out. One day it was kicked in the head by a mule and went crazy, snapping at everybody, running round in circles and constantly falling down. Bernardo wanted to get hold of it, even though it didn't seem to recognise him, and someone had to drag him away by force. Eventually, a sack was thrown over the dog, and one of the men caught it and broke its neck.

Bernardo was heartbroken and hardly ate for a week. His father offered to get him another dog, but he didn't want one. One of his uncles brought him a handsome hunting dog which he gave to someone else. He said he never wanted another dog but preferred to remember the one he'd had, and while most of the boys went about with dogs at their heels, he went alone. Arturo teased him for his devotion, but in some things, Bernardo was steadfast, and he never kept a dog again.

II

Childhood goes so quickly, and to Dionisia Zabaco, it seemed that in no time at all, Arturo was packing his bags and leaving home, a young man anxious to make his way in the world. He had no regrets about leaving and was eager to go, chiding his mother for her last-minute warnings and reminders. Even though he was never an affectionate boy and she had grown used to his long absences from home in his school days, this time she felt an empty space in her heart when he was gone. She knew that he would never want to come back; he had been longing all his life to escape the narrowness of the village, yearning for success since childhood. His parents were proud of him, and only his father realised that Arturo was somewhat ashamed of them and that this secret shame was his main stimulus to success. Hadn't he felt the same himself at Arturo's age, out of step with the rustic family he had been sent away from as a child?

His father had run off to Cuba while hardly more than a lad but returned twenty years later with pockets literally full of gold. He married a young widow who had inherited lands from her husband and gave him three daughters and one son. Determined to ensure that his son had the best possible start in life, he sent him to be educated by the Jesuits from whom he eventually returned home with his head full of knowledge but estranged from the family affection his heart had longed for throughout his childhood and youth. It was this homesickness that brought him back to Los Pinos after completing his medical training when he could have stayed in Madrid and probably have done much better for himself.

Whether doctor or shepherd, Pedro de Rosas would have been a success. Caring by nature, he had empathy for the sick and helpless, those beaten down by circumstances, which in either walk of life was a major qualification. In his youth, he had been all that Bernardo was, but the sensitive grey eyes had blurred with study, the sight of pain and brutality, and too much wine; his innocence had been warped by experience and the years when only faith in his original ambition kept him to his course had made of him a doctor well-loved but deeply disillusioned. His face was blotchy, his humour inclined to irony. Below the surface, he hardly cared any more about the people he served, but he had to pretend just because they believed in him. Bernardo's warmth had been in his own before time cooled it, and all that Arturo had inherited from his father was the ambition which had long ago made him venture to Madrid to be a doctor and, perhaps from his grandfather, that youthful ambition that had taken him to the Americas before Spain lost its empire. Bernardo seemed to have inherited no ambition at all.

His wife was comfortably plump, less well-dressed perhaps than a doctor's wife should be, the mourning she had donned for Adriana her customary attire. Arturo had only vague memories of his mother gaily dressed, Bernardo none. But the artless sparkle of her eyes was all one ever noticed. The mourning had gone from her heart long since, and she was a busy, cheerful little woman, cheerful perhaps because her life was in her sons and she was unaware of her husband's unhappiness. She was fond of him, but she had never tried to pierce the surface of his character, had no curiosity to know his inner self. And he had given up expecting or hoping that she would be urged one day to seek for something more. His life was the village and its sickness, hers the rearing of her children and the keeping of the house.

But still he loved her in a way that she never knew, unable to free himself from the bond that had inextricably drawn him to her from the day he had first encountered her, caring for a sick father who needed his frequent administrations and made him a regular visitor to the isolated farmhouse. It wasn't any beauty that attracted him; she wasn't even particularly pretty; but there was such a sparkle of life in her simple, uncomplicated, childlike acceptance of everything in her spartan existence, something like a fountain of fresh, clear water that danced before his eyes and demanded that he satisfy his thirst in her. He had never come across such innocent honesty and lack of self-awareness in a woman. He gave her his heart and married her as soon as her father died, before they had even exchanged a kiss.

She was twenty-one, ten years his junior, hardly more than a happy-go-lucky child in spite of the responsibilities she had borne for years in that motherless household and she the only daughter, quite willing to go from daughter to wife at her brothers' encouragement, surrendering her share of the lands in exchange for an annual rent which in good years gave her a more secure income than her husband who often received little, and sometimes nothing, for his services. She was utterly malleable in her marital duties, gave him pleasure, never refused him, but there was none of the responsive ardour he needed and longed for. She loved and cared for him as she'd loved and cared for her father and brothers, as she loved and cared for her sons; willingly, devotedly, unquestioningly, a better daughter, sister and mother than she was a wife. He taught her to read, and she dutifully learned, without seeing much point in it, although she was inordinately proud of her sons' education, especially Arturo's. He was so clever!

They never talked about Adriana. The doctor was unable to forgive himself for her death, although he could hardly be blamed. So many children, and even adults, died during the smallpox epidemic of 1914. He was with the sick all the time, night and day, never pausing for rest, and it was hardly surprising that he brought the disease into his own house. The only wonder was that he never went down with it himself. Both parents loved her dearly, but Dionisia was more able to accept her death than was the doctor.

Over and over again, he said, 'I should have been able to save her. If I can't save others, surely I should be able to save my own child, my own flesh and blood. I didn't take enough care. I was so tired, so many were sick. I just didn't care anymore. I'd seen so many children die that I didn't feel anything when I tended her . . .

not until she was dead. She was suddenly still, and I realised, "But this is my own daughter." And I loved her so much.'

Dionisia always felt that her husband loved Adriana and his memory of her more than he ever loved his sons. Although Arturo recovered after lying very ill for several weeks, the doctor never congratulated himself on saving him. All he could remember was that Adriana had died, and he never ceased to blame himself, although his wife never once reproached him. She didn't know how much the little girl reminded the doctor of her mother when he first fell in love with her, so innocent and sparkling and undemanding, and how in his grief he felt it was his fault that Dionisia seemed unable to respond to his needs; that he had failed her even as he had failed his daughter. When he tried to tell her this, she didn't understand and went on believing that he had loved the little girl more than the boys.

Bernardo was fifteen when Arturo left home. He had finished school a year earlier and showed no inclination for further education, and neither jealousy nor resentment when he was told that his brother was to go to Madrid and that because of this, he would have to do military service in his place, for one of the doctor's two sons was bound to be conscripted, and Arturo's university education would exempt him. With the help of an older cousin, Frumencio, he became responsible for the produce grown on the only piece of land still remaining to his father, and when it was learned that the carpenter needed an extra pair of hands, he was quite willing to be apprenticed to him, quickly learning the skills of the trade, as able at turning wood as tending the soil and the vines.

He didn't seem to miss Arturo. The two were never close, and Bernardo had many friends. Most of the lads of Los Pinos were his companions at one time or another. They roamed and idled about together and from time to time would come under attack from the boys of Quintera, or make the assault themselves, throwing stones or trying to dodge them, until one group was chased off by the other, both sides boasting of their cuts and bumps and bruises. Bernardo never got involved in these skirmishes. He couldn't see the point of wanting to hurt and insult anyone or being hurt and insulted himself, and just shrugged his shoulders if he was called a coward.

His only special friend at that time seemed an odd choice to his mother, Fidel Martínez of Quintera, the grocer's son. They were often in each other's company from young boys upwards, probably because they both liked reading and poetry, but all who felt affection for Bernardo wished that he could have chosen someone else to be a regular companion.

There was always a lot of talk about Fidel. People said that he was not normal, and the doctor said that the poor boy had been born with characteristics more feminine than masculine and that he couldn't help being what he was. But this didn't make it any easier for Dionisia to know that Bernardo seemed to like his company so much more than that of the others. Once, she asked him why.

'It's not that I like him more. It's because we like the same things. I can't discuss books and ideas with anyone else but him. The other boys only talk about—well, girls, and it gets monotonous after a while. Fidel understands poetry. He even writes it! And when we're reading together alone, and everywhere it's silent and empty, the words aren't on paper any more but in the air. They come alive. You can feel them.'

His mother remained uncomprehending and dissatisfied. Bernardo was impervious to what people might make of his relationship with Fidel, but she minded very much. She even thought she would rather he came home with a bloody head than with books tucked under his arm. The neighbours were gossips and took advantage of any occasion to slight a person's character, and she didn't want to hear their insinuations or know that they might be thinking that her son was the same as Fidel, although in appearance they were so different.

At fifteen, Bernardo was already a young man. His work in the fields had darkened his skin, toughened his hands and developed the muscles of his body. His mother was proud to see him so strong-looking, and there was many a girl that glanced at him even then, although he didn't seem to notice them. For all his physical appearance, he was still a boy at heart, whereas the girls of his age were young women.

Dionisia was glad when his friendship with Fidel came to an end.

She didn't know how it happened, and he never mentioned it himself. All she knew was that one night he came home late. He had spent the afternoon with Fidel, and his mother had expected him home a long time earlier as he had promised to go after crayfish with the next-door neighbour's son and a few others. They came calling for him and went off without him, impatient and unwilling to wait any longer. He returned very late and, wanting no supper, went straight up to bed, with words for neither of them and not even a kiss for his mother. Dionisia felt then that something must have happened between the two boys, and her suspicions were confirmed when she learned that they no longer went about together.

It wasn't just an ordinary quarrel. Bernardo was not a boy to bear malice against anyone, and he would have made up the argument the very next morning, even had the other been in the wrong. Dionisia did no probing, waiting for him to speak, but he never said a word on the subject or mentioned Fidel's name again. It was the first time that Bernardo did not confide in his mother, and it was a little wedge between them for a while. But time passed by, and the pain of the memory faded.

III

There are lots of little things that Dionisia Zabaco remembers about Bernardo in those few years when she had him more or less to herself when Arturo went away and before he was conscripted and came back to devote himself to Elvira. She remembered the battle she'd had with him over his first Sunday suit when she showed him the cloth she had saved for and bought with pride.

'I don't need a suit to go to mass,' he protested.

'Yes, you do. You're a young man now, not a boy, and you're the doctor's son. You must have a suit for special days. I want to be proud of you, my heart.'

'You can be proud of Arturo. I'm sure he wears a suit every day, not only on Sundays. And a collar and tie.'

He eventually surrendered to being measured all over when he realized how much it meant to her—his father didn't care; he never went to mass anyway (and Bernardo only went to accompany and please his mother)—and, the first time he wore it, patiently endured the approbation of family, neighbours and even the priest, his only consolation being the admiring attention of the younger females. But he drew the line at a collar and tie.

He was never interested in his appearance, not even when he began courting Elvira, and was always ill-at-ease when dressed for special occasions. Shirt, trousers and rope-soled sandals were all he needed in summer, plus a thick winter jacket and boots when the cold set in.

The first lovely thing he made out of wood was the cradle for Arturo's third child. He spent hours and hours on its design, and it was a cradle fit for a prince by the time he'd finished it: birds and little animals carved in the wood, laced by a pattern of corn ears. Fidel's brother, Gustavo, was going to Madrid and agreed to take it with him to make sure that it didn't get damaged or lost on the journey. And he amused himself by making wooden toys, little animals and dolls, which he gave to any child he happened to meet as well as sending a number to Arturo for his children.

Dionisia watched her son grow up in those few years, changing from a boy to a young man whom everyone liked and admired for his good nature, his kindness, his willingness to please. Having only one son at home, she had plenty of time to watch him, and, as many a mother remarked to her, he was a son to be proud of. But, for all that, he was no angel, and Dionisia gathered through gossip that he'd had his face slapped more than once for being cheeky with the girls. He was often among the other lads who stood in the plaza of an evening or a Sunday afternoon, generally parading their masculinity and making remarks to all the girls who passed deliberately by. But that was all part of growing up, and the girls would have been disappointed if they hadn't been noticed or spoken to.

When Bernardo had to report for military service, his mother began to understand what loneliness was, the inner loneliness that one can feel though surrounded by people. She and her husband had privacy again, such as they had never known since the children were born, but they were so used to being without it that they had little to say to each other. When they talked, it was of Bernardo and Arturo. There was nothing else to talk about.

He could have escaped conscription if his father had been willing to pay some other lad to take his place, but the doctor refused to participate in this abuse of the system on both political and moral grounds. Dionisia needed some persuading, not understanding why he should pay for Arturo's education but not for Bernardo's release, especially since it meant more work for Frumencio and less income for them.

'Just be glad it's now only two years instead of three,' the doctor silenced her for at the time of the Primo de Rivera dictatorship, conscription had been reduced, and the dread of being shipped to Africa was a thing of the past.

Letters from them were longed for but infrequent. Arturo rarely thought of them, and Bernardo was lazy. He returned home on rare occasions to delight them both, and Dionisia lived for his coming, realising that she wanted Bernardo's company more than that of her husband. She supposed that it was wrong, but some thirty years of marriage dull many emotions and the doctor was a man of few words. He saved his conversations for his sick patients, he discussed local affairs with the leading men at the casino in Quintera, there read the newspapers that came from Madrid, and when he went home, he had little to say to his wife, much as he loved her. He would tease and caress her and then sigh, "Ay, Noni, Noni," with a shake of his head before getting on with his dinner while she related the doings and gossip of the day.

Now she had no one to read to her or tell her anecdotes or try to educate her, and she longed to have at least one of her sons by her again. She knew Arturo wouldn't come, but she was determined and certain that she would keep Bernardo.

She hadn't missed Arturo in the way she now missed her younger son. Although intensely proud of everything about Arturo – his quick mind, his handsome features, his ability to get his own way with a charm that had no warmth in it and yet which somehow always worked its magic from a very early age—she couldn't understand him and was almost half afraid of him. With inexplicable primitive instinct, she knew that this hungrily anticipated firstborn was not really hers to possess. Like a cuckoo, he was a stranger who had invaded her womb and in whom no traits of husband, father or brothers could be recognized, and she was fiercely protective of him because she knew she wouldn't keep him for long. She prolonged weaning him for as long as she could, ignoring his rejection of her still full breasts until she was pregnant for a second time. Adriana was definitely her own, her smiles and laughter filling both the home and her parents' hearts with sunshine in a way totally alien to Arturo. And then Bernardo came along, his personality even more open than his sister's, and Dionisia was satisfied.

She had it all planned that Bernardo would marry a Los Pinos girl, and they would set up a house nearby, and she used to watch the girls as they foregathered in the plaza and at mass, wondering which one of them would suit Bernardo most. She so much wanted to have him quickly settled with a nice girl. He would be almost twenty-three when he completed his military service, old enough to start thinking of marriage at least, but the doctor only laughed at her when she mentioned the subject.

'Leave the poor boy alone,' he said. 'Let him enjoy his freedom. He'll miss it soon enough when he's married.'

Bernardo came home for a week one spring, in time for the pilgrimage, which was lucky as it was always a very special event and preceded an evening of gaiety and dancing. The doctor's family joined their relations and travelled the bumpy road in a crowded waggon. When the ceremony was over, they ate the food they brought, and Bernardo had to talk to everyone who came to say hello, hiding his impatience to get to his friends. Dionisia didn't want him to go off, knowing that she wouldn't see him for the rest of the day if he did, but a young man can't be stopped from enjoying himself, and she tried not to appear too disappointed when he abandoned the family group. They returned home without him, using the oxcart again, and Bernardo still hadn't come home when they went to bed. Dionisia wanted to sit up for him, but the doctor said no.

'He's capable of getting himself to bed, woman, so leave him to it. He'll probably come home half-drunk, maybe completely drunk, and he won't want you to see him if he does. You'll spoil what he's enjoyed already.'

A lot later, Dionisia learned that it was on this day that Bernardo first met Elvira—and she had thought it lucky that he should be home for the occasion!

PART TWO

The morning of the pilgrimage was sunny, and the day promised well. April was usually uncertain with unexpected showers, high winds and dull skies, and many a time, the spirits of the pilgrims were dampened by a mixture of rain and cold. Bernardo, when he stared up at the sky that morning, noting its blueness, its lack of cloud, knew that he was going to enjoy himself. He had been lucky to get leave that week, for the pilgrimage was not a thing to be missed. It was very religious at first but, once the prayers and procession were over, things would get livelier with wine and food and dancing, and in the general confusion of so large a gathering, the young people always managed to escape parental eyes for an hour's kissing and cuddling behind the ruins.

Bernardo only hoped that he would be able to escape. His mother clung to him since he came home. She sent him off to visit various relations, to eat and chat with them, but she seemed to watch over his every movement and gave him little real freedom. He hadn't been aware of this before he went away, perhaps she hadn't been so possessive before either, but since his return, since he had tasted independence far from home, he was impatient of his mother's effusive affection and uncomfortably afraid of showing it.

While he was examining the sky, his parents and most of the neighbours were forcing themselves into their best clothes. They were all going to be uncomfortable until the effect of the crowd's eagerness for pleasure took over and made them forget themselves, but they wanted to be respectable for the morning's worship and prosperous in the eyes of their neighbours. Bernardo had decided to go in uniform. He was never comfortable in a suit, but if he were badly dressed, his mother would scold and nag him into changing. He could insist that it was obligatory for a soldier to worship the Virgin of the Light in uniform, and at the same time, experience had taught him that a uniform had an interesting effect on the opposite sex. Soldiers nearly always managed to find a girl to flirt with.

The doctor's son was right. He was the only man in uniform at the gathering, apart from the Civil Guards, and caused a flutter among the younger females. As he had been away from home for quite a while, he was called from one group to another, all of which were anxious to know how he enjoyed his new occupation, glad to welcome him back.

'Here comes the soldier!' they all shouted in turn, and some of the older men even shook his hand and heftily patted his shoulders, half affectionately and half in jest, congratulating him for the stripe he now wore on his sleeve. 'You'll soon be a general!' one of them exclaimed.

Bernardo, while agreeably returning the greetings and answering the same repeated questions, watched unobtrusively the reaction to his appearance by his neighbours' daughters. It was almost as unvarying as the questions. They would stare, refuse to meet his glance, some would blush, and then one of the cheekier ones would suddenly cover her mouth with her hand and whisper hurriedly into the ear of a companion. Then both would burst into giggles, quickly silenced by stern parental eyes, but Bernardo knew that he wouldn't be lacking female companions later.

The thing to decide was which ones to go after. He intended to try for three or four at least. Later he and his friends would compare their adventures. Bernardo knew that half of them were imagined and that if he wished, he could outdo them with his own inventions, but the afternoon's play was a thing in which deeds were better than words. He would shortly be back in barracks and with little to live on but memories.

The Virgin of the Light was brought in procession from Quintera on an ox-drawn cart, led by the priest and acolytes and followed by most of the inhabitants of that village who were joined at the crossroads by the pilgrims from Los Pinos. At that point, she was removed from the cart to be carried on the shoulders of the men who had volunteered for the honour. There was a mile or more of rough track, and when the monastery was reached, she completed a full circle, following a pathway worn by countless feet over the years gone by. Penitents followed her, carrying lighted candles whose hot wax dripped on their fingers. Some walked barefooted, keeping a covenant they had made personally with God or accepting the advice of the priest in the confessional. She was brought to a halt before an improvised altar at which the priest and his acolytes performed the ritual mass.

This Virgin looked nothing like the original, which was locked away in the storeroom of Quintera's church, slowly succumbing to the deterioration of forgetfulness. For all its historic and aesthetic value, the Church knew full well how little emotional impact it would inspire among a crowd of excited pilgrims escaping their drab, uneventful lives on a special occasion. Her replacement was a goddess adorned with a crown of gold and robes that shone like silk. Carried on a throne, surrounded by tall lighted candles and the smoke of incense, she was greeted with the appropriate enthusiasm by those who had arrived beforehand. Men removed their berets, women fell to their knees with bent heads, all crossing themselves as she passed, her sightless eyes staring beyond them into the limitless countryside.

Bernardo was no longer moved by the occasion. As a boy, the Virgin of the Light had left him breathless. Her dazzling raiment, her slow, uneven movement and the incense that spiralled about her impassive face made her a mythical creature in his imagination. But he had seen her so many times, always the same, that his illusion was gone. He knew that beneath the paintwork and the petticoats was a piece of wood. Her jewels no longer dazzled him. For a person feeling the urge of life as much as he did that morning, he saw nothing but a statue. He mentally apologised to the Virgin of the Light for thinking so disparagingly of her and, while gravely saluting her as she passed, wondered whether he should try for Quintera or Los Pinos girls first.

He disengaged his mind from girls for a while to participate with more sincerity in the mass that followed the procession. The beliefs in which he had been educated since early childhood made most of his reactions automatic, for he wasn't a person to trouble himself deeply about religion. Arturo had tried to form his mind, first into a fanatical devotion and later an equally fanatical atheism, but Bernardo was spiritually contented and cared too little to be influenced either way. His god was intrinsic to the earth, the sky, the baking heat, the aching cold; the words that rooted him to all these things and made his imagination soar; the mystery for which he sought no explanation and took for granted as being part of life itself. If the religion of the church stirred him at all, it was only because of its rhythmic patterns. Ever sensitive to the shape and sound of language, the simple words of the Latin liturgy formed an innate rhythm to which he instinctively responded.

When the mass was over, the meeting broke up into groups of friends and families. They had all brought food, including lambs which were killed, skinned, barbecued and eaten within the next three hours. These three hours were devoted to eating, drinking, laughing, talking and sleeping. Children shrieked and ran from group to group, ignoring their scolding mothers, escaping their older sisters, accepting titbits and flattery from all and sundry. Women gossiped, men laughed loudly and crudely, dogs hung hopefully about. The Virgin of the Light was carefully replaced on the ox-cart and forgotten. Even the priest seemed to have deserted her. He was invited to share every picnic and judiciously did so.

Bernardo ate with his family. Uncle Juanito had brought a lamb, and Uncle Luis supplied the wine. He had the best vines in Los Pinos and was proud of his wine, which was dry and not too sharp. It left the palate hungry, and food there was in plenty. Apart from the lamb, there were big potato omelettes, smoked ham, chorizo and blood sausage, sheep's milk cheese and bread to satisfy even the greediest. There were sixteen people in the doctor's group, and to eat that quantity of food while laughing and joking and sharing gossip took a couple of hours. The doctor was called away several times: a child was choking on a chicken bone; an old woman had collapsed in the excitement; a boy had fallen from a cart and perhaps broken his wrist.

'Poor Pedro,' sympathised his wife. 'He never gets a chance to relax and enjoy himself.'

'That's what comes of being a doctor. He should have been a shepherd like me, independent, my own boss.' This was Uncle Juanito.

'And smelling of sheep,' added his wife. They all laughed at this, but the shepherd was not dismayed.

'Better than smelling of medicine.'

'But better to smell of wine,' added Luis, widening his lips to receive the rosy jet poured from the skin which he held at arm's length.

No one disagreed with this, and they fell to eating and drinking with more gusto. They encouraged Bernardo to take the choicest pieces. He was popular among them and had been away from home for a long time. They all insisted that he was looking much thinner and reminded him of the fare awaiting him when his leave was over. This was from the women. The men hinted lewdly at the afternoon ahead, remembering their own youth, and warned him not to eat too much. They began to recall their adventures until their wives broke in upon their conversation with pretended anger, and their daughters blushed.

When they finished eating, they threw the scraps to the dogs, searched for a bit of shade beside the wagons or the walls of the monastery, and the majority of them fell into a doze. There was a certain amount of scattered, drowsy conversation, but inertia had spread over the whole gathering, and silence almost reigned for an hour or so. Bernardo threw himself down for a while also. He rested with his hands tucked under his head and stared up at the sky, watching the unhurrying clouds, well content. Soon his eyes closed, and he slept.

By five in the afternoon, everyone was on their feet again, noisy, bustling, with a few arguments breaking out. The children were lively once more, dancing round in circles and chanting rhymes, falling to the ground with delight, then clambering up to start all over again. The musicians who had been hired for the evening's entertainment began to produce a few sounds from their instruments to amuse them; both men and women energetically started preparing the area for dancing; everyone was more or less occupied in one way or another, and it was now that the young couples began to slip away. Girls without partners were more openly wandering off together, pretending they were going to examine the ruins, glancing at nearby youths and hoping they would follow.

Bernardo followed one such couple, but he couldn't persuade them to separate. Almost frightened by their own daring, no more than fifteen years old, they had made a pact to keep together, trusting in the safety of numbers. All they did was giggle when Bernardo tried to pay them compliments and grow haughty when he suggested something bolder.

'Three are too many,' he complained, at last, wearying of conquering either the one or the other.

'Then why don't you go away?' retorted one of the girls.

'If I do, you'll be sorry. I shan't come back.'

'We should worry!'

'Then I'm off. Goodbye. I'm not a man to snatch babes from their cradles.'

He returned to the crowd, hoping for better luck next time. He knew really that he would get nowhere with any of the girls. They liked to pretend they were bold, they liked a little excitement, and they made as if to offer everything but a man who believed them would get his face slapped. Still, it was nothing ventured, nothing gained, and later the young men would invent wild tales which none of them believed but which greatly entertained them. It was a way of getting their own back on the hypocritical girls. They would besmirch their characters, disparage their figures and generally make fun of them.

He joined with two of his friends, and they sallied forth to hunt together, encountering three girls from Quintera who also seemed unwilling to separate.

'Look at these three oafs from Los Pinos,' began one who seemed the leader of the group, a wiry, alert young creature, dark with almost a gipsy's darkness and brightly dressed.

The other two giggled.

'Oafs! Who's calling us oafs?' returned Cándido.

'They're only kids. What more can you expect? Run away home, girlies, before you get lost.'

This was Bernardo. He stared challengingly at the girl who had spoken, determining upon her for himself. The others were poor bait in comparison, tubby and red-faced, almost children still.

'Huh! Listen to the soldier. He thinks that just because he wears a uniform, he knows the world,' she responded, boldly returning his look.

The girls linked arms and walked off with their heads held haughtily. The lads joined arms and followed. Their comments were far from complimentary and occasionally far from decent and loud enough for the girls to hear.

'The dark one, she's too skinny,' said Bernardo.

'But look at the way she moves her hips!'

'I like the fat one myself,' opined Gerardo, 'that little blonde. She may not have much in the head, but what goes in front and behind . . . ' He shook his fingers as if he had touched something hot and whistled.

So they continued, the girls leading them farther and farther from the gathering, pretending deafness and a complete lack of interest, but the dark one swung her hips promisingly and dragged the others on. They reached a cluster of trees that overhung a gully. The girls scrambled down into it, and the fellows behind nudged each other. Cándido and Gerardo were about to break the pace, but Bernardo held them back.

'We can play their game too,' he said.

They flopped down with their backs to the trees and began to talk about things in general. Cándido talked about his father's mules, fine beasts that he bred mainly for the military; Gerardo pulled out some tobacco and began rolling himself a cigarette; Bernardo described his life in barracks where, consigned to clerical duties because of his level of literacy, he was bored and frustrated. They were keener to know about his off-duty activities but, his mind engaged with the dark girl somewhere in the gully, he left them guessing.

Some ten minutes later she came back, as he had felt certain she would, followed by her now panting companions.

'Look at them,' she sneered. 'Worn out already! And then they try to pretend they're men. What a soldier is that one! Don't they teach you how to march?'

'No. Maybe you'd better teach me. You seem so good at it.'

'You'd drop before you'd gone half a mile.'

'We'll see then.'

He pointed to a distant landmark, a huge slab of granite that dwarfed all the boulders about it.

'Are you game to walk as far as that?'

'And get there before you.'

Bernardo jumped to his feet and dusted his trousers.

'Let's go then.'

The other girls cried out in complaint.

'You're not going to leave us here alone, Elvira, with these two bears.'

'You know your way back to the monastery. Get them to take you there,' and she was already scrambling down into the gully to cross to the other side. Bernardo decided to let her have a head start. The chase would be part of the fun. Cándido winked at him, Gerardo cried, 'Good luck,' and he forgot them both in an instant as he finally went after Elvira, who was running as fast as she could without looking back.

II

Bernardo soon caught up with her and reached for her arm. She had slowed to a stride and shook herself free as she felt his fingers.

'Don't touch me,' she snapped with panting breath and such antipathy that he pulled up startled.

'What's the matter? Isn't this what you wanted?'

'I just wanted to get away, and if you don't like it, you needn't come with me.'

She marched ahead without looking at him, and he followed, somewhat puzzled. He stared at her thick, glossy hair, almost blue-black as the sun glinted upon it.

'What lovely hair—' he began.

'Save it for someone else,' broke in the girl ungraciously. 'If you've come with only one idea, you'd better go back.'

'Why did you encourage me then? Don't pretend that you didn't.'

She was silent.

Bernardo put himself in front of her. She tried to push past him, but he jumped backwards and kept ahead. He stared into her face, pretended to be startled by the defiance he saw there but began to believe she was serious.

'Don't act the fool,' she said irritably.

'What's the matter? You look ready to eat someone. I hope it won't be me.'

'Perhaps.'

'I can see we're going to have a very pleasant walk.'

'If you don't want to . . . '

'You invited me.'

They continued in silence for a while, Bernardo puzzled, his agreeable surprise at her original temerity challenged by her now aggressive responses. He recalled that he hadn't noticed her at the mass or among any of the families afterwards.

'Who did you come with?' he asked.

'Nobody.'

'You came alone! From Quintera! How did you get here?'

'On my feet.'

'It's a long way. And now you want to walk more? Why don't we stop for a while?'

'You're tired already?'

'No, but you must be.'

Elvira tossed her head. It was a habit of hers, as Bernardo was to learn. She had so much hair, thick and wiry. At the moment, it was tied with a black velvet ribbon, but when it was loose, it hung heavy about her, and she would shake it back with defiance in the gesture.

They were silent again. Bernardo found it difficult to talk to her. She almost bit off his words before he could finish them and replied with such finality that he was left with nothing to say. He decided to wait for her to open the next conversation and walked a few paces ahead as if he'd forgotten her, alternately surveying the sky and the empty, stone-strewn countryside around them while wondering how far she might let him go if he could break down her resistance. He couldn't make up his mind about her at all.

At last, they reached their destination, and Elvira dropped into the shadow of the rock with a groan.

'I can't walk another step,' she sighed.

Bernardo sat down beside her, and she immediately jumped to her feet.

'What's the matter? What do you suppose I'm going to do to you?'

'We're a long way away,' she said.

'You agreed to it.'

Elvira suddenly looked anxious. She stared about her and saw that there was nothing but boulders and empty plains stretching to the horizon. The monastery was nowhere in sight. Not even a bird seemed to be within hearing. All her boldness vanished. A chill wind was getting up, adding to her sudden fear.

'We'd better go back,' she said, rubbing her bare arms and hugging herself.

'So soon? You can if you like, but I'm staying here. This soldier confesses himself defeated,' and he stretched out comfortably.

Elvira hesitated, stared at him for a moment, tossed her head again and started walking.

'Come back,' called Bernardo, jumping to his feet. 'You must be crazy.'

She stopped but shook her head.

'Don't worry. I'm not going to touch you. Come and sit down for a while and tell me what's the matter. Why did you come to the pilgrimage on your own?' Another thought suddenly occurred to him. 'Have you had anything to eat?'

She shook her head again.

'You are crazy then. Utterly.'

Elvira retraced her steps and sat down again beside the rock, as far from her companion as was possible, her face turned away as she replied, 'My father wouldn't let me come on the pilgrimage because I did something he disapproved of a fortnight ago. He thinks he can treat me like a baby. But I won't let him.'

'What did you do?'

She angrily exploded, 'I let some boy carry the water-jar back home for me. He was saying stupid things to me, like you all do, and I was listening. I didn't know my father was watching, but even so, I wasn't doing anything bad. He acted as if I were about to yield everything and called me a hussy. I could have killed him. He made me feel as though I really had been doing something wrong.'

'Now I understand,' said Bernardo with a grin. 'You decided that this afternoon you would behave like a hussy to get your own back, only you got cold feet at the last moment.'

Elvira would not meet his laughing eyes. She was ashamed of herself and still afraid. She had never been so completely alone with a person of the opposite sex before, and the memory of her mother's warnings filled her with alarm.

'We'd better go back,' she said. 'It'll be getting dark.'

'Where shall we go back to? The monastery?'

'No. My father will see me.'

'Shall I take you home?'

'I can go by myself.'

'You still don't trust me? I can guess what your mother's told you. Look, why don't we stay a bit longer? You must be tired, and we've only just arrived. I don't even know who you are.'

'My father is Faustino Martínez.'

'Fidel's sister?' Bernardo hadn't expected that.

'Yes, Fidel's sister. And you are Bernardo, the doctor's son. The soldier.'

'I'm not really a soldier. Only for another few months.'

'And I'm not really a hussy,' she said.

III

They stayed talking in the shadow of the boulder until the sky grew dark, illuminated only by the fading sunset. Bernardo was captivated by the girl's vivacity and her independent spirit. Physically she was more refined by far than the average village girl, perhaps a bit thin, but her features were alive and eager, though her manner—now that she was no longer afraid—was less aggressive. And Elvira was attracted by Bernardo's friendliness, which she could sense was now entirely innocent. He wasn't handsome, like his friend Cándido for instance, but his features were honest, and his eyes were serious as he listened to her complaints about her life with her father.

At last, they rose to go. Elvira was shivering, for she had come in a short-sleeved dress, and the night was cold. He offered her his jacket, but she shook her head.

'They'll be dancing now,' she said, staring in the direction of the monastery.

'And with a big fire probably. Shall we go there?'

'My father might see us. I'd better go home.'

They began walking in the direction of Quintera, not speaking. Bernardo suddenly broke the silence, softly reciting, *'In the darkness of a night, Love's longings reaching to great height—O venture of delight—I went out by all unseen, The house asleep where I had been.'*

'What's that?' said Elvira sharply, somewhat disturbed.

'It's a love poem.'

'I didn't know you made up poetry.'

'I don't. I only remember it. That was San Juan de la Cruz.'

'And how does it continue?'

Bernardo recited the whole poem, and Elvira wished she hadn't asked. She blushed in the darkness and hoped that Bernardo wouldn't think she already knew the words and had asked him on purpose to recite them.

They covered the rest of the distance with little conversation. Elvira couldn't forget the poem and was no longer comfortable in Bernardo's presence. He didn't touch her or come too close, and for that she was glad, but she was happier still when the village was reached, and she told Bernardo he need go no farther.

'Someone might see us together and tell my father.'

'They're all at the pilgrimage.'

'You don't know. Please don't come any farther. I must hurry.'

Bernardo didn't argue. He could see that she was in earnest. He wished her good night and let her run ahead, losing herself among the shadows of the narrow street almost immediately. He had wanted to kiss her but decided not to try.

IV

Bernardo and Elvira saw nothing of each other in ten months. The former returned to barracks at the end of the week, and on the odd occasions that he came home for a day or two, he found no opportunity to see Elvira, although he did think of her from time to time. She wasn't easy to forget.

Helen Griffiths | 29

Elvira thought of Bernardo more. Her life in Quintera was so narrow, so strictly governed, and so uneventful that her only escape from it was in daydreams, and her daydreams were of marriage to a man handsome, kind and wealthy. She knew that in the end, she would be like everyone else and make do with what she could get, but in Quintera, she could find no young man that appealed to her.

She was seventeen when she first met Bernardo, not ready to be thinking of marriage seriously but old enough to be thinking of a man romantically. Until now, the prince of her dreams was only shadowy in features, sharing the characteristics of whatever romantic hero was known to her and very similar to that of all her friends as they shared the same cheap stories.

But after her adventure at the pilgrimage, her prince began to take on Bernardo's features, his dark wavy hair, his clear grey eyes, his Roman-blunt features and sun-browned skin. She imagined him more handsome than he was; she knew that he was kind. If only he had gone to Madrid to become a lawyer instead of his brother! But she knew he was poor by her family's standards, even though he was the doctor's son, and that if she wanted the life she dreamed of, it would be no good marrying Bernardo.

Her sister Sole was engaged to marry a grocer in Burgos, a man that her father did business with, and she asked her if she were in love with him.

'Well, he's nice,' she hedged. 'He's quite good looking.'

'He's a lot older than you.'

'Only eight years.'

'But will you be happy with him? Do you want to marry him?'

'It's better than marrying someone in Quintera. At least I shall live in Burgos, not this dead hole. I shall have a decent home, with water and a bathroom. We're going to buy lots of furniture. It'll be very exciting.'

'But do you love him?' insisted Elvira, wanting to put her own conscience at rest.

'I suppose so. He's a bit of a bore sometimes, but I shall get used to him.'

She seemed quite contented, but Elvira knew that she didn't love him, at least not as she imagined a woman should love a man, as she wanted to one day. But then she thought of spending a lifetime in Quintera, like her other sisters, married to a neighbour's son, never knowing what existed outside the village, and she knew she would do the same as Sole if the chance presented itself. She could dream about Bernardo, but she would marry someone with better prospects. So she decided when she was seventeen.

She was eighteen when she met him again. He was no longer a soldier with a uniform to make him more attractive. He had gone back to being a carpenter and a dreamer, and she met him by accident on Quintera's market day. He had brought some kitchen chairs to sell and various other wares; she had come from curiosity and was alone.

'What! Have you escaped again?' Bernardo greeted her with a grin. 'You seem to make a habit of it.'

'No, this time I have permission.'

They stared silently at one another for a few moments, Bernardo agreeably surprised to discover the girl again, who seemed more attractive, with dark eyes warmer than he remembered. Elvira was suddenly shy. She recalled the evening they had walked home together, so close in the darkness, and that poem between them whose words she didn't remember but whose sensuality she couldn't forget, and she was faced with her dream prince in reality.

'How about another walk?' suggested Bernardo at last.

'No, no. I can't. I must go home soon.'

'But not just yet.'

He tried to keep her with trivial questions and remarks, but she grew anxious, knowing that eyes would be watching them, neighbours who had nothing to do but gossip, and her father would soon learn that she had been in conversation with a man from Los Pinos. Bernardo tried to make her promise to see him again, but she would do no such thing. He attracted her in a way she couldn't define, and she was almost afraid of him.

'I must go,' she said shortly. 'I can't stay any longer. My mother will be wondering where I am.'

She looked about, pushing her hair back from her face, which that day hung loose and fell thickly over her shoulders.

'People are watching us.'

'And so? What does it matter?'

'My father . . . If he finds out . . . I must go. Goodbye.'

She went hurriedly, pushing her way through the crowd, again disappearing quickly. Bernardo tried to keep track of her but lost her suddenly behind a mule. He thought of her hair, so thick and black, and for a while, thought of nothing else.

V

Sometimes they saw one another in church, sometimes on a market day, but she deliberately kept her distance while somehow seeming to draw his glances. Her brother Gustavo went to Madrid on business for his father, and he took with him a cradle that Bernardo had made for one of his nephews. Elvira saw the cradle. She thought of Bernardo working on it, imagining his cheerful face serious for once. She smoothed her fingers over it, thinking of his hands on the wood, and when Gustavo took it away, she felt as though it was something of hers that he had taken.

Two years after they first met, they danced together at the pilgrimage. Bernardo tried to persuade Elvira to come away with him for a while, but she refused. She danced with several partners that evening and had little conversation with any of them. Her mother and a sister were watching her. She had to behave with propriety, which meant that she must only dance with persons her father would approve of. She was cross with Bernardo for insisting that she dance with him. She knew she wanted to but was afraid of her father's censure. She discouraged his conversation, kept him as distant as possible and hurried into the arms of another before he could ask her to dance again.

After the fiesta of Corpus Christi, with the bull caping, another dance was held, and this time Bernardo was determined that

Elvira shouldn't escape him. Perhaps her interest in him was negligible, but after each occasional meeting, he found himself thinking more of the lively creature who encouraged but eluded him. She was among a group of gaily dressed, giggling companions, surrounded by an outer circle of youths whose compliments were resulting in so many giggles. Bernardo pushed his way through them, grabbed Elvira firmly and dragged her away from her friends. There were startled squeals from the girls, laughter and bawdy remarks from the youths, and Elvira was very angry.

'What do you think you're doing? Let me go.'

'Not until you promise to dance with me for at least an hour.'

'I shan't do anything of the sort.'

She dragged her arm free and rubbed her wrist. 'I didn't know you were as much a brute as the rest,' she complained.

'That's your fault for being so tantalising. Why must you stick yourself with such a silly crowd when you know I'm longing to talk to you? Do you detest me so much that you won't even dance once with me?'

'Let's go somewhere else to talk. Everyone's watching us.'

They moved away from the press of people and slipped between the farm carts that still lined the square, and stood in the shadows to talk. Other couples had found their way there already and were close together. Elvira kept at a distance so that he shouldn't mistake her reason for following him, but her anger was dying, for it was rather exciting to do something bold.

'Well?' demanded Elvira, pretending an annoyance she did not feel. 'What do you want?'

'I want to talk to you and dance with you. I want to tell you that your hair is beautiful—you've never let me tell you so, and it is.'

Elvira laughed. 'If you think you're the first one to tell me that!'

'Perhaps not, but it's true. And none of the others means it as I do.'

'How do you know?'

'Because . . . ' Bernardo hesitated. The shadows, the other couples, Elvira's taunting closeness, so near and yet so untouchable, made him lose his head a little. 'Because I love you,' he said at last.

Elvira was too surprised to think of a suitable reply. She had been ready to make fun of him again, but what had started as a light adventure had become more serious than she could have supposed.

'We'd better go back,' was her only comment. 'They'll be missing us.'

Bernardo shook his head chidingly. 'You're always the same, always anxious to run away. You still don't trust me.'

'How can you love me when you hardly know me? It's silly.'

'Perhaps, but it's true.'

'You only say it because you want me to dance with you.'

'And will you?'

Elvira looked at Bernardo. She didn't know whether to take him seriously or not. It was difficult to decipher the expression on his face, half-hidden in the darkness. His voice seemed a little strained, but it might not have been because he loved her. He had not attempted to kiss her, but she knew he wanted to.

'All right. I'll dance with you. But only because you force me to. I've plenty of other fellows to dance with, don't think I've not.'

'But you've only one who loves you.'

Elvira gave a snort of contempt. 'A lot of good your love would do me!' and she moved away, escaping from the shadows to the crowd again, the music catching at her heart and feet. She turned to Bernardo to dance with him, her eyes a little mocking but not unkind.

He tried to hold her close, but she wriggled away.

'My parents are watching,' she warned him.

He tried to tell her that she was beautiful, but she scorned his remarks. At last, he remained silent and as distant as she had wanted, and Elvira was disappointed and wanted him to be closer. She was afraid that perhaps he didn't love her after all. He danced very correctly and didn't even speak.

'What are you thinking about?' she asked at last.

'You.'

She waited for more, but he said nothing. The dance ended, and she expected him to drag her into the next. But he dropped his arms, thanked her and left her standing astonished and bewildered in the middle of the plaza as the music started up again. She saw him take hold of another girl. He said something to her, and she laughed. They began to dance, indecently close, and even as she watched, an unattached fellow of Quintera grabbed Elvira and forced her into the first few steps. She tore herself angrily away and ran from the crowd. She hid herself in the shadow of the carts, where no one she knew could see her, and she caught a glimpse of Bernardo now and again as he danced first with one and then with another.

Elvira was very, very angry. Some other sentiment troubled her, too, but she couldn't define it. She didn't know why she should be so annoyed if Bernardo chose to dance with someone else. After all, she hadn't wanted to dance with him. But he had said that he loved her, and if it were true, he couldn't have left her as he did to make himself so popular with other girls. Elvira knew that she was angry because she had believed him.

The evening was danced away, and gradually the villagers began to make their way back to their respective homes. There were fewer girls about now, called home by their parents, and the young men were gathering into groups, laughing loudly, singing and generally acting the fool. Elvira had kept away from her family, longing for an opportunity to talk to Bernardo again, waiting until now when the dancing was petering out, and there was nothing left to do. She moved about in the shadows, behind the remaining carts, evading any who might be looking for her, and kept a watch on Bernardo's movements, catching him at last when he flopped down alone at one of the tavern tables set out in the square.

'Bernardo,' she called and beckoned to him.

He came at once, but whatever he might have felt for her, he kept disguised. She saw only his usual friendly face and could read no particular emotion into it.

'What do you want?'

'How could you leave me like that?' she began. 'I think you're the most awful person I've ever known.'

'That's why I left you because I knew what you thought of me.'

'You're no better than the rest,' she declaimed bitterly.

'Did you expect me to be?'

'Yes. After what you said . . . '

Bernardo laughed. 'You didn't believe it?'

'No, of course, I didn't believe it.'

'Then what's the matter?'

'Why didn't you dance with me?'

'I thought you didn't want me to.'

Elvira wailed, 'And now there are no more dances for ages.'

Bernardo pulled her more into the shadows and kissed her.

VI

For some time, their only opportunity to speak to each other was at the market where, if they were observed, not much significance would be given to their brief exchanges of conversation. Elvira lingered about with various pretences, came and went, snatched a few more words while Bernardo patiently stayed in his place, hardly caring if he sold anything or got any commissions, delighting in this way of passing the time.

If there had been anything meaningful in his first kiss, they both dismissed it, she because she knew her father would never approve of their relationship, and also because she had considered it more a kind of trophy she had won while conceding nothing; he because, although he had declared that he loved her, he wasn't sure if the feeling that had stirred him then was anything more than the impulse of the moment, after an evening of drinking and dancing, and he wasn't willing to repeat the declaration unless it was true. He was very aware that a casual relationship with this desirable yet tantalizing creature was out of the question. Elvira was a respectable girl with an influential father, and she was too innocent, anyway, for him to take advantage of her, but who could resist responding to her coquetry?

He knew she was playing with him, but he enjoyed the game, contenting himself with teasing her in a brotherly fashion, determined to provoke that haughty toss of the head which had at first attracted him and was now beginning to bewitch him. When finally, one market day, he persuaded her with many promises that he would do no more than hold her hand if they found an opportunity to slip away from the crowd, Elvira couldn't resist. Instinct told her that she was playing with fire by doing something quite forbidden, but the desire to break free from the narrowness of her daily life was stronger than any fear of the consequences. So they separately found their way beyond the last houses on the other side of the village where no one could see them and where Bernardo, as promised, only took her hand.

A flame seemed to scorch through her whole body at that instant, making her want to melt into him. It so shocked and frightened her that she immediately dragged herself free, snapping, 'Don't touch me or I shan't stay!' and he put up his hands in merry surrender, willing to obey because he was certain now that one day she would be his if he wanted her.

From then on, they found opportunities to meet, though not very frequently. Although it was a handicap, distance of itself would not have kept them apart, for Bernardo would happily walk the ten miles to Quintera and back for the chance of a kiss or two and the hope of sinking his face into her hair. But Elvira, for all the fire in her eyes and the quickness of her blood, remained determinedly cool towards him and put limits to the number of times she was willing to risk being in his company and for how long. She could only find so many excuses for being absent from home, but the challenge was irresistible. At long last, there was some excitement in her life, something to look forward to!

She knew what boundaries she had set for herself, regardless of others she had already broken, and had no intention of going beyond them. When she felt him growing too friendly, she would pick a quarrel, her defence from his amorous approaches being in sharp words and mockery. She was afraid to encourage him in anything but the mildest flirtation while not knowing how she could keep him from losing interest in her, unaware that her inner conflict was for Bernardo a major part of her attraction.

However, what he had unthinkingly responded to as little more than a light-hearted flirtation had deceptively and imperceptibly become something different, at least for him. Before he realized it, before he had time to draw back, he found himself caught in an inescapable web of desire and restraint. Each time he saw her, he wanted her more, but this wanting had somehow grown beyond the mere physical into a deeper and more profound longing to possess her completely, to make everything that she was his own. His physical need warred with his romantic nature, nurtured on the literature that shaped his ideals and emotions, and he was as much challenged by conflict as she was, the difference being that he was aware of hers, but she not of his.

And in this, she had the advantage. Her desire for him was coquettish, self-centred and contradictory, and she could satisfy it by letting fly with that wild temper of hers, the fire in her body transformed into sharp arrows of hostility. His only defence was his incorrigible good nature and a willingness to accept her rebukes. Until he was ready to marry her and she had given her consent, he had no right to lay claim to her.

Placid by nature himself, her vivacity and unpredictability both fascinated and disconcerted him. As a boy, he used to catch butterflies, patiently waiting for their flutterings in his cupped hands to cease so that he could examine them more closely. Experience had taught him how fragile they were, how easily damaged, but the wonder of having something so delicate and beautiful just resting quietly on his palm although it was free to fly off remained in his memory.

Elvira was like a butterfly, dancing around him, tantalising, full of colour and fascination, afraid of the hands that reached out to her and yet unwilling to withdraw from danger. And when she let herself be caught, just for a moment, he was flooded with delight as well as desire.

These moments were always brief, for she was as quickly alarmed by her own feelings as by his. The Church's teaching on the duties and restraints of procreation had been well instilled, making no allowances for the flesh outside of marriage, nor even within it for a true Catholic, and she was less free than the butterfly that followed its God-given instincts; less free perhaps than a labourer's daughter whose expectations were more limited and more easily satisfied. Bernardo understood all this and didn't want to hurt her. But the mixture of tenderness and desire was a heady one, not always easy to control.

She liked it best, and it was safer for both of them, when he told her stories. He knew or invented so many tales that were funny, scary or romantic and filled her hungry mind with colourful dreams, and she would sit with her back against the outside wall of the cemetery where no one was likely to pass, and whose tall trees threw a protecting shadow across them, he a respectable arm's length away, she living every moment, quite forgetting that the person who told her the stories was Bernardo. He was no more than a voice that stirred her imagination and her senses, like someone on the radio. Her heroes were those of the novelettes she devoured and shared with her friends, along with daily serials she faithfully listened to on her father's radio, but more and more, these unreal characters began to merge into Bernardo.

Poetry she was slower to appreciate. She liked Bernardo's voice, and he recited well. Machado's haunting ballad of the brothers who murdered their father was a favourite which she demanded again and again, but she had not yet experienced the passionate emotions expressed by Bequer and others. They made her feel uncomfortable; unlike the stories, they affected her in a way that she felt to be dangerous, threatening her confidence that she could keep Bernardo's growing desire for her at bay. So she eagerly agreed when one day he offered to read *Don Quijote* to her, knowing it was a very long book.

'A hundred and twenty-six chapters,' he told her. 'I shall get tired if I don't get a reward.'

After some lively argument, she agreed she would give him a kiss in exchange for each chapter, calculating that he could hardly read through more than three at any one time. She didn't reckon on his blatant cheating. After the first session, the chapters not only got shorter and shorter, but he insisted that she had misunderstood the agreement. What was meant was that the number of kisses related to the chapter number, six for chapter six, seven for chapter seven and so on. This gave rise to lengthy analysis and debate—what kind of kiss, just a peck on the cheek, for example, sisterly fashion (Elvira's choice) to Bernardo's much bolder suggestion which earned him a slap. And so on … Between arguing and demonstrating length, intensity and location, *Don Quijote* was forgotten until Elvira decided that it was time to go home and that she didn't want any more chapters.

'If you married me,' he suggested, 'you could hear the whole story, and we could kiss and cuddle between chapters all night long.'

'And I could read the book for myself without having to spend the rest of my life with you,' was her caustic reply. 'I want more than that from a husband.'

'It's all that I have,' he said, 'a whole sea of love but nothing else. I know you'd like it once you tried it.'

'You're disgusting!' she exclaimed and ran off, suffused with a sense of shame. He didn't follow her, but she filled his thoughts all the way back to Los Pinos.

In spite of her upbringing and her general ignorance, she had an inquisitive mind, and it amused him to find out how much nonsense she would believe just because he said it was true. But old customs, superstitions and religious traditions were too firmly embedded to be easily dislodged. When he told her she was an old-fashioned reactionary and not fit to be a member of the new republic, she retorted that a king was more romantic than a president, and she hoped that one day the king would come back.

'My father says he will,' she insisted when he said he thought it unlikely. 'I heard him say so. He hates the Republic. Do you?'

'Why should I? Unlike your father, I have nothing to lose. And nothing to gain, either,' he added with a laugh.

'But don't you wish you had more?' she urged crossly for, as a prospective husband, he had little to offer.

'I wish I had more of you,' was his instant response, reaching for her hand to pull her close, but she swirled away, exclaiming, 'Animal!' a favourite insult which, whether she realized it or not, had more sensuality in it than rebuke, and usually resulted in a kiss to which she surrendered with pretended reluctance.

One day she asked what being a soldier had been like. Had he ever had to kill someone? And he told her about peeling thousands of potatoes, parades, sentry duties, endless paperwork, his adventures and misadventures with a typewriter which had seemed to take a dislike to him, along with the aching boredom of it all and the longing to be home.

'What about girls?' she asked. 'They say soldiers have lots of girls.'

'Decent girls don't ask such questions,' he jokingly rebuked her, 'but if you give me a kiss, I'll tell you whatever you want to know.'

'You're shameless,' she spat at him, suddenly hostile because she found herself on dangerous ground. She wanted to know, as curious as any young woman shut out of a man's world, and how could she find out if he didn't tell her? But his words burned, though he hadn't meant them to, because she felt the weight of the guilt of ignorance with its corresponding desire to know. Perhaps he would tell her in exchange for a kiss, but … She was having trouble enough already at confession without adding to her sins.

Sensing her troubled mind, Bernardo mollified her by describing the bookshop in Burgos he had come across whose owner, Don Jacinto, was happy to let his customers read his books when he knew they couldn't afford to buy them and through whom he discovered new poets and writers. Don Jacinto had invited him to join his literary circle, which met in a large café just a few doors down where, in spite of the tensions this sometimes provoked, only literature was discussed and politics were banned. This place was his home from home, his main consolation, where he could sit for hours with one of Don Jacinto's books or enthusiastically discuss his passion with like-minded men, some of whom were writers and poets, others just lovers of words like himself. It was the only thing he missed from his army days.

'And is that all you ever did?' she persisted, not really interested in his literary pursuits. 'I don't believe you.'

She had recovered from her initial humiliation and was still angry with him. She was always ready to quarrel, and he enjoyed annoying her, just to see the fire in her eyes, followed by that imperious toss of her head.

'Well, let's see then,' he began, screwing up his brows as if making a tremendous effort to remember. 'The first was . . . No, I can't remember her name. But the second was definitely called Amalia, or was it Eulalia? Then there were several Mari this and Mari that and—'

'You're a big liar!' she interrupted him furiously.

Then, unable to resist the merriment in his eyes, she held out her hands to him as a sign of peace, but even as he stretched out his own to take hold of them, with a saucy toss of her head, she swiftly turned away and ran off, laughing. He didn't immediately chase after her as she had expected, so she stopped and looked back, disappointed. He was standing where she had left him, lost in thought.

What would happen if he told her about Claudia? It was one thing to rag her about non-existent encounters which, after some sanctimonious hostility, she might well accept as the norm, the making-up afterwards being a delight to look forward to. He enjoyed her provocative little games, aware of the fire that simmered beneath the fear-ridden surface, but he wasn't certain enough of her feelings for him to be totally honest with her just then. Men only talked explicitly about women among themselves, and certainly not with a serious girlfriend. So he decided he couldn't tell her about Claudia, who had flagrantly seduced him, inviting him to share her bed whenever he had a weekend pass.

Although most of the regulars in Don Jacinto's literary circle considered themselves to have broken away from their traditional conservative background, none of them really knew what to make of this flamboyant woman who imposed herself on them and whose lifestyle seemed to them as surreal as her poetry. They admired and despised her. She embarrassed and tantalized them. Those who propositioned her, she snubbed. Those whom she propositioned rarely resisted. Bernardo was one of them, his attitude being, 'Why reject her generous offer?'

He had no appetite for the kind of woman he could afford on his pitiful pay, but with his very limited experience of the opposite sex, he didn't know how to classify Claudia. He had never come across a woman who sat and argued among men as their equal, chain-smoked and drank. She was neither a decent woman nor yet a whore. He paid for an evening meal for them both. She gave him his breakfast. It was a purely physical relationship. Neither of them talked or thought about poetry when they were in bed. She was at least ten years his senior, and although he had enjoyed the experience while it lasted, he wasn't sorry when it ended and easily let it go.

'You can't catch me!' Elvira taunted defiantly, breaking in on his thoughts when he didn't move.

She radiated desire, wanting to be chased. Did she really understand just how seductive she was? Was she able to distinguish between flirtation and love, he wondered as he called back, 'That's what you think. And when I do catch you, I'm going to eat you up with kisses. You've been warned!'

She squealed and started running again, not looking back, and he did chase her and catch her and kiss her with rising passion, and then very reluctantly but with determination told her to go home.

VII

The whole summer of 1934 went by in this in this fashion, when Elvira was nineteen and Bernardo twenty-four, and it was only a matter of time before they were seen together by this one and that one and gossip began, light remarks dropped here, an exclamation there, until there was hardly anyone unaware of the fact that Bernardo and Elvira were spending time alone with one another. When their respective families became aware of the association, neither of them was happy about it. Faustino Martínez was determined to put a stop to it. He didn't know how they had come to meet, but someone told him that they had been seen wandering hand in hand in the fields, and he himself saw them dancing together at the various fiestas.

He wrote a letter to Dr. de Rosas, preferring to keep the matter private rather than confront him in the casino, suggesting that his son should desist from his attentions to Elvira, for as far as he could recall, the people of Los Pinos and Quintera had never intermarried. The surnames found in Quintera did not exist in Los Pinos. They were two different peoples, and in the opinion of Faustino Martínez should always remain so. It happened, however, that some twelve years earlier, two youngsters from the different villages fell in love. At least, Martínez knew that the girl of Quintera was serious in the affair, though the lad from Los Pinos was only out to enjoy himself. He got the girl into trouble and refused to marry her. There was a terrible scandal. The girl's reputation was completely marred, and she'd had to leave Quintera. Martínez didn't want that to happen to Elvira, and he wrote to the doctor because he feared it would. He knew there could never be a marriage between the two villages, he knew there could only be a scandal, and he hoped that between himself and the doctor, they could avert it. The doctor did not reply, and the grocer was very annoyed.

He was a man of below-average height, dark, unprepossessing in his looks and with ungenerous eyes. In his youth, he had suffered for being the dwarf among his Viking-like brothers, the runt of the family, his despotic character rooted in the sense of inferiority that had grown with him since infancy. As soon as he realized that money meant power and that he had a seemingly natural talent for making it, he took advantage of every opportunity that came his way.

Patiently, quietly and with a dogged and ruthless determination, he began to accumulate some capital, but fortune really smiled on him when he met Eugenia in Aranda, where he was living at the time. She and her brother had been orphaned in early childhood and interned with nuns by an only relative unable to take care of them. A small inheritance was due to them on reaching adulthood, although in Eugenia's case, she would have to wait until she was twenty-five unless she married sooner. The brother, a reckless and headstrong sort of man whose character Elvira must have inherited in her father's opinion because the sister was a mouse, emigrated to America, leaving the sixteen-year-old girl to Faustino's care. He had done well by investing in a couple of Faustino's ventures, so it wasn't too difficult for him to believe that Eugenia would be safe with him.

Although he didn't love her, he felt a kind of affection for her at first and was grateful for her money. She was reasonably attractive and well-trained by her convent upbringing to be submissive and obedient. Knowing nothing of the world, she was the first person to respect and fear him, totally dependent on him and easily persuaded to surrender her inheritance to his keeping. He brought her back to Quintera, to his father's small general store, preferring to be a big fish in a small pond, and it was only a question of time before his acute business acumen began to produce results.

His arrogance grew with his success but so did his contempt for his wife's meek and scurrying ways. He hardly noticed that he treated her more like a servant than a wife, and her almost constant pregnancies were an irritant even while his growing brood occasioned him pride. Of the seven who survived to adulthood, only Fidel and Elvira gave him grief.

The doctor's seeming slight by not responding to the letter put him in a towering rage. 'I can't believe that he's forgotten it,' he exploded to his wife. 'He's just completely ignored it for all that I used most generous terms. I wouldn't be surprised if he even encourages his son. She would be a good catch for him.'

Faustino could not forget the doctor's attitude to the previous case, that of amused indifference, and therefore he was uneasy when he learned that the son of such a man should be going about with his daughter, creating gossip. He deprecated his general attitude, the politics expressed in his refusal to wear a collar and tie, his contempt for the church. He accepted that the doctor was a person of equal standing with himself in the two communities and that his competence and dedication could not be denied. Doctor, surgeon, apothecary, even a veterinary at times, he was rarely idle. He had been called in the middle of the night to deliver Elvira and had willed life into her when all had given both mother and child up for dead. He had previously advised the grocer and his wife to have no more children.

'Your wife's finished for breeding,' he had said roughly and had come in a very bad-tempered fashion to save her life and the child's, accusing him of being worse than an animal with no consideration for his wife.

'Look at this thing,' he growled, pointing at the squalling, blue-faced baby. 'A runt, fit for nothing, and its mother with an empty breast. How do you expect it to survive?'

But still mourning the loss of three sons during the smallpox epidemic, Martínez welcomed Elvira in spite of the doctor's warning. They had done their best, with all the attentions that money could buy. She grew into a pretty child and an attractive young woman, but with the years, she grew defiant, too. Eugenia said that if she hadn't been born with a spirit of defiance, she would never have lived. Sometimes he wished she hadn't. She was so obviously sent as a trial to him. Along with her father's strictures and narrow upbringing, she had always had everything she wanted. She had been extravagantly indulged by him in her early years, but when the childhood tantrums grew into violent outbursts, he was at first bewildered and then both offended and deeply humiliated. She seemed possessed of a devil when in a rage, and sometimes Martínez felt that she hated him in spite of his best and sacrificial efforts to guide her into godly ways. She and Fidel were the bane of his life, a cross he had to bear, but he couldn't understand why he should be so afflicted.

Knowing Elvira's character, Martínez was certain that he would need the doctor's help if he were ever to keep the pair apart. He was sure that Bernardo was the weaker of the two and that if pressure were brought to bear on him, he would renounce her. His main reason for objecting to the match he kept to himself.

He could not forget the memory of a sunny evening some eight years earlier when Fidel had come home, his shirt splattered by blood which had fallen from a split lip and a dislodged tooth, almost hysterical when his father began to question him.

'What's happened? Who's done this to you? I want to know.'

'It's nothing. Leave me alone. I don't want to talk about it.'

'But I do,' and at his father's insistence, terrified by the hand which lifted threateningly, he broke down and began to sob.

'It was Bernardo, the doctor's son. He did it.'

'Why?'

Fidel averted his eyes. He couldn't face his father's wrath with the agony of that incident still burning deeply within him.

'Out with it. What have you been up to?'

'He, he . . . '

'He what?'

'He wanted to . . . He wanted me to . . . to do indecent things with him, and when I wouldn't, he hit me.'

'My God, if this is true, I'll, I'll . . . ' He stopped, doubting even as he raged. 'Get out of my sight, miserable thing,' he shouted at Fidel, 'and don't let me see you in any trouble again.'

He grabbed the boy by his shirt, buffeted him about the head, then threw him to one side. Fidel scrambled away, blubbering like a child, and looked for his mother to clean his swollen face.

The grocer withheld his desire to denounce Bernardo, afraid to start delving into something whose outcome he couldn't ascertain.

He had to let the matter lie, knowing how people spoke of Fidel, believing him only because it was better than disbelieving. Knowing that a certain something had passed between the two lads that day, he could never hear mention of the doctor's son without a sense of nausea striking him. Maybe the two boys had done things together—they were always in each other's company—and to think that Bernardo might now be encouraging Elvira to similar things was something he could never tolerate. Any man under the sun, but not Bernardo.

VIII

Some weeks after sending the letter, Faustino decided it was time to confront his daughter.

'Are you still seeing that fellow from Los Pinos?' he began.

'I see him when he comes to Mass here, Papa,' she responded as lightly as she could, wanting to deflect his icy mood with pretended nonchalance, which instead he took to be insolence.

'You also see him in the market and go about the fields with him like a whore. Everyone's talking about you. I won't have it. That a daughter of mine should be so shameless!'

'We don't do anything wrong,' she protested.

'Wrong!' he shouted. 'Just being alone with him is wrong.'

'We only talk. I've no one else to talk to. He tells me stories, and he makes me laugh.'

'If you don't care what people are saying, I do. There'll be no more of it.'

'I'll not stop seeing him. You can't make me.' Defiance made her recklessly continue, 'I love him, and I want to marry him.'

'Has he asked you?'

'Not yet, but he will.'

'Don't be so sure. What has he asked you?'

Elvira creased her dark eyebrows into a frown, pretending puzzlement. She did not answer.

'Has he tried to make love to you? Tell me.'

Martínez saw the stubbornness creeping across her face, her lips tightening, her eyes growing hard. She had the same expression now as she'd had at two years old, and his sense of impotence when thus confronted goaded him beyond endurance. Again he demanded, 'Has he tried to make love to you?'

'You're not Father González to ask me such things, and I wouldn't even tell him.'

She gasped as her father hit her across the mouth and was dazed for a moment.

'I'm your father,' he shouted. 'You'll tell me everything I want to know and do everything I tell you. There'll be no more sneaking away, and if I ever hear of you being seen alone with him again, I won't even let you out of the house.'

'Do you think that will stop me wanting him?' she retorted wildly, looking at him with hate-filled eyes.

'Perhaps not, but it might well cool his ardour for you.'

He heard her sobbing in her room that night and was satisfied. He was determined to control that wild spirit of hers whatever the cost, and he decided to look about for a suitable husband for her. When one wishes to take a dangerous toy from a child, finding another to replace it helps to avoid screams and tantrums. Elvira was a young woman now and probably feeling the need of a man. He would supply her with one, as he had with her sisters, and within a couple of years, with a child and a home as well as a husband to care for, she would probably be content, her longings satisfied, her turbulent spirit properly controlled. He didn't think he would have any difficulty in arranging a match as she was an attractive girl, with a spirit that any man would enjoy wrestling into obedience and a reasonable dowry to make up for any shortcomings of character.

Jaime Segundo was not married. He farmed chickens on the outskirts of Quintera and had a monopoly in eggs, chicks and table birds for miles around and as far as Aranda. He would make a very useful son-in-law and was not unattractive either, although he was nearing forty. Of course, he was a lot older than Elvira, but Martinez considered that an advantage, if anything. A young man would never teach her to respect him, and Elvira had not yet learned to respect anyone, not even her father, though that was due to her inherent defiance rather than through lack of encouragement on his part.

If she didn't like Jaime Segundo, there was a younger fellow whose father owned the only transport service which connected the villages with each other and the nearest towns. He was a man of prospects and good temper, and an amalgamation with him might eventually help the grocer reduce transport costs or open up a new line of business.

He gave Elvira the choice, and she turned them down. He invited first the poultryman and then the other to see her, but neither of them made sufficient impression upon her. At first, she even refused to acknowledge their intentions and laughed when her father suggested an alliance with either one. But secretly, she was afraid that this might be the end that awaited her, a marriage of convenience to a not particularly attractive man, and, without loving him, she clung to Bernardo as her only escape from such a fate.

'I'll marry Bernardo de Rosas or no one,' she insisted. 'Maybe my sisters and Faustino will sacrifice their lives to you, but not I. I hate anything connected with shops and taverns and chickens and buses and counting money. I want to marry for love, not sell myself to the highest bidder.'

'No one marries for love, and if they do, they soon regret it, especially a woman. Do you think your brother's happy with that common girl he married in Madrid, someone little better than a gipsy? And do you think you would be happy for long with a man who couldn't support you and the children you'd have year after year?'

'Bernardo can support me.'

'How? His father has nothing. He might be the doctor, but what money he ever had went on sending that elder son of his to university. The other hasn't even had a decent education.'

'The school in Los Pinos is as good as ours.'

'But it doesn't take a man without money very far. Even his grandfather's flocks don't come to him. His father sold his share to go to Madrid. Your Bernardo's got nothing but his hands to work with, and the job he does will never earn him more than enough for bread and chick-peas.'

'And even if we do live on bread and chickpeas, at least we'll be happy.'

'You, happy on chickpeas!' His face was contorted with scorn. 'You eat the best of everything, every day, thanks to me. You have no idea!'

She braved his ridicule, insisting, 'He's a good man, Father. I wish you'd believe it. I wouldn't waste myself on a man who wasn't worth it. He's good and kind, and he loves me,' her father's sneer provoking her to add petulantly, 'and he'll give me more than chick-peas. I know he will.'

'Bah!' he exploded but said no more, recognising the dangerous look in his daughter's eyes and leaving the room before a storm broke.

'Happiness is an elusive quality, Elvirita,' said her mother when he had gone. She had been listening in silence to the conversation, seldom voicing an opinion in her husband's presence. 'When you're weary from washing and cooking and having babies, happiness might seem a long way away. And if you look miserable and worn out, your man might start searching for more cheerful company elsewhere. Then you'll wish you had a richer man who'd give you less worries and some pretty clothes now and then.'

Elvira did not answer. It was a long speech from her mother, and she looked intently at her, suddenly seeing her life in a new light, so much child-bearing, so much work, so little comfort, and so little love. She had never seen any sign of affection between her parents. Her mother only came to life when she was outside the home. Indoors, where she spent most of her time, she was a thin and mostly silent shadow, her only pleasure the radio serials which even this her father begrudged and quickly curtailed if he happened to come in, ranting about wasting the batteries. The shock of this discovery made her all the more determined to escape the possibility of a similar fate.

Her father tried earnestly to make her change her mind, but he might have guessed that it would be useless. As she had been stubborn as a toddler over refusing to say grace or pick up a shoe she'd thrown down in a tantrum, so she was stubborn about Bernardo, regardless of the consequences. But still, he would not wash his hands of her. While she was under his roof, he was determined to do all he could to guide her wisely. If the mule will not be led, it must be forced, and he forbade Elvira any further communication with the doctor's son, hoping he might lose interest with the passing of time.

IX

A mother can be more or less certain that the girl her son first mentions at home is the girl he intends to marry. This, at least, was Dionisia's experience. Arturo wrote a letter to his mother in which he described Paquita, and a year later came another to say that they were married. They knew nothing about the wedding until, in a letter addressed from a hotel in Santander, he told them he was honeymooning with Paquita and that when opportunity permitted, he would take her to meet them.

The whole family was incredulous at the news, the neighbours too - for they all had to be told - and it was more than Dionisia could bear. She was as crushed and bewildered as a child, and the doctor ached with her hurt, for he had never seen her so distressed except for when Adriana died. Nothing would comfort her, and the doctor struggled to forgive his son for so cruelly wounding her simple heart. In her deep pride in his achievements, she had forgotten what he was like. The very day after she had first heard Paquita's name, she began to embroider her initials alongside Arturo's on the bed linen she had already put aside for a future daughter-in-law, unthinkingly expecting that they would marry in Los Pinos and spend the wedding night in the family home. It was still in the linen chest, stiff, white and smelling of rosemary.

Many a mother would have been consoled to discover that Paquita was the only child of well-to-do people, likely to have a good dowry, but all she could understand was that this son she was so proud of, and for whom all the family had made sacrifices, had blatantly rejected them.

'He's so young,' she had moaned, 'and women can be very cunning when they're out to get a man,' determined to blame the unknown Paquita for the offence. 'She put him up to it. She wants him to forget his family. We're not good enough for her. Men can be made to do anything. They only see what they want to see when they fall in love.'

'And you're forgetting what he's like. Could you really imagine Arturo falling in love?' the doctor had mused sardonically, recalling how self-contained had been this son of his since early childhood. 'Do you really think she could make him do something like this unless it suited him?'

He folded her into his arms. 'Come on, woman. Don't cry any more,' he urged, kissing and kissing her tear-stained face. 'Stop worrying. He knows what he's doing, and she's probably just the girl you'd choose for him yourself. You'll see.'

So when Bernardo one mealtime, as if casually between one mouthful and the next, asked them, 'What do you think of Don Faustino's daughter, the youngest one, Elvira?' Dionisia guessed that she was intended as her second daughter-in-law.

She had heard the gossip that they were keeping company but hadn't wanted to believe it. In the fields, in the glare of the sun and at a distance, it was easy to mistake one girl for another. Surely, it couldn't be Elvira?

'Is it true then, what they're saying?' was her troubled reply.

'Yes, Mother. And she's a decent girl, whatever people might be thinking. She's different from the rest. That's why I like her.'

'Why don't you bring her home then, so we can meet her?' she asked.

'It's too soon. She's not ready. I'm not sure what she wants.'

'And what about you, son?' asked his father. 'Are you ready? What do you want?'

'I want the moon, Father. I want the moon.' He shrugged his shoulders, adding, 'But you know how it is . . . '

They went on eating silently for a few moments until the doctor said, 'Be careful, son. Think of her reputation.'

But Bernardo would say no more just then, and they both understood that if he had spoken, it was because his heart had been captured.

'If they get married,' said Dionisia to her husband when they were alone, 'we shall have to see about finding a house for them here if they don't want to live with us.'

'It's too soon to do anything until we know what they want. They're not officially courting, or he would bring her home. We don't know it will come to marriage, and if Martínez has any say in the matter, it certainly won't.' The doctor continued dogmatically, 'Elvira's not the right girl for Bernardo. I've seen her grow up. She's stubborn and likes her own way too much. I hope Martínez wins. Bernardo's too easy-going, and Elvira will run rings round him.'

Neither of them was very keen on his choice, she mainly because Elvira was from Quintera. A girl likes to be near her family, even after she's married, and to have Bernardo living in Quintera would be almost as bad as if he were in Madrid like Arturo.

Dionisia wanted Bernardo to marry a local girl whom she could relate to and love. Elvira was good-looking, but looks didn't last, and already beginning to feel somewhat left out of her son's affections, she was hard put to think of something positive. He was really too good for that saucy girl. What was she doing, behaving the way she did, making people talk?

'At least the family is of good standing,' she conceded, trying to find something in favour of the girl her son seemed to have chosen, then adding, 'But no better than ours.' After all, if Elvira's father was addressed as 'Don,' wasn't her own husband, also?

The doctor grunted. 'If having a father with a monopoly in everything and several businesses that wouldn't bear too much looking into were enough to ensure their happiness, I'd give them both my blessing tomorrow.'

He recalled his own passion for Dionisia so many years ago and how, in spite of all his efforts, she had never been able to satisfy it, good wife though she was, and he saw himself in Bernardo and wondered if it would be the same for him. As far as he could judge, Elvira was a spoilt child and as calculating as her father. Yes, there was fire in her, but if Bernardo was like himself, he would want more than what any woman could give. He would want her very soul.

But for all that neither the doctor nor his wife approved of their son's choice for different reasons, they agreed not to oppose him. Bernardo was always slow to make up his mind about anything, and, as their relationship was still unofficial and might yet come to nothing, it was better to wait and see. However, Dionisia quietly made plans, determined that Bernardo at least would have the best wedding they could afford and that no one in Quintera would be able to find anything to criticise. Once again, she busied herself with making sheets and pillowcases, and the doctor came home one day to find her carefully ironing the pattern of her son's initials on them.

'What's the hurry?' he asked with amusement, enjoying her pleasure.

She had never learned to write, but she could embroider exquisitely.

'These things take time, and I want everything to be ready and well done. I don't want that family to put us to shame.'

'It won't be like that, woman. But don't get carried away. Nothing is certain yet.'

'But he will marry one of these days, won't he, whoever it is, and while I sew, I can think about it and have something to look forward to, even if it is Elvira in the end.'

'Well, but don't talk about it with the neighbours. There's too much gossip already.'

It wasn't gossip but the letter from Martínez which began all the trouble. Until then, Bernardo and Elvira had been seeing each other whenever the opportunity permitted, and reasonably innocently. They hadn't talked about a formal engagement or marriage, and when the doctor showed Bernardo the letter, he just laughed.

'If I want to see her, I shall,' he said, not angrily, but with the calm certainty with which he faced every setback in life.

His temper was rarely ruffled, but that didn't mean to say that he would allow himself to be pushed in any direction that he didn't choose to follow. Mainly he didn't care which way he went, taking each day as it came, but when he did, he was as stubborn as a mule.

Dionisia, listening to his response to the letter, watching the determination suddenly forming in his eyes, remembered that as a girl, she had once seen a man beat his mule almost to death because it wouldn't cross a rickety bridge. It had always been the most docile and willing of animals and never contrary, but it got it into its head that day that it wouldn't cross the bridge it had already crossed a thousand times, and it didn't. The farmer was so surprised and so furious when all the usual beatings made no difference that he started kicking and punching, throwing stones. He even broke a loose plank from the bridge and hit the mule with that, cursing all the saints in the calendar, but the mule wouldn't go over the bridge, and in the end, the farmer left it standing there and went back to the village for a drink.

She knew that Bernardo was like that mule. As willing and as docile as could be until some principle stirred him into taking a stand, and when he added that he intended to see Elvira for as long as she wanted and marry her if she would have him, his mother's heart sank. It was in the context of strife when for the first time, he talked definitely of marriage, and it seemed to her a portent of sorrows to come. Faustino Martínez was a stubborn man, too, and their fate was more or less sealed from the moment that the letter was written, as she knew that neither of them would give in.

X

The harsh Castilian winter did more to keep Elvira and Bernardo apart than any family disapproval or pressure. No one could wander about that frozen plateau, however enamoured they might be, so the talk died down, and Faustino was satisfied. It wasn't until the following year that he began to concern himself again, thinking of the forthcoming fiestas where they were bound to meet unless Elvira were strictly chaperoned or kept at home.

His severity towards her only made her the more determined to escape his tyranny. Had he been less implacable, less heartless, she might have been more docile, but he would not bear contradiction, and she would not be broken. For the first time in her life, she had found affection, someone who really cared about her, and she clung to Bernardo as she might have clung to one of her brothers had any of them ever done anything but provoke her.

Sometimes she wished he were just a brother, so afraid was she of her body's response to his look or his touch, which made her recoil even while she longed to be entrenched by his arms. She was ashamed of such feelings, though she indulged them when she was alone, ignorant of everything but the church's teaching, which was as rigid as her father's, effectively reducing the marital act to a husband's right and a wife's duty, and which she ought not to pleasurably anticipate even in her thoughts. It was all very well to whisper about these things with her equally ignorant friends, but how could she confess the sinful desire that too often drew her to Bernardo as a moth is drawn to the light? If she were married to him, it would be all right. But she was clear-headed enough to know that she wanted other things as much as she wanted Bernardo, things that he could and would make no promise to give her.

Because of and in spite of all this, she took advantage of every opportunity to escape for a couple of hours in total defiance of her mother's pleadings. She knew she wouldn't dare tell her father that she couldn't restrain her. Eugenia was almost as cowed by her daughter as by her husband. But it was mainly through letters that they kept in touch, which Elvira almost preferred because it was safer than being alone with him and more like the kind of romance that she found in her novelettes. She spent hours dreaming over his words, and parts of her replies were copied from the stories she read.

This correspondence was made possible by Bernardo's friends. Both Gerardo and Cándido were happy to be drawn into the necessary subterfuges to help the unhappy lovers. Having tired of trying to persuade him to abandon Elvira and join them in their occasional escapades, they decided to help him instead. There was little enough to entertain them, so that finding ways of secretly delivering letters to both parties was a great joke. Quintera was enemy territory, and if a man from Los Pinos could steal one of its girls, especially that particular one, daughter of one of the local big men, so much the better. In their wilder moments of hilarity, they would have been willing to kidnap her for him if he gave the word.

But if Elvira was consoled by their secret communication, Bernardo was not, and he couldn't disguise his frustration and unhappiness from his mother, who knew him so well and felt his need almost as if it were her own. Until he began to take Elvira seriously, he had been the most contented person anyone could meet, but once he gave his heart to her and determined to win hers in return, he was restless and moody, 'Like a dog with an in-season bitch about,' grunted the doctor when his wife remarked anxiously on the change in him.

She tried to make him see the senselessness of his love, especially when she both feared and hoped that it would come to nothing. She had heard that love was a painful business, but it seemed to her that after a lifetime of marriage, those that started off passionately were no more in love with each other than those that arranged a match for more material reasons. In the end, they got used to each other, and love became companionship, nothing more. She grew very fond of her husband once she married him but, thinking it over honestly, she knew that she wouldn't have minded if he hadn't married her, had there been someone else one day to take his place.

In her opinion, the most important things in marriage were for a girl to have a man who could support her and treat her with respect, while a man needed someone to take his mother's place and satisfy the animal in him at the same time.

All this she told him, ending with firm confidence, 'Love is all very well in stories, but it doesn't bring happiness, except for a little while.'

'What do you know about it, Mother?' was his impatient response.

Although she had initially agreed with her husband to leave the subject alone, she couldn't help trying to persuade Bernardo to forget Elvira, to settle with someone in Los Pinos, certain that for all he might suffer at the moment in losing her, he would be happier in the future than he could ever be with that demanding creature in Quintera. Pained by the heart-sickness he was unable to hide from her and determined to turn his attention elsewhere, she found excuses for inviting this or that neighbour to come in with a daughter for a chat round about the hour Bernardo was likely to return from work. It didn't take him long to realise what she was up to, and he told her to stop.

'You're giving them ideas, and I'm not interested in any of them. There's only one woman I want.'

'There's many a girl who would love you as much as she does, if not more,' she insisted. 'Good girls, too.'

He resented the implication expressed in the last words but held his tongue, and she went on, 'Suppose she stops loving you one day? Love doesn't always last.'

'She won't stop loving me,' he replied. 'And even if she did, I would still love her. You don't understand. For you, love is only the feeling that mothers have for their children. That's the only lasting love to you. You can't imagine anything higher than that because you've never felt it.'

'Perhaps not, but I do know that mothers always love their children, no matter what they do or become, and that love between a man and a woman can easily turn to hate. It's better to have less at the beginning than lose all later on.'

'Not for me it isn't. I'd rather have one hour in heaven and the rest of my life in hell than never taste of either.'

'You don't know what you're talking about,' she told him crossly. 'You read too much poetry. Life is on earth, not in books, and there's little romance in living together day after day, year after year, knowing everything about each other, having nothing to talk about except the neighbours and the children. You listen to what I'm telling you. I might be an ignorant woman, but I know about marriage and people's feelings, and I tell you that keeping up this passion for Elvira won't bring you anything but misery.'

<h2 style="text-align:center">XI</h2>

The summer of 1935 was altogether a worrying time for the doctor and his wife. As if Bernardo's frustration and unhappiness were not enough, Arturo suddenly decided to return to the village for a while and brought with him a sense of uncertainty and indefinable discord instead of the happiness that his parents had looked forward to.

They had talked a lot about Arturo going to Madrid. He had been only twenty at the time, and to his mother, he seemed very young to be living so far from home. It wasn't as if they had any relations there to keep an eye on him. Pedro had the addresses of a few friends he'd made while he was there, and Arturo had promised to look them up. He kept his promise, too, and within five years was married to the daughter of one of them.

They had a baby every year, all boys, and when they arrived in Los Pinos that summer, they brought the three children with them, and Paquita was expecting the fourth. They didn't stay long enough for any of them to form much of an opinion of this attractive young city woman, daughter of a surgeon. She was out of place among them though she did her best to conceal it, and Dionisia didn't really know how to treat her. She had long since forgotten her original hostility, accepting her for the children's sake, and now honestly warmed to her when she saw that she was very much in love with Arturo, who took her love for granted as he had always taken that of his mother.

Arturo was a complete stranger to them all. After some ten years away from home, with only rare letters and the infrequent week's holiday which ceased entirely after he married, the bonds which had united them had been severed completely, and he was no longer the son who had so eagerly left them when he was only twenty. He was looking much older than his years, already losing his hair, and his handsome features creased by responsibilities whose nature he never revealed. He had always been thin, but now he was positively gaunt, and Paquita said that he worked too much and often didn't come home for weeks at a time without ever explaining where he had been. Although she didn't say anything in actual words, they gathered that beneath her composed exterior, she was torn with anxiety and frustrated love. When pressed about what kept him so busy, he explained he had a good deal of government work as well as his own private clients but added abruptly that he'd come for a holiday and didn't want to talk about work. It was all legal stuff they wouldn't understand anyway.

Dionisia was left with a feeling of apprehension, and even Pedro sensed that all was not well between them. They both assumed that they were having marital troubles, but they were afraid to say anything because Arturo seemed such a stranger to them, and Paquita was polite but withdrawn and beyond frank questioning. For his part, the doctor didn't want any political talk in the house, aware as his wife was not of the instability of the times. He wanted to enjoy this unexpected visit and not get embroiled in their personal affairs or know what his son might be involved in.

His own situation was becoming more delicate for, although he was cautious about airing his unacceptable socialist tendencies, the fact that he made no concessions to the church was held against him by some. Only his good relationship with Father Gonzalez, with whom he regularly played chess, and his high standing as a dedicated and skilful doctor, as well as respect for the memory of his father, saved him from open censure. He was relieved that Bernardo seemed as careless about politics as he was about the general opinion, ploughing his own furrow.

In his years away, Arturo had forgotten what village life was like, that the nearest fresh water was a long walk away at the stone troughs where the women did the laundry in ice-cold water; that the toilet was a pot under the bed or the stable behind the house with its audience of chickens and a pig; that there was no electricity.

'But your father's a doctor. Surely he could afford to live better?' Paquita wondered when he voiced his complaints to her.

And he irritably replied, 'Perhaps he could if his patients paid their bills and if he hadn't spent his inheritance on me.'

'Then why are you so angry?'

'I'm not angry with him. My father's a socialist. He's always been a socialist though he might never call himself one. He doesn't talk his beliefs. He lives them, and that's why he has no money. That's why he spent it on me. He wants me to change things, don't you see, not just for himself but for Spain.'

'And your brother?'

'What about him?'

'Well, isn't it unfair? You've had everything, and he—well, he has nothing. That's not socialism. Is it?' Her gaze was troubled. Arturo's indifference towards individuals, even his own family, deeply wounded her.

'Half of the house will be his one day, the vines and so on. He's happy enough. I'd have him in Madrid if he'd come—I could use him there—but he's only got one thing on his mind right now.'

'And what's that?' she asked, and his flippant reply, 'To bed that girl of his,' did not mollify her because she knew how little he cared.

Not for the first time, she struggled to understand, even to make excuses for this man whom she loved with passion. From the day she first met him, when her father, happy to take under his wing the clever and ambitious young man whose father he remembered with warmth, she fell under the spell of his magnetism.

She was eighteen years old, the only child of a comfortable, professional family who considered her ready to take the first tentative steps in the career she had been groomed for—marriage and motherhood. She had been escorted here and there by several young men who had her parents' approval, all of whom were good-looking and fun to be with, and she enjoyed the light flirtations, encouraged by a mother keen to see her well married, following the rules with an untroubled heart although aware that at some point she was expected to make a choice. She had discussed with her friends the pros and cons of each one as a prospective husband, but none of them sufficiently attracted her.

But with Arturo, there was no flirtation, no frivolity. She wanted him from the moment he was first brought home by her father and became a regular visitor. He was always polite and correct and coolly charming but seemed unmoved by her attractiveness and unaware of the desire he provoked in her. Afterwards, he told her that he had known all along how much she wanted him but that it hadn't been part of his plan to rush things. It was her father he was cultivating, using deference and charm to play on the surgeon's affection for an old friend, as well, perhaps, a frustrated desire for a son. Don Rodrigo was an open-hearted man, not unlike Arturo's own father, happy to reminisce and not put off by the young man's honest description of his father's general practice.

'Ah, he could have done so much more! Your father had talent. He could have specialised, as I did. He was too romantic. But a good man,' he said one night at the dinner table. 'I'll make sure you don't make the same mistake.'

Even before Arturo was licensed, he used his influence to open the right doors for him, both he and his wife beginning to consider him as a future son-in-law, well aware of Paquita's feelings and wondering somewhat at Arturo's lack of response. It was the right moment for him to respectfully ask Don Rodrigo for permission to court his daughter, and he was unimpressed by the father's pretended surprise and caution.

After that, things moved swiftly. A wedding to which all the right people were invited, an apartment in a good quarter of the city as a wedding present for the young couple, and for Paquita herself the utter joy of surrendering herself to the man for whom she had hungered far too long, within a twelve-month finding herself the mother of her first son and pregnant with the second. Arturo had, with deep regret, presented very convincing reasons for his family's absence from so significant an occasion but later confessed to Paquita that he hadn't invited them because their presence, especially his mother's, would have embarrassed him.

He never lied to her. He respected her enough for that. Mostly, he just didn't tell her things, never letting her into the life he lived outside the home, that life to which all his true passion was dedicated. They were worlds apart, except in bed, but with time Paquita came to realise that this was because Arturo was proficient in all his undertakings. The love he neither needed nor wanted from her she poured out on her children.

Some days before they were to return to Madrid, Dionisia began to complain that her grandchildren were leaving her too soon, just as she was getting to know them, just as they were beginning to look red-cheeked and healthy.

In the few weeks that they had been in the house, everyone grew to love them, especially the eldest, Arturito, who was a merry little boy, much like Bernardo in both character and looks. Bernardo forgot his own problems for a time and spent many an hour with the children about him, telling them stories, wrestling with them and letting them clamber all over him. When he had work to do among the vines or vegetables, he took four-year-old Arturito with him and told him how things grew, for the little city boy had never been in the fields before. He showed him his carpentry tools and gave him bits of wood to bang nails into, and all of them would watch with wide-eyed wonder as he turned a piece of wood into a donkey or a bird. He was glad of their company which helped keep thoughts of Elvira at bay. There was rarely a moment when he wasn't ready to play with them, and perhaps only Dionisia realized the pretence put up by Paquita as she watched them to disguise an inner resentment towards their father, who had so little patience with and even less empathy for his sons.

Arturo suddenly said, 'Would you like us to leave them here?'

'Leave them? For how long?' asked his father, sensing more behind the remark than did his wife.

Arturo hesitated, glancing first at Paquita as if expecting dissent.

'I don't know. A few months. Perhaps longer. It would do them good to get more country air. The summer in Madrid is stifling. It would do Paquita good to stay, too.'

'And I agree,' joined in his mother, longing to have them. 'They can stay as long as they like and welcome. It would give Paquita a rest. She'll have enough to do when the new one arrives, which won't be long, I can see.'

'No!' said Paquita, her voice taut. Round the big table, with five adults and three children eating, talking and squabbling at the same time, she had remained almost unnoticed until now, for she rarely made any contribution to a conversation. They all looked at her simultaneously. She was white-faced and defensive, in total reversal to her previous passivity.

'Why not?' demanded Arturo, and, quick to anger as always, the first signs of annoyance were creeping across his face.

'Because my place is with you in Madrid, in case you need me, and the children are all the company I've got.'

'But you could manage without them for a month or two, surely?' Dionisia tried to persuade her. 'At least leave Arturito here. He'd love to stay, wouldn't you, my little heart?'

The little boy hesitated, staring at his mother, next at his father and then looking down at his breakfast bowl. 'I want to stay with Mama,' he almost whispered, growing red about the ears. He hated to be singled out for attention.

'I still say they should stay here,' insisted Arturo. 'You know it would be best.'

'No,' replied Paquita with the same taut determination, and the others sensed that they had already argued on this subject before.

The doctor suggested that they could perhaps come another time if they wanted to and that it would be wrong to keep Arturito if he didn't want to stay, and then he changed the subject abruptly before they could argue any more.

XII

The two brothers had only one private conversation. They went up to the bodega one evening at Arturo's suggestion, drank some wine, and smoked almost silently together as each searched to rediscover a certain bond that had once existed. The bodega was no more than a dug-out in one of the few hilly areas not far from the village, big enough for two people to enter, deep enough to be always cold, and there the family wine was stored from year to year; there the occasional piece of meat was kept fresh in the summertime; there a man went to have a drink when he didn't feel like the sociability of the tavern. Several of the families in Los Pinos had their own bodega, and the low hillside was dotted with the locked wooden doors that had been built into it.

Bernardo had been hardly more than a boy when Arturo left home, but even the little affinity they had once shared then seemed to have disappeared. He was at a loss as to how to find a way to re-establish a relationship with him, recalling how he had always been somewhat in awe of the big brother with whom he had shared a bed in the coldest months of winter when they were children; not that Arturo had ever wanted to share, determinedly turning his back to avoid contact but always finding when he woke the next morning that Bernardo, while they slept, had somehow got an arm and a leg round him, keeping them both warm. Arturo sometimes pushed him right out of the big bed, but Bernardo would just laugh and climb back in, his cheeky grin infuriating the much older boy.

'Do you remember how you used to throw me out of bed?' he mischievously asked Arturo, as the odd memory unexpectedly returned, whose astonished response showed that he didn't remember at all and didn't find it funny.

'You were always a little snot-nose,' he said.

'I'm a bigger one now,' Bernardo laughed in reply.

They continued in this vein for a while, the distance that held them apart gradually reducing as they felt more comfortable in each other's company. For all his fastidiousness, there was a magnetic quality about Arturo which drew people to him and made them like him, even while he somehow kept them at a distance. However, he found it harder to keep Bernardo at bay, whose carefree nature disarmed even while it irritated him.

He moved him away from personal matters by suddenly enquiring, 'So, where do you stand politically? I know the general mood of this place and wonder if you share it.'

'Don't let's talk politics, brother. I'm not interested,' was Bernardo's reply after a short pause.

'But you must know what's going on?'

'And you must know a lot more, so why ask me? You know I never look for trouble. Let every man think for himself.'

'Well, you may be no knight errant, but surely after those years in the army, you must have some idea of the thinking of the Burgos command, their loyalty to the Republic?'

'All I learned from those "gentlemen" was to keep my mouth shut, obey orders and go with the flow. I did so well, they even made me a corporal,' he added with a laugh.

Arturo knew his brother well enough not to pursue the matter. He would get no more out of him. He questioned him instead about his love affair. He had heard something of it, of course, from their mother, but the subject had been touched upon lightly, and he had guessed that there was more to it than the usual caution on the part of the girl's family.

'Tell me about this girl, then. Our parents don't like her. Mother has three or four local girls lined up for you who'd give you no trouble at all. You've heard her,' he laughed. 'They, or their mothers, can't wait to get their hands on you.'

They spent a few minutes joking about these girls and their eager mothers until Arturo cut in, 'So, what's so special about this unobtainable Dulcinea of yours?'

His half-mocking enquiry only encouraged Bernardo to defend his choice with an enthusiasm he made no effort to contain and which amused Arturo because it made no sense to him for whom one woman was as good as another and had only reluctantly tied himself to Paquita for the advantages it would bring him.

'So why don't you marry her?' he interrupted

'The father won't let us.'

'What reason does he give?'

Bernardo shrugged. 'He doesn't like me. He wants someone better for his daughter, someone not from Los Pinos. Someone he can control, perhaps. How do I know? He's used to getting what he wants.'

'Do you really want to marry her, tie yourself down?'

'Of course, I do.'

'Then I can't see the problem. Just up and marry her. What can the father do then?'

'If it were as easy as that, do you suppose we wouldn't have done it? Elvira's not twenty-one yet, and, even then, how do you suppose we can be openly married in either Quintera or Los Pinos without the father's permission? If the churches aren't in ruins, it's only because Don Faustino pays generously for their upkeep.'

'Ah!' exclaimed Arturo contemptuously. 'What have churches got to do with it? The Republic has changed all that. In Madrid these days people don't get married in church. In fact, you don't need to marry at all. Marriage is an outdated bourgeois institution. Have a civil wedding if the girl insists. It's just as legal and preferable, anyway, as people showing too much religious fervour are frowned on.'

'But we're not in Madrid, and religious fervour's very fashionable here.'

'So? That's easily remedied. Come to Madrid. I can find you a job better than the one you've got now. You could use your brains for a change instead of your hands.'

Bernardo was silent. He had never been anxious to leave the village as had his brother, the harsh seasonal rhythms of his vast, severe surroundings and his books both challenging and satisfying his imagination and his soul. It was where he instinctively belonged. He had been forced away for a time against his will, and now, having found the girl he loved and was determined to win, there was nothing to stir him to action beyond this one desire.

'What's the matter? Wouldn't you like to see Madrid?'

'What would I do there?' he objected.

'Come and see for yourself. I promise I can find you any work you fancy.'

'I don't think I'd be happy in a city. I like space, silence.' He stretched out his arms as he spoke, indicating the sky and the earth, the one brilliant with stars, the other softly reflecting their light. 'This is my place.'

'But you also want to marry Elvira,' Arturo responded dismissively. 'Ask her if she'd like to go to Madrid. She'll tell you yes like a shot.'

'Do you really care if I go or not?'

'Of course I do! You're just rotting here in this village. Are you going to waste your whole life on cartwheels and digging potatoes? I could set you up in a good position, doing something worthwhile, something with a future. I need a man I can trust. There aren't many people one can trust these days. You could earn enough money to have a home of your own, enough to keep a wife and raise a family. You'd be independent, and Elvira could put her attractiveness to some use. She's wasted here, too. From what you say of her, she's too vivacious to be appreciated only by the louts of Quintera and Los Pinos.'

'It's enough that I appreciate her. She's not at all wasted,' retorted Bernardo, a little ruffled.

'Wouldn't you like to be able to give her pretty clothes, see her dressed in the latest styles?'

'I like her as she is. I don't want her to change.'

Arturo laughed. 'You're afraid that someone might steal her from you?'

'No, but . . .' he hesitated. 'She might start wanting more than I can give her. City life might go to her head. She might not be satisfied after tasting new wine, and I want to be able to make her happy.'

'Bring her to Madrid,' urged Arturo, 'and you'll see if she'll be happy. It's here that she'll get tired and dull and fed-up with being a housewife. What on earth will you do together?'

'The same as what you and Paquita seem to do in Madrid,' said Bernardo, with the invariable mischievous grin that had always annoyed Arturo when they were boys.

The conversation ended on a less serious note, and the brothers returned to the house. Three or four days later, they were gone, and the house seemed big and silent without them. Dionisia's heart ached for the little grandson she had grown to love so quickly, for some instinct told her that he should have stayed with her. She didn't know why she felt like this. There was nothing to warn any of them what the next five years would bring, but perhaps Arturo's insistence and Paquita's white-faced refusal had fed her fears.

XIII

Faustino Martínez was under the impression that he had broken off the association between his daughter and the doctor's son. They were never seen in each other's company; Elvira was chaperoned by an older sister on every occasion that she was likely to be absent from home for more than an hour, and she was kept at home as much as possible. Soledad was expecting her first child, and Elvira was set to making the christening robes as well as embroidering cot sheets and blankets. She wore a sullen face throughout the whole period and rarely spoke to anyone. Contrary to the anticipated habits of frustrated lovers, she did not lose her appetite and ate as well as ever. Her mother was suspicious and had begun to watch her figure, but then, with Sole expecting, she had the subject very much in mind, and her suspicions were unfounded.

It was towards the end of the year that Bernardo went to see Martínez. He put on the rarely-worn suit, having shaved very carefully, scrubbed his fingernails, and even polished his rarely-worn shoes so that his mother, watching him, found no difficulty in guessing what he was up to.

'It's too cold to go over there tonight,' she protested, thinking of the long trek ahead of him, but it wasn't the temperature she was afraid of as she begged him, 'Don't go.'

'Why shouldn't I go, Mother?' he calmly replied. It wasn't really a question but an objection to her plea.

'Because if you go, I know what will happen. You'll marry her, whatever her father says.'

'But I must ask him first.'

'She's not for you. She won't make you happy. Listen to your mother. Give her up,' she pleaded.

She clung to his hands and would have knelt before him in her intensity, but he wouldn't let her.

'For my sake, son, if not for your own,' she begged, and again, 'She's not for you.'

She knew he would take no notice. There was that look about him that she had known from his childhood. He had made up his mind, and nothing would change it. The best she could do was to fetch the warmest blanket and fussily insist on wrapping it round his shoulders, scolding while she did so until he silenced her with a kiss.

He did not time his visit well, arriving while Martínez was still in the shop, even though it was closed to customers. The grocer had spent most of the day stock-taking and was weary and worried as the figures were not tallying. Fidel had been keeping the accounts for some time now, so he eventually left him there to sort things out, feeling the cold and wanting to get home to dinner.

Faustino lived next door to the casino, which his brother Vicente managed for him. He also had been checking stocks that day, so he went there first to tell him to call in later with a report on the figures. The doctor's son was one of the few customers. It was so cold a night that not many had ventured from their homes. Faustino didn't know how long he had been sitting there, but Vicente told him he had drunk three cognacs in the last hour, getting himself warm.

He stood up as the grocer passed his table and said, 'Please, Don Faustino.'

'You want something?' The grocer made his voice as cold as possible, having no wish for conversation with Bernardo, but the latter was not deterred.

'Would you do me the favour of speaking with me for a few minutes, sir?'

'If it's necessary, yes. But if it's about Elvira, you know my answer already.'

'At least allow me to talk to you,' he urged, and as he seemed respectful enough, Faustino could think of no reason for refusing.

He made him wait while he spoke to Vicente for ten minutes or so, then he motioned Bernardo to a corner table, having no wish to invite him into his home where he might come into contact with Elvira. He told Vicente to bring them a bottle of wine—the cheapest.

'Well, continue,' he said, drawing up a chair. 'What do you want?'

'Don Faustino . . . ' He paused, knowing immediately from the man's expression that his petition was hopeless and suddenly startled by the coldness of those hard dark eyes, in which he unexpectedly found a glimpse of Elvira in one of her defiant moods.

He immediately shook this off and bluntly said, 'I want to marry your daughter.'

'And when did you decide this?'

'I was sure of it when you put a stop to our seeing each other.'

'And why wait until now to come and tell me?'

'Because . . . ' He shrugged his shoulders. 'I knew you wouldn't approve. My father said you wouldn't be keen to have me as a son-

in-law. You've as good as said so yourself. I'm only a carpenter. I
don't make much money and—'

'You make more now that you come to see me?' interrupted
Martínez sneeringly. 'You have better prospects?'

Bernardo maintained an even temper. 'No, the same, but my
desire to marry your daughter has increased, and so I've come to ask
your permission.'

'You know very well that I must refuse, that I don't wish Elvira
to have any connection with you whatsoever.'

'But why? What have I done, sir, that you treat me like this?
I have a home to offer, a secure profession, as much as any other
man.'

'A home, with your parents? A secure profession? Suppose
you have an accident, lose the use of a hand at the slip of one of your
tools, anything? If you can't work, what then? You've nothing to
offer my daughter except a share in your own insecurity. You have
everything to gain, and she everything to lose. Do you think I love
my daughter so little that I could sacrifice her to you?'

'If you really cared about her, you'd let her do as she wished.'

'You haven't seen her in months. How do you know she still
wishes to marry you?'

'Because I know she loves me, sir, and will marry no one else.'

'Not Don Jaime or Teodulo Martín's son? They both have
more to offer, and Elvira's a sensible girl.'

'Neither one nor the other. She will marry me or no one.'

He swallowed the wine Faustino had poured for him without
even being aware that he did so, and the grocer was glad that he'd
given him the cheapest. Why give hay to a mule that's accustomed
to straw? The grocer stood up, wishing to terminate the
conversation. After three cognacs and a glass of wine, a man not
used to drinking is liable to become heated, and he didn't wish to
involve himself in a scene on his own doorstep.

'I don't think there's any point in continuing the conversation,'
he said smoothly. 'I've given you my time, and you have been unable

to convince me of your worth. Finish up the wine if you like. It's yours. But leave my daughter alone.'

For a moment Bernardo was silent, and the earnestness in his grey eyes changed to determination.

'Please, Don Faustino, I don't think we've said everything yet. At least, I have more to say. Would you be kind enough to sit down again?'

This time Bernardo poured them each a half glass of wine and, not anxious to appear unjust or overhasty—aware of the eyes upon them, few though they were, and also a little worried as to what Bernardo's reaction might be if he refused—the grocer consented.

'Don Faustino, I hoped it would not come to this,' said Bernardo firmly. 'I hoped you would see reason and give us permission to do what we both desire above anything else. You know Elvira's not interested in any other man. I give you my word that we haven't seen each other since you forbade us to meet, but we have been exchanging letters.'

'Deceiving me!'

'Not intentionally. You gave us no choice. You have no right to keep Elvira a prisoner in your house.'

'She's my daughter.'

'But she's not a child. She's a woman, and she knows her own mind. We shall be married, whether you allow it or not, Don Faustino, and you won't be able to stop us.'

'You're talking stupidly. Elvira is only twenty, and do you think Father González would marry you against my wishes?'

'No, but with the Republic, it's no longer necessary to marry in church. Have you forgotten that? Next August, Elvira will be twenty-one. We shall wait until then, and we shall give you the opportunity to be generous, sir.'

'And if I refuse to be blackmailed into acceptance?'

'We shall still be married. Don't talk of deceit, Don Faustino, because I am speaking plainly. If you love your daughter as you say you do, you will not let it come to that.'

'My daughter obviously has neither love nor respect for me. Why should I care for her feelings?'

'She doesn't want to hurt you. You're her father. But if she has to choose between us, she will choose me.'

This time Bernardo stood up and pulled some money from his pocket.

'I'd rather pay for the wine, Don Faustino. Good night.'

Faustino watched him as he collected the blanket he had thrown across a table and walked out, noticing how he had dressed up especially for the occasion, the suit sharply creased and obviously rarely worn.

'The suit he will marry in,' was the contemptuous thought that crossed the grocer's mind.

He knew Bernardo was determined. He recognised the sensitivity of expression, which reminded him that this was the doctor's son, not just a poetry-reading peasant but the kind of man who would love a woman with his soul, wasting the love that should be reserved for God alone. In the grocer's opinion, a man needed a woman to supply a home, children and physical satisfaction. He should reserve his soul for higher devotion, not expend it on unnecessary emotions. Bernardo de Rosas was a fool, and Elvira would get nothing but children out of an alliance with him. After this conversation, with its insolent and outrageous proposal, Faustino was more than ever determined to prevent their marriage.

XIV

Martínez repeated Bernardo's threat to his eldest son, saying: 'Perhaps you can talk to your sister. She might be prepared to listen to a brother rather than her father. She's only defying me on principle, the way she's always done—you know what she is.'

The younger Faustino nodded with a grin. 'A wildcat,' he agreed.

'You might be able to make her see how foolish she is. Make her see that I'm only thinking of her when I refuse to allow them to marry.'

Faustino was doubtful. 'I don't suppose she'll listen to me either. She's always been an independent creature and, after all, there's a big age difference between us. We're not really close.'

'Then she should feel that you've almost a fatherly interest in her,' suggested the grocer. 'See what you can do anyway. Talk to her.'

'And if I get nowhere. What then?'

'Then you can go and see Bernardo.'

The younger Faustino, from being always a big lad, had become a powerfully built man, about the tallest and broadest between the two villages. A contented marriage had started something of a paunch, but, apart from this, he was all muscle. However, he was not a quick-thinking man and needed most details to be set out clearly for him to understand their meaning. Now he frowned.

'And what shall I say to him?'

'Words won't be necessary. Use this,' and the grocer held up his clenched fist. 'Reasonable conversation won't dissuade him from his purpose, but more forceful reasoning might. A man has every right to defend his sister's honour, and that's what you'll be doing.'

The younger Faustino grinned. It was the kind of argument he was best at, and the fact that his victim was of Los Pinos pleased him all the more. But even as the grocer suggested the idea, he had a feeling that nothing would deter Bernardo. When he had said that he intended to marry Elvira, Martínez could tell by the tone of his voice and the expression in his eyes that he meant what he said. He seemed to be the type prepared to suffer anything in pursuit of an objective.

'At least,' he added, speaking his thoughts aloud, 'if he intends to have Elvira, I'll make his path a stony one.'

He talked again to Jaime Segundo, urging him to pursue his suit with more fervour, and even persuaded Elvira to spend a day at his chicken farm in the hope that the man himself might be able to influence her. But she remained stubborn in everything, as rude to her brother as she had been to her father, showing Don Jaime that she was plainly bored by his chickens and even more so by him. Her insolence outraged her father, yet neither time nor events seemed to curb her spirit.

It was late on a Friday afternoon that the younger Faustino called on Bernardo. He had spent the best part of the day in the fields and had only just sat down with a book, offering to read something to his mother while she set about preparing the evening meal. He was surprised when she told him who was at the door.

'What does he want? Did he tell you?'

'He said he wants to talk to you. I told him to come in, but he said he'd rather talk to you outside.' She was anxious. 'Don't go, my son. I don't trust him.' For all that he was solidly built, Bernardo was a slight figure beside that hulk of a man.

Bernardo only laughed. He gave his mother a kiss as he went out. 'You worry too much, and you shouldn't think the worst of everybody.

Faustino had suggested a drink while they talked, but not in the bar where anyone might overhear the conversation. Dusk was falling as the two men walked silently to the bodega. Although it was easy for Bernardo to guess who was behind this visit, the miller seemed placid enough, so he was not unduly wary as he filled two tumblers from the barrel and joined him on the hillside.

'Well,' he said, handing Faustino a glass. 'What do you want?'

Faustino responded slowly. 'Elvira,' he said. 'I want to know what you're up to with my sister.'

'I'm going to marry her.'

'Why don't you leave her alone? You know she's not for you.'

'No, I don't know that.'

Faustino made as if to drink from the glass, but instead, with a rapid movement, he threw the wine into Bernardo's eyes.

The latter stepped back with a gasp of surprise, and Faustino hit him with all his powerful force in the stomach. Bernardo doubled with hardly a sound, and, as he fell, the other brought up his knee and cracked him under the chin. From the first moment, the miller had the upper hand as Bernardo never recovered from the first blow. He was a rag doll in the assailant's hands and had no protection from the blows and kicks which fell upon him. Faustino eventually tired of his sport and, exhilarated by the exercise, set off for home, leaving his victim crumpled on the hillside, groaning and only semi-conscious.

A shepherd found him and fetched help from the village to carry him back. His mother gave a cry of fear as she opened the door and saw Bernardo between two men, huddled and unable to walk, and sent half a dozen children running to find her husband. She was afraid to touch her son until the doctor came but began preparing water, searching for bandages and cotton wool. Most of his injuries were deep bruises, however, and there was little blood for her to wipe away. The doctor was afraid of some serious internal injury, but luckily there was none. The buffeted ribs and kidneys caused Bernardo agony for a week, but he was tough and against complaining.

'They say that men in love are fools,' said Dionisia later to her husband. And sadly, she added, 'Bernardo certainly is that. All that poetry he reads is no good to him. Why can't he just settle for someone who would marry him tomorrow and without any fuss? I'm sure he'd be a lot happier.'

The doctor just grunted, having no clear view of what made anyone happy or if happiness was even an achievable state of being.

If the Civil Guards didn't get to hear of the matter, Father González did, and one day, he decided to call on the grocer and broach the subject.

Father González performed his duties in three villages while living in Quintera. He had been priest there for some fifteen years, was respected by the people who treated him with reasonable affection, and to Faustino Martínez was a close friend. He often went to chat with him and play a game of chess, and the grocer liked to think that he was the only man in the district to have the priest fully in his confidence. He was proud of this trust and rarely abused it, and Father González appreciated the financial help Martínez gave to the church from time to time.

The grocer explained his desire for Elvira to marry well and voiced his doubts as to Bernardo's suitability as a son-in-law, but even from the priest he guarded his most potent reason.

'He seems a sober young man,' argued Father González, who did his best to remain unprejudiced, not wanting even a close friendship to cloud his judgement. 'He's a good son to his mother, attends mass regularly, and everyone in Los Pinos speaks highly of him. He's a likeable fellow, intelligent, fond of books. Given a chance, he'd have probably made a good civil servant. You could help him, you know.'

'Help a man who's determined to seduce my daughter, who threatens to marry against my wishes and not even in the church!' Martínez was righteously indignant. 'What are we coming to these days? I knew the Republic would encourage every kind of immorality, and this law about civil weddings threatens the very sanctity of marriage. It's a deliberate slap in the face of the Church. I agree with you. With the present government in power, he'd make a very suitable civil servant indeed, bursting with outrageous ideas and disrespect. I shall never agree to this marriage, Father. It's impossible. On principle alone, I couldn't change my mind now and let him think he'd frightened me into doing so. Perhaps you could speak to both of them, Father, and persuade them of their folly. Neither of them will listen to me.'

'I've already spoken to them,' he said.

Martínez was surprised.

'Yes. They've both been to me at different times, asking for advice. I've reminded them both that to marry into a hostile family is a bad idea. I've warned them of the dangers of turning against the Church. I've tried to instil patience into them and . . . ' He paused and smiled slightly. 'I promised to talk to you.'

'Tell me, Father,' began Martínez anxiously, 'have they done… have they confessed to anything serious? You know what I mean.'

'I couldn't tell you that even if they had but put your mind at rest. Young Bernardo's very much in love with your daughter, but he has a great deal of respect for her. I imagine that, like any other man, he wants a virgin in his bed on his wedding night.'

'That's what worries me most. Elvira's a hot-headed girl, always has been. She might be persuaded to something foolish and regret it for the rest of her life.'

'So why don't you let them marry now and get it over with? Then you'll have nothing to fear.'

'That's what they want. That's what they're trying to force me into!' cried Martínez petulantly, 'and I won't have it. They haven't even got anywhere to live.'

'The doctor's house is big enough, or they could soon put a home of their own together. The neighbours would help.'

'In Los Pinos, of course.'

'Probably.'

'And have my grandchildren brought up as strangers to me! You know the people of Quintera and Los Pinos don't mix.'

'There's always a first time.'

'There was a first time in 1921, and look what became of it. No!' He slammed his fist on the table. 'I'm against it, completely against it, and nothing will ever persuade me to change my mind. You can tell them that, Father González, if they come to you again and you can remind Elvira of the respect she owes to me, her father. You wouldn't marry them against my wishes, would you?'

Father González paused for a minute and then said, 'No.'

XV

Elvira's mother was looking through her daughter's belongings one morning while the girl was elsewhere and came across Bernardo's letters, proving that they were still somehow managing to communicate with one another. She dared not conceal her find, unable to withstand her husband's daily interrogations regarding Elvira, but wordlessly handed them over. He read them all, regardless of the intimate nature of some passages, intermingled with poems whose substance shocked his strictly narrow interpretation of life, and gathered that they had even been able to meet occasionally without anyone's knowledge.

'Some of the poems are downright indecent,' he told his wife. 'They're no doubt the works of these new writers, and God only knows what kind of effect they have on her mind. They ought to be banned.'

He confronted Elvira with the handful of letters that night as they sat down to eat, deliberately choosing to add to her humiliation by the presence of her mother and brother.

'Listen to this trash!' he cried, taking phrases at random from the various pages, his eyes glittering with malicious pleasure. To her relief, he refrained from exposing Bernardo's own expressions of love, which she could not have endured, but she was shocked into silence by his ruthless mockery. Relentlessly he carried on, battering her with words that had been her consolation for so long.

'"*Have you not felt in the night, when the shadow reigns, a muted voice that sings and an immense sadness that weeps?*"' he quoted. 'Have you no shame, girl, that you can allow that oaf from Los Pinos to send you such rubbish?'

Fidel until now had been enjoying his sister's wretchedness, his lips curled with satisfaction, but on hearing Becquer's words so badly recited, so abused, he suddenly recalled the poem and an uncomfortable memory stirred within him; a summer's evening, a long time ago now, when in his own desire he had believed that Bernardo loved him. Ever lonely and often made fun of and bullied, he would long for his company, treasure his presence and thrill to his voice. On that last day of their friendship Bernardo had recited this very poem. And now all these beautiful words, these emotions so perfectly expressed, were for Elvira. They had never been for him.

A coldness came over him. It twisted in his stomach. After so long a time, could he still feel the agony of that rejection? Yes, he could and did, because of all the many rejections in his life, it was the one that had mattered most.

Martínez sought out the doctor, showed him the letters and told him to restrain his son from sending such filth to his daughter, but he derided what he saw as the grocer's religious prejudice and philistine views.

'They only describe human emotions,' was his retort. 'Elvira knows what it's about already, or if she doesn't yet know how the world is populated, it's about time someone enlightened her.'

'I think you'll agree with me that that is the responsibility of her mother and the priest, not your son. You're treating this matter far too lightly, Doctor, and if anything happens to Elvira, you'll be as much to blame as your son.'

'Look, Martínez,' answered the doctor impatiently, 'this is no concern of mine. I've told Bernardo he's wasting his time. Elvira could never make him happy, anyway. I've no more wish to become related to you than you have to me, but the lad's old enough to know his own mind. If he's prepared to sacrifice his family and to get himself beaten up by that ox of a son of yours, he's obviously intent on his purpose. You're only holding him up, not stopping him.'

'I'll stop him,' fumed Martínez. 'If I have to put Elvira into a convent, I'll stop him. You can be sure of one thing. Your son will never marry my daughter. Never!'

He took the letters home, showed them again to Elvira, tore them up in front of her and threw them into the kitchen stove. Elvira pretended disinterest, but secretly she was heartbroken. While she couldn't see Bernardo, the letters were all she had, her most precious possession. She would smell them and kiss them and even guiltily hold them to her breasts to somehow bring him close, aching for his presence.

The doctor mentioned his conversation with Martínez to Dionisia.

'But Bernardo would never write anything indecent to a girl,' protested his mother. 'What did they say?'

'I don't know. I only scanned them. It looks as though he's been copying poems. One of them was something about a gipsy making love with a married woman who pretended to be single. They weren't indecent. It was good poetry. Martínez is too old-fashioned and bigoted to appreciate it.' Then he laughed. 'I wonder what it was that disgusted him most, that the woman was committing adultery, that she told a lie or that she was cheap enough to make love with a gipsy? I should have asked him.'

He told Bernardo that the letters had been found and advised him not to write any more, or at least not to offend the taste of Don Faustino, who might afterwards want to read them. Then changing to a serious tone, he said, 'Look, son, it's silly to ask if you've done any kissing and cuddling but have you gone further than that?'

'No, father.'

'I just want to advise you to be careful, that's all. The way things are, your hopes of marrying Elvira are pretty remote.'

'I'll marry her,' vowed Bernardo.

'But it might take you years. She's not even of age, is she? All I'm going to say is this. If you sleep with her now and still have to wait a long time to marry, you might find yourself getting tired of waiting. After all, you will have had the thing you want most. It wouldn't do you much harm to give up afterwards, but where would that leave Elvira? Who else would have her?'

''It's not what I want most, father. I want her. Her. Not just her body, father. All of her.'

'Ah, son,' the doctor sighed, shaking his head with a wry smile. Bernardo's longing reminded him of his own all those years ago when he gave his parched and thirsty heart to a girl who could never satisfy him even though she held nothing back.

'Don't you believe me?' insisted Bernardo, not knowing his father's thoughts but wondering at his expression.

'I believe you. Of course I believe you, but believe me, too. We don't always get what we want. If Elvira is her father's daughter, she'll want more than you can give her and perhaps give you less than you hope for. Open your eyes, son. And listen to your mother. She knows you inside out.'

'But she doesn't know Elvira or understand how I feel about her.'

'Perhaps not. And maybe she's a little jealous. Be patient with her. Try not to hurt her feelings. Think about it, son. Between you,

you and Elvira have stirred up a hornet's nest, and there's always a price to pay when you flout the rules. You learned that at school - and from the miller!'

He looked earnestly at his son. 'You are both playing with fire, but she's the one likely to suffer most if it all goes wrong.'

'I'm not giving her up, Father. Elvira is my life. I know what she's like. When I'm with her, sometimes she tears me apart, but . . . how can I explain it . . . she's my life, Father, my life. One day she'll know that she loves me, and then—then she'll be truly mine.'

'May it be so, may it be so,' the doctor agreed though unable to repress another sigh.

Bernardo laughed. 'You're an old man, Father. You've forgotten what love is.'

'No, son. I haven't forgotten. Your mother is a constant reminder.'

And he left Bernardo to wrestle with this characteristically equivocal remark.

XVI

Martinez decided to send Elvira to her sister in Burgos. He wanted to get her right away from the village to a place where Bernardo couldn't find her. Soledad was expecting her first child any day and would need some help around the house, and Elvira would be company too.

'Don't tell anyone where she's going,' he said to his wife. 'Gossip in Quintera soon becomes gossip in Los Pinos.'

He himself escorted her to Burgos and to her sister's house. He spoke privately with Sole for a while, but it wasn't difficult for Elvira to guess what he was saying. He was telling her to act as a chaperone, perhaps even as a spy.

'Watch for any letters she might receive. Don't let her get too friendly with anyone unless you can be certain he's of a good family. Keep her busy. There must be plenty to do with a baby in the house and your husband needing you in the shop.'

Elvira went to stay with her sister in February 1936, and he took his leave of her with a sigh of relief. The annual pig-sticking was coming round, and there was work for everybody. There wasn't a person to spare who could keep an eye on Elvira from dawn till dusk. It was altogether a good thing that she went when she did. He was even more contented to learn a couple of weeks later that Bernardo had gone to visit his brother in Madrid. Perhaps at long last, he had put an end to their relationship.

The Popular Front had just been voted into power in the General Election, but in spite of the elation and the hopes and dreams of half the nation engendered by the victory, from the very first days, the new ministers—socialists, communists and every kind of leftist imaginable—seemed incapable of agreeing on policy, or of uniting in a common cause, while right-wing elements watched and waited and made their own plans. No one in February could have imagined with what rapidity the euphoria of the first days would descend into discontent, strikes, recriminations, murder, revolt and then war.

It was a volatile time for some, but life in Quintera continued more or less as usual, the Popular Front having no foothold in that part of the country, but Martínez liked to have a finger in local politics, and he was glad to rid himself of the worry of Elvira. There was ongoing political discussion at the casino, in which he was determined to take a leading part. Agricultural reform was top of the new government's programme, and there was some anxiety about what it might mean for them. It was all very well to break up the unproductive lands of the south and put them into the hands of the unemployed labourers, but their own properties, which returned good yields when the weather was favourable, should be left alone.

Father Gonzalez was worried about the people of Peña Alta, the third village in his parish. It was little more than a hamlet of labourers who lived from hand to mouth, more or less dependent on Faustino Martínez and Don Pedro for even the air they breathed. It was there that the smallpox epidemic had started, the people being too poor to call the doctor until too late. Having lived without horizons and resigned to the labour that made them old before their time, Father González said that the majority were now out-and-out anarchists and made no secret of it. For the few who actually wanted his ministry, it hardly seemed worth his while to go there, and his efforts to persuade the rest to wait patiently for the promised reforms that would eventually change their lot made him unpopular. The word 'reform' meant nothing to them, the anarchists having filled their ignorant heads with revolutionary ideas, and as he walked among them, it was no accident that he overhead their mutterings about ridding the country of priests and bosses.

He still faithfully fulfilled his duties there, however, while there were those who needed him but he always returned to Quintera in a shaky state, the mule that carried him receiving the brunt of the stones which they sometimes threw after their retreating figures. Martínez, whose mules he borrowed and who wasn't happy when they came back cut or lame, tried to persuade him to denounce his attackers to the authorities, but he refused, knowing it would go badly for them if he did.

'A few cracked bones will quickly silence them,' he insisted, enraged. 'How dare they, the scoundrels, when without the help of the church, some of them wouldn't survive the winters! They need to be taught a lesson.'

'No, no, Don Faustino. Broken heads won't solve anything. On the contrary. Are we not to forgive our enemies and do good to those who hate us? And I am to give in to their threats? Who can blame their impatience?'

Martinez admired his courage while deprecating his gullibility.

'Don't admire me,' the priest replied. 'I'm sick with fear every time I go there. But I'm their confessor, not their accuser. This is a test for me, mild in comparison with that which our Lord had to face, and I must not fail.'

He continued his visits to Peña Alta until war was declared and they almost killed him. Apart from this unreported hostility towards Father Gonzalez, there was little to worry about in

Quintera, so Martínez was feeling pretty contented, the trouble gone from his house.

XVII

When Bernardo announced that he was going to spend a few weeks in Madrid, Dionisia sensed something odd. First came the news that Elvira had been sent away from Quintera, and Bernardo hadn't seemed very surprised. Some said that she'd gone to stay with her sister in Burgos. Others said she was living with an aunt prior to a marriage with some farmer or another. No one really knew, and if Bernardo had better information, he kept quiet about it.

His sudden decision was so much out of character that her suspicions were aroused. She had always been able to see through her sons' pretences, and she couldn't help feeling that there was more to it than he was willing to admit. She probed casually at first and then more openly but gained no sure answer. Bernardo said he was going to see the capital for himself and perhaps look for work there if he liked the place.

'Arturo invited me, don't you remember?' he said. 'He promised me a job. Perhaps I can make a home for Elvira there. It seems to me that we'll never be able to live peacefully either here or in Quintera. Perhaps it's best to go right away.'

Had he known how much his words would hurt his mother, he would have probably not made the remark, or at least not so bluntly, but she hid her feelings and her disbelief, and he went from home a few days later unaware of the unhappiness he had caused her. There were tears in Dionisia's eyes as she watched him go, following his hasty hug, the first of many she was to shed for him from that day on.

He returned three weeks later with a mood that his mother couldn't define. He didn't want her to ask questions, perhaps because he didn't want to lie. He was hardly able to control his impatience at her probing and was withdrawn in a manner totally out of character.

'What's the matter, son? Is something wrong?'

How many times did she ask him, only to have him shrug his shoulders and say coldly, 'You imagine things. Nothing's the matter,' and, the most hurtful of all, 'Mother, stop asking questions. Leave me alone.'

That he was ill-at-ease with himself was all Dionisia could understand, and he had never been like that before. He had been unhappy and frustrated for months, but somehow this was different. He seemed to have lost confidence; she didn't know how to explain it to her husband, but something wasn't right with him, and she was unable to help him. He didn't talk about Madrid or his brother, and this convinced her that he hadn't been there or seen him, but such was the unnatural estrangement between them that she dared not ask or even mention Elvira's name. Perhaps their relationship had finally been broken.

PART THREE

Dionisia's intuition had not failed her. Bernardo took the train to Burgos, not Madrid. He had the address of Elvira's sister in a confused letter delivered by Cándido, to whom she had entrusted it, in which she begged him to come to her, or she might never see him again.

'*My father will make me marry some horrible man but I'll kill myself first,*' were the dramatic words remembered from one of her tales. '*If you don't come I'll know you don't really love me. If you do come I'll show you how much I love you. You said you'd come if I asked you.*'

He didn't really believe that she would kill herself, but her last words were too promising to resist. Remembering his own avowal to follow her wherever she went should ever they be separated, desperate to see her again, to hold her in his arms and make her his own, he gave no thought to any consequences and within a few days was standing outside her brother-in-law's establishment after finding a cheap boarding house just a couple of streets away.

The house porter told him that Soledad Martínez lived on the first floor, above the shop, which was double-fronted and undoubtedly prosperous. When he rang the bell with a fast-beating heart, Elvira opened the door. She hadn't been expecting him, and she drew back, startled.

'You!' she gasped. 'So soon!'

'Aren't you pleased?'

'What a question!' She didn't know what to say, aware of the heat rising in her cheeks.

She stood staring at him for a few moments, smoothed her hands over her hair which hung round her shoulders, then nervously began to remove the apron she was wearing.

He wanted to drown her in kisses, but instead, his heart now beating more steadily, he said, 'Can I come in?'

The discomposure she could never hide at first sight of him, however much she pretended unawareness of her desire for him, and immediately suppressed, enchanted him as always, and it was as if he hadn't been separated from her for so long a time. He felt as natural with her as he'd always been, and her reaction was also the same as ever.

She led him to the dining room where a large chandelier overhung a polished table surrounded by stiff, hard-backed chairs, while a sideboard and a show cabinet filled with glasses and coffee cups took up most of the remaining space. There was no time to speak personally, for, at that moment, Soledad herself came from the kitchen to see who had called. She was huge, her baby already overdue, but she was quite unselfconscious of her figure and proffered Bernardo her hand, less taken aback by his presence than was Elvira.

'You must be Bernardo. It's a great pleasure.'

'Enchanted,' he returned politely.

There was silence.

'How's everything at home?' Soledad asked.

'The same as ever.'

'Have you got somewhere to stay?'

'Thank you, yes.'

'I'm sorry you can't stay here, but . . . My husband must know nothing of this, you understand? If he were to find out . . . '

'Don't worry, Señora. We are both very grateful to you and wouldn't dream of causing any embarrassment.'

Elvira had disappeared into the kitchen and came back with a bottle of anise and another of cognac. She hurried off again and reappeared with some biscuits arranged on a plate, needing this regulation etiquette to calm her nerves. Her heart was pumping madly. She took some small glasses from the cabinet and arranged them. She almost ignored Bernardo, and her back was towards him most of the time. He longed to take her in his arms.

The drinking of the anise and the cognac was very formal. No one knew what to say. Bernardo asked after Sole's husband, she asked after his parents and brother, Elvira remained silent. Then Sole finally said that she must return to the kitchen.

'Don't be long, Elvirita,' she warned. 'Paco will be up soon.'

She was hardly out of the room when Bernardo pulled Elvira into his arms and, almost crushing her, exclaimed, 'My heart and soul, how much I've longed for you. I love you, I love you, and I love you.'

He pressed his mouth fiercely to hers. But she didn't relax as he'd expected nor respond to his kiss. Instead, 'Be careful,' she warned as he drew back. 'Sole might hear you.'

'What does it matter? She knows why I'm here,' and he kissed her again.

Elvira struggled free.

'You don't seem very pleased to see me,' remarked Bernardo, puzzled and disappointed.

'It's not that, but . . . We must be careful.'

'Be careful of what? If you knew how much I've been thinking about you, longing for you, you wouldn't talk of caution.'

'But you've only been here five minutes.'

'What difference does that make? I've been away from you for five centuries.'

'There's time to make up for it.'

Bernardo was exasperated. He sat down on a chair and sighed.

'Perhaps it's my fault, Elvira, but I don't understand. Are we supposed to start from the beginning again, as if we'd only just met?

When you begged me to come here, you wrote as if—as if our love should be fulfilled. Now you treat me as if I were a stranger.'

'Bernardo, don't try to rush me. Of course, I wanted you to come. You know that. And I've been longing for you just as much as you have for me. Haven't I persuaded my sister? But….'

'Then no buts. I'm here, and we're together. There's no one to keep us apart.'

He rose as he spoke and took Elvira into his arms again, covering her face and ears and neck with kisses. He buried his face in her hair, and she was all that he had remembered, dreamed of and desired ever since he had first declared his love for her.

Elvira, at last, was caught up in his passion. She yielded with sudden recklessness and returned his kisses, remembering the too few occasions that they had been able to enjoy each other's touch. She knew that nothing could happen—Sole was in the kitchen, Paco was coming—and so she gave herself up to this man who desired her so greedily, confident in her security.

It was Bernardo who brought the moment to an end. He, too, recalled that Sole was nearby and that Paco was coming. He must stop before stopping became unbearable. There were many days ahead; they would have many hours alone. This was no way to satisfy hunger. Elvira was disappointed when she felt him slacken. Her eyes were closed. She was almost in a trance and had been unaware of the sideboard against which her back had been pressed uncomfortably. She awoke to find him pouring himself another cognac.

'Why did you stop?' she said petulantly.

'Didn't you want me to? Your sister . . . Paco . . . '

'Kiss me again,' she pleaded, closing her eyes and drawing closer, but he pushed her away.

'No, you were right. We've plenty of time. When's your sister going to have the baby? Is anybody coming to stay here?'

'No. There'll be lots of relations on the day itself, I suppose, but they'll soon drop off. Paco's like my father. He doesn't like the expense of entertaining. She should have had the baby already.'

'You won't be so free then.'

'I'll manage it. Sole will leave us alone together, and Paco's always in the shop. But you mustn't come too often, or the concierge's wife will begin to talk. We must meet outside.'

She laughed. 'If my father could see us now! Fancy him thinking that Sole would be on his side. Without knowing it, he supplied us with the best opportunity for being together.' The idea delighted her.

'Will you come out with me this evening?' urged Bernardo. 'We'll eat somewhere together.'

Elvira shook her head. 'Paco would wonder where I was.'

'What time does he go to bed?'

'About eleven. Why?'

'Couldn't you sneak out? We could walk round the streets.'

Elvira thought the idea sounded romantic. 'I'll try,' she promised. 'Where shall I meet you?'

'I'll be waiting on the other side of the street. You will come?'

'I'll do my best. Now you must go. Paco might come up while you're still here.'

'Kiss me once more,' he said.

Elvira kissed him, and any awkwardness she had felt towards him, caused by their long separation, had melted away.

'I'm glad you've come,' she said.

II

They wandered through the cold and deserted streets that night kings of the universe. There was no one to see them, no one to disapprove. Elvira had never known such freedom in her life. Bernardo's arm was about her, and she didn't feel the cold. Every now and again, they stopped in the shadows to embrace and kiss. They smiled at each other, and they laughed about silly things, Elvira feeling very daring. What would her father think if he could see her now, and half the pleasure of being with Bernardo that bitterly cold night was due to her successful defiance of him?

Helen Griffiths | 93

Bernardo's pleasure was entirely in the girl he was walking with. There was no separation, no irate father and doubting parents, no coldness, no darkness, no existence outside Elvira. This was all a dream, one that had occurred many times in his sleep, and all his body, soul and mind was a fusion of delight. Soon she would be entirely his; the desire that he could hardly contain would find its outlet, and every moment he must stop to kiss her, touch her face, run his fingers through her hair, fill her ears with words of love.

At last, Elvira said she must return home. She was beginning to worry. Delightful as all this was, supposing Sole were to start having the baby now? She would be called for, and no explanation could be given for her absence. Bernardo regretfully agreed that she was right, and they wandered slowly back to the grocer's, stopping often along the way, not wanting to lose this silent, eyeless world that was theirs that night.

Bernardo clapped his hands for the night watchman, and they exchanged more kisses while waiting for him to come running with his jangling keys and long truncheon to open the door.

'Will you come tomorrow?' said Elvira.

'Nothing will stop me. Good night, my life.'

The night-watchman locked the door again, and Bernardo was left in the street, wistfully longing for the time when they could share the whole night together, and every night, when nothing would separate them again. The night watchman, who had been asked to wait, broke in on his thoughts by impatiently rattling his keys and then walked him to his lodgings, where he was also let in and locked up, to console himself with the delightful thought of seeing her again the following day.

Elvira found it difficult to get to sleep. No one had missed her, the house was completely silent, and she had crept into bed without even switching on a light as if she'd never been out. She lay for a long time just thinking about Bernardo. He was good-natured, entertaining, forgiving, and she was extremely fond of him, but she wasn't absolutely sure in her own mind that she loved him. To anyone who asked her, she would say that, of course, she loved him, but in truth, she hardly knew what love was. There was none in her home or in her sister's home either, at least not the kind of love she craved for and yet knew to be sinful outside of marriage, outside the blessing of the church.

She believed from all the novelettes she had read that to be in love with a man meant not caring about anything else. She would accept him exactly as he was and be prepared to die for him. But Elvira couldn't accept Bernardo exactly as he was. For all that she wanted to escape her father's tyranny, she hated to think she might have to live in Los Pinos, in his parents' house and with his mother. She hated the plain living, which with Bernardo was sure to be her lot. He never spoke of wanting to improve himself. Even though she had suggested on several occasions that being a carpenter wasn't good enough for him and tried to encourage him in thoughts of doing better, like his brother, he had only replied that he was happy enough as he was and told her not to nag him.

When he began writing letters to her, she felt herself caught up in a romance as intense as any she followed on the radio or read in comics, and copied her heroines' ideas in replying to them. When she told him that she was being sent to Burgos, and he had said he would follow her there if she gave the word, she gave it. But now, she was beginning to have misgivings. The letters that had intoxicated her in her loneliness and their long separation had made her only half remember how Bernardo's actual presence disturbed and overwhelmed her. The afternoon in the dining room, the night they had celebrated, had stirred her powerfully, and she was stunned by the stark realization that there was an ocean of difference between the live lover and the one on paper.

Lying in the dark, even blushing in the dark, she was tossed about with fear and uncertainty, and something else she didn't want to think about as she relived the hour or so they had just spent together. In all their previous moments of intimacy, she knew that she had held the upper hand. In her ignorance, she had even taken pleasure in leading him on, only to rebuke him with her favourite insults. But now . . . now she sensed that she had lost that control.

Bernardo had clearly assumed that she had told him to come to Burgos for a particular reason. It seemed to her that his every word and action held an assurance, an expectancy, an implicit inference that their relationship was to be made complete.

She wasn't quite sure why she had told him to come. The challenge had been too strong to resist. She longed to be revenged upon her father, and the excitement of being loved so fiercely, of knowing that Bernardo would do almost anything she asked him, had forced her to prove that it was so. Extravagantly indulged throughout her childhood, she expected to get her own way, and it always had been so with Bernardo, who was too good-natured to resist her whims and fancies for long.

She couldn't remember the wild words she had written that had brought him there, but now that he had arrived and she saw how much he desired her and expected her to reciprocate his desire, she was frightened. She knew she could never go through with it. Her mother's warnings, her whole upbringing, had filled her with a terror of anything so dreadful. She wasn't terribly religious, but she had a healthy respect for purgatory and hell—just in case—and was afraid she might go there for thousands of years were she to give herself to a man before she was married to him and had the act sanctified by the Church.

Bernardo obviously believed that she was willing. How to tell him now that he was mistaken? How to tell him that she invited him to Burgos to defy her father and to enjoy a romantic adventure? How to tell him that she didn't really love him enough to abandon herself completely?

She knew she couldn't tell him any of these things. He did truly respect her, but she knew that she had led him too far to disillusion him so completely. No, it was best to let things continue as they were for the time being. After all, she probably would marry him if no one more appealing crossed her path. He would see for himself by her actions that she intended to remain a virgin until then, and words would not be necessary. He would behave like one of her honourable heroes because he knew she was a decent girl. With these muddled thoughts, sleep finally overtook her.

The very next day, the baby was born. Within a few hours, the whole street was aware of the fact so that when Bernardo arrived, buoyed with expectation, he had no choice but to turn away. He paid a visit to Don Jacinto, trying to assuage his frustration as he had so often done before with books and conversation. The literary circle had been suspended as it was now impossible to keep politics out of it, and neither Don Jacinto nor the owner of the café where they used to congregate wanted any trouble. He spent the best part of the next few days catching up with old associates and with the latest literary publications but ignored the newspapers freely available for the price of a cup of coffee. He was relieved to learn that Claudia was no longer around. No one seemed to know what had happened to her. But he wasn't interested, filled with the ache to be close to Elvira.

As his money dwindled, he began to wonder whether he should ever have come to Burgos at all and how much longer he could stay there. Every morning he passed by the grocery store half a dozen times, heart beating fast as he imagined himself accidentally bumping into Elvira. There was a bar on the opposite side of the street, just a few doors down where he also whiled away the time, discreetly watchful, and at long last, certain that Sole's husband had returned to his usual routine, he made up his mind to call.

Elvira opened the door. The startled look she gave him, as if he were the last person she was expecting, or perhaps even hoping to see, caused him to draw back for a second, but he was so hungry for her that he just pulled her into his arms and covered her with kisses.

'Don't, don't,' she managed to gasp out as she struggled free. 'Someone might see us.'

He pushed them both into the hall and shut the door with his foot, again enfolding her in a passionate embrace from which he reluctantly withdrew as Sole called out, 'Who is it, Elvira? Don't stay at the door.'

Without a word, Elvira signalled to Bernardo to follow her to the kitchen where Sole sat with the baby on her knees, a picture of maternal contentment.

'Oh, it's you, is it? You haven't gone home then?' Her tone was friendly enough, and after the usual salutations and Bernardo's obligatory admiration of her sleeping son, she invited him to sit down and told Elvira to make some coffee.

It was just as well that all Sole wanted to do was talk about the baby. It was the barrier they both needed, Elvira to regain a semblance of composure, while Bernardo wondered what his next move should be. The whole situation was so irregular that he was more out of his depth than either of the women seemed to be, or perhaps they were more adept at simulation than he was.

At last, Elvira said, 'Sole, could we go out for a while? Paco won't know, and I'll be back before he shuts the shop for lunch.'

Sole gave her consent after laying down some strict ground rules for the game her sister was playing, and once they were out on the street, the tension that had built up between them began to diminish. They walked and small-talked, then for half an hour, they sat on a bench in a nearby square, watching toddlers at play, but there was still a space between them, a space that Bernardo ached to fill but which Elvira was afraid to relinquish. She kept her hands tucked under her arms and rejected his playful efforts to break down her resistance.

In the end, somewhat exasperated, he exclaimed, 'Tell me what's the matter. The way you act is driving me crazy. I'm out of my mind, I want you so much. I'm here because in your letter you promised—'

She cut in sharply, 'But how can I be sure that you really love me, not only when . . . if . . . I want you to love me always, as your wife, not just . . . '

She trailed off, suffused with the desire to melt into the embrace she knew he was struggling to restrain because they were in such a public place, mind and body battling against each other, with as yet no room for her fearful heart. In her confusion she at last let him crush her hands in his and fill her ears with passionate endearments.

'If you don't know by now how much I love you, you never will,' he concluded. 'I swear by all that's sacred that I love you more than my own life. You are my life! Without you, I'm nothing. I can't breathe or think or live. I promise you we'll be married as soon as the law allows. What more can I say? If you don't believe me, if you don't trust me, then I'll get the next train back home. You decide.'

He violently shook his head and ran a hand through his hair before adding, 'I can't go on like this. Tell me what you want me to do. But don't play any more games.'

'Don't go. I don't want you to go.'

Afraid of losing him before she could make up her mind, the words unthinkingly escaped her. Then she hurriedly jumped up, exclaiming, 'I must get back before Paco shuts the shop,' and she was halfway across the square before he caught up with her.

'Elvira,' he began, but she silenced him with, 'We must hurry!' and parted from him two streets away from home, promising to spend an hour with him in the evening.

III

When Sole's baby was a fortnight, old Paco insisted that she should take it to visit some relatives of his who lived in a village outside Burgos. She wasn't keen to go. It was cold, she was afraid the baby might catch a chill on the journey, the road was a very bumpy one, and it might be sick.

'Elvira will help you. It's not as if you'll have to go alone, so what are you complaining about?'

Sole still wasn't happy about the idea, but Elvira persuaded her, saying that Bernardo could come too. While Sole spent the day with the relatives, they could picnic in the countryside.

'No, no. It's bitterly cold. You'll catch pneumonia.'

Sole was getting cold feet about sharing her sister's conspiracy. She had agreed to it in the first place on the understanding that they should only meet in public places or in her own home when she was there. There was some entertainment to be got from frustrating their father's efforts to keep them apart, and surely no harm could come of it. But alone in the fields . . . However, Elvira's pleadings and promises wore her down, and when Paco began to wonder at her reluctance to do what he wanted, she at last agreed but not without showering her sister with dire warnings.

'I'm experienced in the ways of men,' she said, considering that two years of marriage was enough to teach a woman all she needed to know, 'so be guided by me. Just don't let him start any nonsense because once it's started, it's difficult to stop. You'll be thinking, "Just a little, just a little," and then before you know what's what, it'll be too late. And it's not him that'll pay the consequences of it.'

'Oh, Sole,' exclaimed Elvira in exasperation, 'you're like an old woman! You're worse than Mama. I'm not a baby. I can look after myself. Bernardo respects me.'

'Don't be so sure,' returned Sole. 'He's a man like all the rest.'

All the way to the bus station, she continued to fill her sister's ears with warnings so that, should the worst happen, she herself could not be blamed. Paco, already in the shop, hadn't offered to see them off, which relieved the sisters immensely, although they pretended disappointment, and Sole complained. Bernardo was waiting for them and, for the benefit of other passengers who might be from the same village and would be sure to gossip, he and Elvira deserted Sole and travelled together as if she were unknown to them. It wouldn't do for Paco's relatives to find out that Sole had come with a sister who had mysteriously disappeared before reaching their door.

The bus that took them to the village was a ramshackle affair, with uncomfortable seats and more standing room than places to sit. About a third of the travellers emptied out at the first stop, including themselves. Sole enquired for the relatives she sought. Elvira and Bernardo walked off in the opposite direction. A few curious eyes followed them, but no one knew who they were.

They walked a long way until the village was lost from sight, and on every side of them there was nothing but flat ploughed fields, the horizon disappearing into the sky. As they walked, a profound silence fell upon them, each thinking intensely of the other, aware of how alone they were together. They could do as they liked, and no one would ever know. The sky was blue, and the sun shone. It would have been warm had not a relentless wind torn itself across the empty landscape, and Elvira was frozen. She said so to Bernardo.

'Let's run, then. You'll soon get warm.'

He grabbed her hand, and they ran together, she sometimes stumbling in the furrows but kept on her feet by his strong grip. They began to laugh, and soon Elvira was breathless. She slowed, but he dragged her on.

'Stop, stop. I can't run any more. Do stop. I shall fall,' she gasped.

Bernardo turned, swept her into his arms and carried her like a baby. She struggled at first, squealing, but then she relaxed and closed her eyes. It was a heady sensation. She felt like a cloud, weightless, moving without effort. She was quite dizzy and lost all sense of direction.

'Now I know why babies stop crying when they're picked up,' she murmured. 'It's wonderful.'

'But you weigh half a ton at least,' retorted Bernardo as he set her on her feet and then pulled her down beside him.

He had stopped at the skeletal remains of an old dwelling on the edge of one of the fields. Its remaining low stone walls with the hint of a door frame broke the force of the wind, and there was something romantically inviting in its unexpected shelter, attractive to them both as they sat there, the sun shining strongly on them, silently absorbing one another's closeness.

'Why don't you take off your coat?' suggested Bernardo. 'It's not cold here.'

He was already pulling at her coat buttons, in too much of a hurry to undo them properly, so Elvira helped him. She was still feeling dreamy from being carried in his arms. She let him remove her coat, laughing at his clumsiness, and then she laid back again, her head crooked in his arm. He began to kiss her, his lips moving over her eyes, her cheeks, her ears.

Her dreaminess continued. It was all so pleasant, the unexpected warmth of the sun, the sheltering wall, the touch of lips on her face and in her hair, on her neck. This was what the heroines of her novelettes enjoyed, and she didn't want it to stop. Excitement was slowly filling her whole body, right down to her toes. She was aware of Bernardo's voice, soft, almost panting, as he told her over and over again how beautiful she was, and she obligingly moved herself to facilitate his actions, hardly aware that she did so. Somewhere in her subconscious, she heard Sole's voice chanting, 'Just a little, just a little,' and slowly, this incantation seemed to grow louder while Bernardo's voice, so close to her, receded.

'It'll be too late,' she heard Sole warning. 'Too late. Just a little. . . Too late . . . '

She shook her head to drive out the unwelcome words, and the abrupt movement also shook off the delicious coma she had almost fallen into.

'Bernardo!' she cried. 'We must stop.'

'Not now, not now.'

He covered her mouth with his own to prevent her speaking. She felt that he was smothering her. All his weight was upon her. Panic struck her. She tore her head away.

'No, no!' she cried. 'Stop! Leave me alone. You're hurting me.'

Bernardo ignored her.

She twisted and turned, tried to push him away, and at last, in desperation, she clawed at his head, grabbing his hair and pushing against him as hard as she could. She felt she would die if he didn't let her go, and an eternity seemed to pass while she struggled and frantically pleaded with him.

'Please, please don't,' she begged again and again.

In the end he yielded to her, and she relaxed her grip on his hair. He said not a word but stood up and turned his back towards her. Elvira was glad. She was too ashamed to look him in the face. She also silently stood up, rearranged her clothes and put on her coat. Bernardo remained as he was. He had taken off his jacket, and his shirt sleeves were rolled up. They were always rolled up, even in wintertime, and she could see that his fists were clenched.

Elvira, feeling contrite, longing to think of something suitable to say, picked up the jacket and, approaching hesitantly, placed it across his shoulders. He shook himself angrily and the jacket fell at his feet.

'Bernardo . . . ' She hesitated, afraid. 'I'm sorry,' she said, almost with the voice of a child. And again, 'I'm sorry.'

Still he didn't look at her or answer.

'I shouldn't have let things go so far,' she began again, 'but I didn't realise. I . . . ' Her voice faded.

At last, he turned to face her, and his look made her shrink still further, an implacable mixture of anger and scorn. His voice, when he spoke, was completely bereft of any gentleness or consideration.

'What do you think I am? A machine that can stop and start at the touch of a switch? A boy of eighteen to be satisfied with coquetry and little girls' tricks?'

She began to apologise again, but he broke in without listening to her.

'So you've got me like a little bird on a string, fluttering at your command. When you tug the string, I come, and when you're tired of playing, you stick me back in the cage.' He shook his head. 'Well, now the little bird is getting weary. I've endured it for a long time. All the promises that lead nowhere! I'm sick of it. I'm a man, Elvira. I need a woman, and I want you.'

They were both silent, Elvira unable to meet Bernardo's gaze, at first mortified by his words and worried by his last ones.

She looked up eventually and said, 'I didn't understand. I didn't mean to give you false promises, but you must realise we can't... we mustn't. Not yet.'

He saw the fear in her eyes but was unmoved by it.

'Don't worry. I shan't touch you again. Keep your precious virginity. Exchange it on your wedding night for a ring with as many carats as possible. But don't expect me to come running any more at the snap of your fingers.'

He picked up the jacket and slung it over his shoulder. Releasing Elvira from his gaze, he coldly said, 'Come on.'

'Where are we going?'

'Back to Burgos.'

'But—Sole. We promised to meet her at the church.'

'You can if you like.'

He was striding swiftly, and Elvira had to run to keep up with him. Her throat was pained with hardly constrained sobs. She couldn't trust herself to speak. Why had this to happen when the day had promised so well? Was it really all her fault? Anger succeeded remorse, and she forgot her tears.

She stopped hurrying and called after him, 'Go on then and good riddance to you. Animal! You expect me to be as shameless as yourself?'

He ignored her and kept walking. She called after him all the scornful, insulting words she could think of, little caring that she sounded like a vulgar shrew, and when he was almost out of earshot added, 'A curse upon the day I ever met you.'

IV

Sole knew. How could she not know when she found Elvira alone outside the church, head sunk in her upturned coat collar? Her question, 'And Bernardo?' remained unanswered, and she knew her younger sister's moods too well to dig any further just then.

Elvira was plunged in darkest misery, having grown colder and colder as she sat in the church waiting for her sister and the bus. In spite of herself, she couldn't help wishing that Bernardo was sat beside her, keeping her warm and making her laugh. And she hated him all the more because she couldn't stop thinking about him, wallowing in resentment.

On the way home, Sole did all the talking. There was plenty for her to say about Paco's relatives, who had given her some very pretty things for the baby, but Elvira hardly listened, staring moodily at the quickly darkening vista beyond the window, her mind a blank. She knew she would have to face a lot of questions but just then, she didn't want to think at all, having exhausted her anger against Bernardo and not daring to probe the depths of her own sense of shame.

She managed to avoid the expected interrogation till the following morning, pleading a severe headache and escaping to bed before Paco came up from the shop. She'd eaten nothing that day since breakfast because the bread and cheese Bernardo had provided for them both were still in his jacket pocket when he marched off, so she was grateful when Sole brought her a glass of milk and some biscuits before retiring for the night herself, but the manner in which she did so boded ill for the morrow.

All night she tossed and turned, unable to escape the web of emotions that entangled her. To see those eyes that had only ever expressed affection and merriment suddenly dark with fierce anger was an unbearable memory that she wanted to tear from her head but couldn't. It implacably stayed with her. Used to her father's rages, hardly moved except to be spurred on to parallel them, she had expected no dark side in Bernardo, and that look, which mirrored the harshness of his accusation, plunged her into deep confusion.

It pursued her, hounded her. She hated herself, she hated Bernardo, she hated her father, she hated her sister. It was bad enough not being able to escape the memory; the thought of having it dragged out of her, of having to somehow describe her shame, was more than she could bear. Even though it was all Bernardo's fault, she knew blaming him wasn't going to be enough. Sole would blame her, too. And it wasn't her fault. It wasn't. He should have respected her. He should have known she wouldn't, she couldn't. He shouldn't have tried to make her. No man would ever have her until she had a wedding ring on her finger, and Bernardo never. She would never marry him, never!

But none of these passionate thoughts could drive away that dark expression he had turned on her, not even the flood of tears that soaked the pillow as she was finally overtaken by the sleep of exhaustion.

As anticipated, the interrogation took place as soon as Paco had gone and the baby had been fed and settled. To salve her own conscience, Sole hardly listened to Elvira's defence, over-riding it with strong accusations and the reiterated reminder, 'I told you so,' and rejecting out of hand her sister's equally insistent denial of any culpability.

'You always want your own way. You won't listen to anyone. What else did you expect? I told you so. You can't blame him when you so deliberately went off on your own with him. Why did you, anyway, if it wasn't what you wanted?'

'I trusted him.'

'Well, you shouldn't have. I told you, but you wouldn't listen. I must have been crazy to listen to you in the first place and let him come here. I didn't think you'd let me down. I'm beginning to think that Father was right about you. He was thinking of your own good.'

'You won't tell him, will you?' Elvira begged.

'How can I? But if anything comes of it . . . '

'It won't. I promise. He didn't. He didn't—'

'Go all the way?' Sole prompted, seeing her sister satisfyingly crushed for once and without words, and when she shamefacedly nodded, added sarcastically, 'You were lucky then.'

After a long silence, when the passions of them both had subsided, Sole, with an attempt at solicitude, moved somewhat by Elvira's wretched appearance, asked, 'Did he hurt you?' and, at the negative shake of the downcast head, changed the subject.

Bernardo had returned to his lodgings, walking all the way for there was no bus until much later, angry with Elvira, angry with himself. He threw his few things into the suitcase, left a scattering of money on the table where the landlady could not miss it, in too much turmoil to realise what he was doing, guided by passion alone. At the station, he had to wait an hour for the last train back to Aranda and spent the time in the railway canteen, drinking cognac and reading the newspapers without taking in a word of the political agitations mentioned in its pages. He refused to think about anything and fell asleep on the train in spite of the bunch of soldiers who were shouting out ditties behind him.

As soon as he returned to Los Pinos, he knew that he had done wrong. He had behaved like a wilful child, and now there was no hope of apologising to Elvira or letting her know how much he regretted his actions until she returned to Quintera. He was afraid to write a letter in case it fell into Paco's hands first and had to live with the burden on his conscience, unable to know what Elvira must be thinking of him, sure that she would never forgive him.

He cursed himself a thousand times for his stupidity and heartlessness and hardly knew how to bear with his own presence. The only gleam to brighten his terrible despondency was the knowledge that Elvira was due to return to Quintera within a few weeks. Perhaps when they could be together again in their own surroundings, he would be able to make her understand his feelings and hope that she would have compassion on him. But he knew that she could be relentless when she wished and had no great confidence in her understanding, so deeply influenced was she by the restraints of her upbringing. She could have written to him, after all, but didn't. Probably her pride wouldn't let her unless she believed that he was still angry with her and no longer loved her. Either idea caused him hell.

Elvira didn't return when he expected her. Martínez managed to postpone the occasion for another month, dreading that the same trouble might start all over again now that Bernardo was back. Elvira fumed, saying that she was bored to death in Burgos and longed to be home again, begging to be back in time for the bull caping at the end of May, and he reluctantly agreed. After all, he couldn't keep her in exile forever.

For Bernardo, two months with neither word from nor sight of Elvira were a torment. With each day, he grew less confident of his ability to win back her undoubtedly lost affection, and the patience which had always been part of his character and had stood him in good stead all the previous summer, deserted him. He had spent too much time waiting. The hours dragged along too slowly, and nothing that he did to keep himself occupied was enough to distract his tortured heart.

His mother asked too many questions, sensing his turmoil, his friends laughed at him. They said he was a fool and advised him to find another woman. Cándido said that his youngest sister had been madly in love with Bernardo for ages—she was only twelve.

'Suppose you wait four years for her? You'll still be able to have her before you get the other one,' he laughed, but Bernardo could find nothing amusing in his suggestion.

Nothing and no one could divert his thoughts, and he wanted only to get away from the village, to escape the misery that entangled him. In spite of his aversion to city life, his brother's promises offered a kind of hope. But he must see Elvira at least once more before he left, needing her assurance to give him courage, or at least to have her tell him whether he could ever count on a future with her or not.

V

Elvira returned to Quintera a few days before the annual bull caping which was celebrated at Corpus Christi. It had long been a traditional event whose initial expense was borne by the mayor and the leading citizens, and pleasure-seekers from miles away turned up for the occasion as it was the one great drama of the year and could keep people talking for the next twelve months. The fiesta was spread over the whole day, with mass in the morning followed by an eating and drinking competition, the caping in the afternoon and dancing in the evening. Faustino supplied the wine and food for the competition, the latter cooked by volunteers; the mayor paid for the hired bull; Faustino's son-in-law, Don Pedro, arranged the orchestra and the decorations, including fireworks, and the doctor attended the caping in his official capacity but always under protest. He considered the event on a par with throwing Christians to the lions, both criminal and barbaric, and insisted on being paid for his services should they be required.

He deplored the mindless animation of the onlookers as with jeers, laughter, insults and applause they obliged inexperienced hirelings to confront the full-strength charge of a heavyweight killer and, artistically using a cape to control its movements, attempt to plant at least one, if not two pairs of darts in its shoulders, and to keep on trying until success, injury or exhaustion brought the ordeal to an end, sometimes as much as an hour later. Facing risks no professional would dream of unless desperate, and all for a moment of glory and a pittance hardly sufficient to keep them alive for a week, these aspiring toreros were lucky if they escaped without serious and sometimes fatal harm.

The bull was the star of the afternoon, and this year's opponent was a wily five-year-old with a split horn which had done the rounds before, knew what to expect, and wasn't going to be deceived by capes, and the doctor's heart sank when he learned its history. He protested to the mayor, who just shrugged his shoulders with the excuse, 'It's all I could get.'

'You get what you pay for,' he flung back heatedly as he stalked off, expecting the worst, not wanting to think of the lads he'd patched up over the years, some of whom might well have died later from septicaemia.

Martínez supposed that Bernardo would come along with his family and was determined to have a careful watch kept on Elvira in case they happened to meet. He warned his wife to chaperone her strictly, and his wife warned Elvira's two married sisters in her turn. Half Quintera seemed intent on watching her, but she pretended to be undismayed, as if nothing could be further from her mind than talking to Bernardo.

She wore a white, flowered dress, as low-cut as her mother would allow. Her shoulders were almost bare. She brushed back her hair into the nape of her neck, tied with a white ribbon, and then draped a long black veil over her head and shoulders so that she would be quite respectable for the mass which started the day.

While the concentration of most was on the eating and drinking competition, Elvira was hemmed in by various family members. They had been well-briefed, and she was obliged to watch, hardly able to turn her head away from the spectacle without someone noticing. Beginning with giant-sized helpings of haricot beans stewed with pigs' ears and highly spiced sausage, followed by fat potato omelettes, each one large enough for a working man's lunch, with as much bread and wine as they could swallow, few men stayed the course. It was great entertainment, even inspiring some betting among the spectators, and the last man standing was rewarded with a young pig and many hearty cheers. The doctor had no sympathy for those who rolled about groaning afterwards but neither did anyone else.

Elvira was surprised to see that Bernardo, with his usual friends, Cándido and Gerardo, was seated with bravado at one of the trestle tables around which were crowding the competitors. It was a thing he had never done before, and she was angry at seeing him there, joining in the conversation that kept the occupants of the table in fits of laughter and causing older women nearby to call shame on the lot of them. She blushed for him and kept well away, not knowing if he had seen her and not wanting him to.

The three friends drank a lot of wine but didn't take part in the competition. They wandered away from the table, leaning on each other's shoulders, eyeing all the girls quite brazenly. Elvira saw that her father was watching them. She noticed the disdain and the satisfaction with which he observed Bernardo, and she hated both of them for causing her so much mortification and sorrow. But he was worse in the afternoon, encouraged by his companions who found his unusual behaviour extremely amusing and urged him on.

Before the actual bull caping, it was the custom for the lads to show off with a heifer let loose in the barricaded plaza. Like the bull, this was often an animal rented out by its owners for these local entertainments. Depending on her experience and character, she might be vicious or cowed. Either way, sooner or later, she would be sufficiently persuaded or tormented into making some sort of attack, at which the lads would scatter with shouts of laughter or remain as close as they dared when she turned round on them, trying to grab a horn or her tail. The idea was to amuse themselves and the spectators at the heifer's expense and indulge their own high spirits, helped along by the admiration, scoffing or squealing of the girls. Confused by jackets flapping about her, jabbed by sticks doing service as swords, callously stabbed by whoever happened to have a knife, punched, kicked, dragged to the ground and sat on if she couldn't escape a concentrated attack, if she was brave, she would get some applause. If not, she would be pitilessly battered.

Bernardo had never taken part in this event, not even as a youth boasting of his manhood and out to impress the girls. The mindless brutality of both the afternoon's events offended him, and he shrugged off his friends' derision. But to the dismay of those who cared for him and the entertainment of the rest, that afternoon he jumped into the circle with Gerardo and Cándido and somehow managed to drape himself over the heifer's head between her horns. Her efforts to shake him off and his efforts to cling on raised a lot of laughter and cheers. He ended up under her belly in the dust and was only saved from a possible horning by the quick actions of his friends.

'What on earth's got into him?' said the doctor to his wife, viewing the spectacle with swelling rage.

Dionisia remained silent, as uncomprehending as her husband. She sensed that Bernardo's unhappiness was at the root of it, although she found his behaviour illogical, for if he were so unhappy, why should he play the clown?

The grocer watched the exhibition with intense satisfaction. Bernardo's behaviour that day entirely justified his opinion of the doctor's son, and he hoped that Elvira was watching too.

'Thoroughly drunk and thoroughly disgusting,' he remarked to the mayor who stood beside him. He spoke in a tone loud enough for the doctor, who was just behind him, to overhear.

'He's too old for such nonsense,' agreed the mayor. 'I would never have thought him capable of it, either.'

'He's capable of anything is that one. The quiet ones are all the same. They break out now and again, and when they do, they're worse than all the rest.'

'It's just as well you've managed to steer your daughter clear of him then. I suppose it's all over between them?'

'No doubt of it. I knew she'd come round in the end.' Faustino laughed with proud satisfaction. 'I thank God I know how to treat my daughters. One mustn't be too soft with them. Women always appreciate an iron hand.'

Dionisia had wanted to interrupt this conversation, indignant at hearing her son so berated, but her husband put a restraining hand upon her and told her not to add to the scene.

'Pray that he won't jump in with the bull as well!' he ironically suggested, but at the sudden dart of fear that crossed her face, quickly added, 'I'm joking, woman. He's not that drunk.' He was thinking, 'not that desperate' while wondering just how desperate he was.

But Dionisia was already praying and crossing herself, alarmed by his words because it did sometimes happen that a drunk or over-enthusiastic spectator would join the fray.

Martínez thoroughly enjoyed himself that day. He saw that Elvira seemed unaware of Bernardo's existence. She kept away from wherever he happened to be, and he apparently ignored her also. His mind was much at rest, especially when he saw her once in conversation with Don Jaime, looking animated and acting the coquette. In the evening, he saw her dancing with the same man and with several others, all of Quintera, and knowing that her mother and sisters were chaperoning her, Faustino left her to it, joining the mayor and one or two others in a private celebration, which developed into a political discussion more than anything else and kept them occupied until two in the morning.

Yes, in the grocer's opinion, it was altogether a satisfactory fiesta, except that one of the young capers was horned by the bull and died on a tavern table, his blood unstanched by the tourniquet and swabs that the doctor vainly held to the wound in his groin. When the mayor announced his death, a lot of the girls cried, but it made their eyes all the brighter for the dancing later on. The other lad, who had been a close friend of the one who died, got himself drunk at the mayor's expense and spent the night in the arms of a free-living widow from Peña Alta who took pity on these lads every year.

VI

The dancing had been underway for nearly an hour before Elvira found an opportunity to escape from the vigilant eyes of all who watched her. Her sisters had joined a group to gossip, and her mother had taken charge of someone's baby and was crooning over it. Bernardo had caught her eye when the band first struck up, signalling for her to follow him. If she didn't get away soon, he might give up waiting for her. She didn't even know where she should find him, having seen nothing of him since he had caught her attention.

She slipped unobtrusively from the gathering, wishing suddenly that she hadn't chosen to wear a white dress, and kept to the lengthening shadows, turning into an alley which led to the outskirts of the village. Would Bernardo have seen her and follow? She hung about for five minutes or more before a figure also turned into the alley. Elvira hesitated, not certain of the person's identity, for the only illumination was that offered by the moon.

'Are you there?' came Bernardo's voice softly, and she ran to meet him.

They clung to each other for a long moment, moving into a corner behind one of the houses. Then they parted to stare at each other, their faces shadowy. The moonlight caught Elvira's face for a moment, illuminating her irresolution, her perplexity. Bernardo missed nothing of her beauty, nothing of her misery, and he folded her in his arms again, his head against hers, castigated by her expression. He hurt her without realising it, crushing her so close, and was unable to speak. He moved his head agitatedly, and then he was crying. She had never heard a man cry before, and the harsh, unexpected sobs frightened her.

Bernardo had introduced Elvira to many new emotions but never had she experienced such distress as she stood in his arms and felt his shuddering sobs. She pulled his head to her shoulder and caressed him with a tenderness alien to her until this moment, her throat too constricted for words. This was a Bernardo she had never understood, never imagined, and for the first time, a realisation of the depth of his love for her was aroused. She had been playing a defensive, frivolous game for so long, constantly rebuffing him, capricious and self-centred, and she must have hurt him many times either unwittingly or deliberately.

At last, he said, 'Do you forgive me for—'

'Ssh!' she almost sharply hushed him. She couldn't bear for that memory to come between them now, but he went on, 'I treated you so badly. Oh God, what a brute I am! But I love you so much. If only you could know. I've been through hell these last weeks.'

'Don't, don't, she pleaded. 'Don't say any more. I shouldn't have let you think . . . I didn't understand . . . '

The moonlight exaggerated the intensity of Bernardo's gaze, and she couldn't trust herself to say any more, hardly knowing what was in her head or her heart, and there was a long silence while they just clung to one another.

He kissed her again, crushing her so tightly against him that she almost struggled to escape. His mouth pressed into her lips, his arms stopped all movement of her lungs. Eventually, he released her, but Elvira had thought that she was going to be suffocated first. She was shaken. Even in Burgos, Bernardo had not begun so passionately as this, and his breath was sour with wine. Elvira felt weak, lost. She was far beyond her depth and knew of no way back.

She let him take her hand and lead her along the alley, which led to the watering-place where a dog was lapping at moonlit water. There were no people, all were at the dance, but their voices were still clear enough to remind them to be careful. Beyond this place, the water became a bubbling stream, stony and deep enough to paddle in. On either side were fields of young corn. The banks were thick with poppies and cornflowers, their colours lost in the darkness, but their scent was heavy in the grass, and the stream gurgled lazily and occasionally plopped as some creature disturbed the rhythm of its flow.

Elvira was unaware of the night's perfume, of the harmony produced by the nocturnal creatures, of the now brilliant moon which kept them from stumbling. She was too much aware of Bernardo to notice anything, realising his intentions and not knowing how much she should concede. She knew he had drunk far too much that day, and hadn't her mother warned her against drunken men? Had he forgotten his promise, made in Burgos, to never touch her again, and should she remind him of it?

She didn't know what to do, the deeply embedded strictures which had protected her while her emotions were not truly engaged, now losing ground to the desire to make Bernardo happy. She had seen him so wretched all day, his tears still seemed damp in her hair, and if surrendering herself to him would bring back the cheerfulness to his eyes and the ever-ready smile to his lips, surely it would be no bad thing that she did? But her mother had always insisted that a man would never marry a girl who said yes, no matter how much he was supposed to love her. The situation was beyond her control, and while the cicadas chorused, the stream bubbled, and sheep bells tinkled in the distance, Elvira heard and saw nothing, greatly perturbed, defences crumbling as these new sensations overwhelmed and confused her.

She put up no resistance when Bernardo stopped to embrace her again, drawing her to the ground. Neither spoke. There was too much emotion between them for words. Bernardo laid back on the carpet of grass and wildflowers and undid his shirt buttons. He began to stroke Elvira's arm, but she sat with her back towards him, feeling his great longing but afraid to allow herself to be overcome by it. He pulled her round gently, untangling her fingers from the grass and placing her hand on his chest.

'Feel,' he said. His heart was thumping wildly. 'It beats like that just for you, but you have no compassion. It could burst for all you'd care.'

He shut his eyes, and Elvira gazed down at him, her hand still clutched to his breast, and she saw clearly for the first time how changed was his face, its lines of happy carelessness lost in frustrated desire. The heavy eyes, the frowning brow had never been part of his features, and again it struck her deeply that his love for her had brought him no happiness, only pain and heart sickness.

'I do care,' she returned at last. 'Don't think I don't care. It's just that—'

'It's just that you care more to go to confession with a clear conscience.' His tone was bitter, impatient. 'You've never told me that you love me. I've told you a thousand times, and you laugh at me.'

Elvira was stung by his accusation. She knew it was true. Those simple words—I love you—had never sprung impulsively from her lips. She read about love, she talked about love, she had told her father she loved and would marry Bernardo to spite and enrage him, but she had never let her heart run free.

She couldn't speak and he, aware of her quandary and weakening willpower, sat up, pulled her close and covered her with passionate kisses that both frightened and excited her.

'Tell me that you love me,' he insisted. 'Show me that you love me the way I love you. You already have my heart and soul. Won't you give me anything in exchange?'

He removed the ribbon that held her hair in check, and as it fell round her shoulders, he pressed his face into its inviting thickness with more kisses, gentler now, while feeling for the buttons that would undo the dress. Elvira, struggling to say those words he longed to hear and yet which somehow she found so hard to speak, hardly noticed.

She spoke his name, but there was that hesitation in the tone which he, misunderstanding, compelled him to interrupt. 'Don't say no. Not now. Don't kill me, Elvira. Don't kill me.'

Distressed by the force of his plea, heart racing, she was unaware that the dress had slipped from her shoulders. All she knew was that she wanted to give herself to this man who had loved her so constantly with the love she had been seeking for so long and yet had not recognised until now. She wanted him as hungrily as he wanted her. She wanted to plunge into that sea of love that he was always promising her and which she had regarded of so little worth. She did love him. She was choked with love for him. It surged through her whole being, insisting on total surrender. There was no going back. But if this was to be her wedding night, she wanted to give herself freely. With or without a priest, she felt it to be a sacred moment.

So, set free from all that had constricted her for so long, she stood up, putting a finger to her lips as a sign for him to be patient, and as a bride coming to that moment of full consecration, she simply slipped out of all her garments before lying back on the grass and with open arms invited him to make her his own.

VII

Later they lay side by side and looked at the stars. Bernardo knew the names of many of them and the legends surrounding them. As a lad, he had spent many a summer night under the stars with the merinos, and his uncle taught him about the constellations, feeding his ever-hungry imagination even while he felt both lost and intoxicated by the vastness of the silent, sparkling glory above them.

He drew her attention to this one and that, adding, 'They're smiling at us. Look!' She laughed at him, so he took her hand and pointed one of her fingers up to the sky, directing it first to this one and then to that, as childishly happy as she was, and it did seem as though they somehow knew and winked at their happiness.

Elvira was too contented to speak. She cuddled closer to Bernardo, resting her head on his shoulder, enjoying the feel of his warm nakedness against her own, basking in sensual satisfaction, accompanied by an instinctive pride in knowing herself now to be a woman, a wife.

'What would Becquer say?' she wondered at last, knowing that Bernardo's oracle usually had a comment for every occasion.

'Becquer had forgotten happiness. Most of his poems are of love disillusioned.'

'But he must have written something cheerful.'

'Yes.' He thought for a moment. 'Listen. *"Today the earth and the skies smile on me; today the sun reaches to the depths of my soul; today I have seen her . . . I have seen her, and she has noticed me. Today I believe in God!"'*

'Is that how you feel too?'

'Exactly.' He fondled her hair.

'Didn't you believe in God before . . . before today?' She sounded both curious and troubled.

'I believe in love, in beauty, in life, freedom . . . If those things are from God, then I believe in God too. If he made the stars and the land and the wind and the rain, then I believe.'

He put both his arms round her, his kisses so gentle they were like a playful whisper on her skin, provoking in her a desire never to be parted from him again. How could they go their separate ways now, he to Los Pinos, she to Quintera? They belonged together.

She sighed deeply and said, 'I wish it really was our wedding night so we could stay together, properly married.'

'We shall be, very soon. In August, as soon as you're twenty-one.'

'But how? Surely my father can still stop us.'

'You'll be twenty-one. You can do as you like. We'll be together in Madrid, and no one shall keep us apart.'

'Madrid!'

'It's the only way. I've been thinking about it seriously. My brother says he'll find me a job. And if I don't like his job, surely there must be room for one more carpenter in a big city. I shall find us somewhere to live, and we'll be married as soon as we can.'

He explained to her about the new law, but still she was doubtful. Madrid was a long way away.

'Shall we see each other again before you go? Must you go soon? I can't bear to think of being without you now.'

'We'll find a way. Don't worry. And in August you must come, too. I'll give you some money before I go and you must hide it where your mother won't find it. Do you think you'll be brave enough to leave home on your own and go to Madrid?'

'If I know you're waiting for me, yes. And we'll be married straight away?'

'Straight away. The very same day if possible.'

'And does it really matter about not being married by a priest?'

'Do you think it does?'

Elvira frowned. 'I don't know.' Till now, she had never imagined that it could be any other way. Wistfully she went on, 'I would have liked to be married properly, like my sisters and my friends, and have a big celebration afterwards with my family.'

'We'll have a big celebration. My brother will help me arrange it. It'll be just like a real wedding. The church doesn't matter any more.'

'I don't know,' Elvira doubted again.

'It's the only way,' insisted Bernardo. 'Your father will never let us marry. And I want you so much.'

He put his arm round her and drew her closer. 'Don't you feel already married? Hasn't it made you feel that we belong to each other, that we're already one person?'

Elvira nodded mutely, rubbing her head against his shoulder.

'The rest is only a device to protect society. Real marriage is two people living together and loving each other. There's nothing sinful in that, and if we were all honest, responsible creatures, like the birds, marriage laws wouldn't be necessary. I could live a lifetime with you without going through any ceremony. Don't you feel the same?'

'Yes, but . . .'

'But you've been brought up to believe that anything outside the sanction of the Church is sinful.'

'If it's not true, why—'

'With you, nothing is sinful,' he comforted her. 'All is beautiful and good, but to oblige society and to satisfy your conscience, I'm prepared to marry you legally, and all the little Bernardos and Elviritas can bear my name with impunity.'

There was a distant, crackling sound, a swish, and a flash of cascading light among the stars.

'The fireworks,' said Elvira. 'The dancing must be over. We'd better get back before I'm missed.'

She started up, but Bernardo pulled her down again.

'There's time. The fireworks have only just begun. You've always been too fond of hurrying away.'

'But—'

'Just once more,' he pleaded. 'Then we'll go. But I can't bear to say goodbye to you tonight.'

Elvira yielded, unable to refuse him anything now that she was his. She proffered herself with a generosity that had never guided a single act in her life, forgetting herself in him, her materialism swamped by love.

VIII

They managed to meet again on several occasions. Elvira, once stirred, was as passionate as her lover, and she recklessly heeded the feverish demands that her heart and body made upon her. There was no sleeping that was not made beautiful by dreams of him, no waking hour in which she was not tormented by her distance from him. How she managed to conceal her desperate impatience and terrible longing from her family, she did not know. She hardly knew herself at all in those days, torn by restless excitement, wearied by endless hours, all of which were haunted by Bernardo. Everything was Bernardo, and the only time that her whole body and mind could be at peace was when she lay in his arms consenting, and they were one person instead of two.

It wasn't easy for them to be together. Only Elvira's determination and recklessness made it possible. She gave free rein to that explosive temper, comparable with her father's, which reduced her mother to silence about the many hours she was absent from home. Saturday was the easiest day because it was the only one on which she could be sure that Fidel and her father would be in the shop until ten, serving and clearing up for the weekend. Also, the village was full of people on a Saturday afternoon and evening, strolling about the square, frequenting the casino, and no one would either notice or miss her particularly.

She met Bernardo not far from Quintera at an abandoned dwelling, its rough stone walls windowless, its thatched roof sinking inwards. Time was too short and too precious for searching farther afield for something better, and when they were together the outside world was nonexistent. Sunlight filtered through many small holes in the thatch, and one was large enough to give them a glimpse of the sky. It was all they needed, that little patch of blue, and it wasn't difficult for them to imagine that it was heaven that they saw, so near and always benevolent.

But Bernardo was not as equally lost as Elvira in the passion of the moment. True that when they first came together, there was nothing but her body and his burning together, but afterwards, he was more clear-headed and she less. She lived only for the moment, for those few hours and for the next time they should meet, but he thought further ahead, knowing that any future life they could have together rested with him and that this was the wrong way to go about achieving their ultimate desire. He knew that for once in his life he must act instead of dream, but to find the courage to leave Elvira now—it wasn't easy. She knew he must go. They both knew it well, but she clung to him fiercely, and his laid-back nature was not strong enough to resist her.

One day she said, 'Are you really going to Madrid?' thinking that perhaps it was only an idea.

'I must. This way, we'll get nowhere, and it will end badly.'

'Couldn't you go and see my father again first?'

'What for? Once was enough, and if he finds out that we're seeing each other now—and like this—it'll be the end. You know it will.'

She shook her head violently. 'Never! My father will never stop me now.' She clung tightly to him. 'I love you. I need you. He'd have to kill me to keep me from you. Why can't I come to Madrid with you now?'

Having flung off all the restraints that had imprisoned her passionate spirit for so long, she was heedless of any consequences. What if she did get pregnant? Her father would then have to let them marry. And they could go to Madrid together.

Bernardo was beginning to realize he had unleashed a volcano and needed to take some control.

'I can't just turn up with you at my brother's house! I'll first have to find us somewhere to live. There must be lots of places in a big city, and he'll help me find somewhere. We mustn't be reckless any more. Don't worry. I'll send for you as soon as I see things clearly, which will be very soon, I'm sure. We must be patient. In two months we can be married. It's not long.'

'It's eight Saturdays long, and I can't live without you.'

'Yes, you can. You can be as hard as nails when you want to and stronger than I am. If we go together, I shall do nothing but make love to you, and that will resolve nothing.'

'But how can you leave me? You say I'm hard, but you must be harder, although you pretend not to be.'

'My heart, do you want us ever to get married or not?'

'Yes, but—'

'Then no "buts". That is how it must be. Staying here will get us nowhere.' He pulled her into his arms. 'Let's forget about it for a while. Why waste the few hours we have in argument?'

He leaned over her and smiled, but she didn't look at him. She was staring up at the little bit of sky, which she could hardly see for the tears that blurred her eyes.

'Elvira!' he exclaimed. 'You're crying. I don't think I've ever seen tears in your eyes before.'

She retorted bitterly, blinking them rapidly away, 'And so that's why you think I have no heart.'

'Silly. I know you've a heart. Isn't it inside me, giving me no peace?'

He kissed away the tears.

'If you cry, you'll make me decide to stay here with you forever, in this little place, until we're hounded out like Adam and Eve from the Garden of Eden. Your father would be the avenging angel with the sword. Could you imagine him, with shining wings and flowing robes—'

'And a moustache!'

They both began to laugh, and then they stopped, their eyes meeting in mutual wanting.

'My heart, why are you so beautiful?' breathed Bernardo.

She drew him towards her without words and closed her eyes.

A strange, sweet sadness seemed to pervade her and, enclosed in Bernardo's arms, unseeing, unthinking, she felt that to die in that moment would have been the utmost satisfaction they could reach. Nothing could be more perfect than this ever. If only this didn't have to be woken up from; if only her father, their separation and unhappiness were all things of the past and the past non-existent, paradise would be theirs. Tears slid down the sides of her face into her hair, loosed from its ribbon. She clung to Bernardo, weeping silently, for the world could never be as sweet again as it was just then.

Bernardo didn't have the courage to see Elvira any more. He knew too well that each meeting with her weakened his resolve and that while he could see her and have her, he would never make the final steps that would take him to Madrid and the freedom to love her as he wished. He wrote her a letter informing her of his decision and enclosing money enough to take her to Madrid also when the time came, but he didn't give it to Cándido for delivery until the very last day, half afraid that she would come storming over to Los Pinos regardless of the consequences.

When he told his parents he had decided to go to Madrid and that as soon as he had found some work and a home for Elvira, he was going to marry her under the new civil law, which didn't require a church wedding, Dionisia was shocked. Her faith in the Church was great, and surely it would be a mortal sin to go against it. And what about the wedding? Was he going to do the same as his brother, turn his back on them, marry without letting them know? Shame them before the neighbours? Arturo and Paquita were at least properly married by a priest, she wailed.

Though the doctor wasn't surprised by his son's decision and cared nothing for the church, he counselled more patience even though he could see no other way out of the predicament, knowing the strength of the grocer's influence in local affairs. He was more concerned about the heightened tensions of the political situation.

'Think about it, son. It's not the best time to go. The newspapers carry reports of gun battles in the streets,' he reminded him.

'What do I care about that? It's nothing to do with me. I'm not going to get into politics.'

A cry had burst from Dionisia at her husband's words. 'My son, don't put yourself in danger.'

'Mother, I'm going to look for a job, not trouble. Arturo will help me.'

'But wait till things calm down. Listen to your father if you won't listen to me. And what about the fields? Who's going to work them if you're not here?'

'That's all sorted with Frumencio. You don't need to worry. You'll still get a fair share.'

Between tears and handwringing and pleading from his mother, and fewer but sober words from his father, Bernardo eventually cried in exasperation, 'I can't stay here waiting and doing nothing any longer. I want to marry Elvira, and I want it to be soon. I'm sick of deception and not being with her. I'll get a job, and we'll marry as soon as she's twenty-one, and we'll have a life of our own with no one to interfere and tell us how to live.'

After what seemed like a long silence, 'Is that how you think of us, as interfering rather than trying to help?' Dionisia asked him, deeply injured. 'If it is, you'd better go. I'd rather you went your own way than believe that we are trying to hinder you.'

And so Bernardo went, and nine months were to pass before his mother saw him again, but then he was in prison and had only fifteen days left to live.

PART FOUR

War came on the 18th of July.

From the 13th, when the assassination of Calvo Sotelo, hero and now martyr of the right-wing, became common news, and while the government daily insisted that it had the situation 'well in hand,' the situation swiftly degenerated.

For days beforehand, when it was realized that things were coming to a head, the battery radio in the casino was kept tuned in to Madrid so that those whose business it was to keep ahead of things could be prepared for any contingency and late on the Saturday night, the place was crowded. Martínez was there, chewing his moustache, his son Faustino bulky beside him; Dr de Rosas looking tired and unhealthy, drinking more wine than anybody; the landowner, Don Pedro; Jaime Segundo, the transport man, the two schoolteachers, all the leading men of the two villages in fact, and also the priest. It was a suffocatingly hot night, heavy with sweat, cigar and cigarette smoke, while the various oil lamps cast a Goya-like glow over the taut, excited or impassive faces.

'It will be war,' stated the mayor, feeling the need to exert an authoritative opinion. Then he added somewhat equivocally, and certainly unwisely, 'The people won't stand for it.'

'Won't stand for what? It's about time this rabble of a government was thrown out. We've been following a downward path ever since the king abdicated. Something has got to be done.'

This was Martínez, surprised by the mayor's unclear sentiments.

'There won't be a war,' disagreed Don Pedro. 'This new lot in government will be all for appeasement. They'll make some concessions, and everything will be forgotten within a few weeks.' He spoke regretfully.

'That's what I mean,' insisted the mayor, excited by opposition. 'The people won't stand for appeasement. They'll take things into their own hands if the government shows any signs of weakening.'

'And which side will you be on?' enquired Martínez coldly.

But the man refused to be drawn, and for all the excited conversation that went on, no one could be certain whether or not the situation had exploded beyond recovery.

However, on the following day they knew, for on that day the government was obliged to admit that civil unrest had turned into outright military rebellion, with insurrections in many provincial garrisons; that the elite Army of Africa and the feared Foreign Legion were spear-heading the revolt; that there was street fighting in Barcelona. But the government continued to have the situation under control, and the same night the government resigned, and a new one was formed. There was confusion, chaos, and in Madrid, a call from the people to be armed.

Within a few days, it was common knowledge that rebel officers had taken command of the garrison at Burgos, having arrested, demoted or otherwise dealt with the loyalists. This event created great excitement in both Quintera and Los Pinos, and those of military age were generally eager to volunteer or return to the regiment where once they had been conscripts.

The mayor felt obliged to call a meeting at the town hall, and the place heaved with emotions let loose. Several of the group were men of property or of substantial middle-class background—the bourgeoisie so hated by the anarchists—but among them were the less well to do farmers who would rather die than lose the fruit of many generations of hard labour. All felt threatened by the new social order the government was determined to push through. They wanted it to fail.

For Martínez, his moment had come. He had never liked the mayor, jealous for the position himself, and if he could cause him discomfort, it would be a triumph he could savour for days. So he returned to his previous attack, not even disguising his antipathy and determined to force a confrontation.

In a commanding tone and with undisguised irony, he over-rode all the voices, putting again the question that the mayor had previously refused to answer at the casino. 'Mr Mayor, we should all like to know your position in this matter. Whose side are you on?'

It wouldn't have occurred to anyone else to ask such a question, but now the doubt was publicly sown, and the mayor found himself the target of every curious eye. Evasion was not an option, so, struggling with his conscience while trying to play it safe, knowing that Martínez, with his son-in-law and ally Don Pedro, held greater sway over the two villages than himself, came down with bluster on the side of the middle party, Spain.

'With my country's interests so much at heart, how can I be anything but as pleased as all of you to know that something, at last, is being done to relieve it of the oppressive influences under which it has been labouring since the king's abdication?'

This was too ambiguous for Quintera's schoolmaster. He was used to boys trying to wriggle out of direct answers and liked a plain reply.

'But whose side are you on?' he cut in bluntly.

'Haven't I made it plain? I was saying—'

'The rebels or the Republic?' insisted the schoolmaster.

The mayor allowed his glance to fall coldly on his inquisitor and the rest. All avidly waited for his reply, wondering if already a traitor among them had been exposed. He opened his mouth, shut it again, and, intimidated by so many accusing or questioning faces, said quietly, for he couldn't bring himself to say it loudly, ashamed of his cowardice, 'The rebels.'

This declaration, forced from the mayor against his will, encouraged the whole gathering to voice their views in favour of the rebels. Someone called out, 'Long live the rebels!' others, 'Long live the king!' and 'Long live Spain!' the whole gathering responding with fervour, and a heated discussion was begun, each one certain that he personally had the best plan for winning the war quickly while the same victorious shouts echoed from outside, women and children among the labourers crowding round the open doors.

'Pain and death,' suddenly growled the doctor, 'that's all it'll be.'

'It had to come,' argued Martínez, assuming by the doctor's attitude that he was in favour of the Republic. He knew he was a socialist. And what was that lawyer son of his up to in Madrid? Again he was glad that the relationship between Elvira and Bernardo had been broken.

'You've got sons of fighting age, the same as I have. What's going to become of them and all the others? They're going to kill each other, and women will be weeping all over Spain. That had to come, Martínez? That's going to solve our political problems?'

'How would you suggest we solve them then?'

The doctor didn't answer. He didn't know. He realised that, in a way, the grocer was right. It had to come. There was no longer any escape from a bloody future. The people had endured too much to surrender their newfound freedom, and the right-wingers were too proud to bow down to them. If the republican government couldn't form a democracy and a united front and put paid to the anarchy on the streets, then one of the two sides would have to be crushed for good and all.

Dr de Rosas wasn't the only heart-sickened one among the triumphant. Father González, for all that he had reason to resent and even fear the Republic, was a pacific man, and he saw the events from the doctor's viewpoint, brother against brother, death and revenge. He listened to the conversation, some of it already savagely vindictive, without comment; noted the mayor's pale face and the doctor's unnaturally flushed one and mentally made separate notes about them both. The mayor had suddenly become a broken man, though none seemed openly to suspect it, and the doctor was killing himself with wine.

The civil guards were present to keep an eye on things but their deliberately blank expressions were unreadable. They represented law and order but now - whose law, whose order? Some of the men there wondered, as perhaps the guards themselves were wondering.

Father Gonzalez decided to hold a special mass in Quintera. He asked for God's intervention and voiced the hope that the powers of evil (without actually naming them) would be overthrown. The following Wednesday, he was called out to a dying man in Peña Alta, and from that village he did not return at the expected hour. He was gone for three days and, while he was gone, Quintera's church was set on fire by explosives planted behind the altar.

It happened at about two in the morning. The inhabitants in the main square were nearly shot out of their beds by the sudden blast, and within minutes everyone was in the street, the men struggling into pyjama jackets or holding on to their unsupported trousers as they rushed to find out what had happened.

Flames were soaring into the starlit sky, shooting up rapidly and devouring what was left after the explosion with amazing voracity. Someone had obviously splashed petrol around the walls of the nave and pews, or the flames could never have taken hold so rapidly, and, later, the bus owner confirmed that several cans had been stolen. There was nothing anyone could do except watch, and some fell to their knees, crossing themselves and praying. Martínez was among those who prayed.

It was soon over. The flames sank to nothing, and by dawn, they were looking upon a smouldering, blackened shell. When it was possible to examine further, it was discovered that all the valuables, few though they were, had disappeared, doubtless stolen beforehand. The body of Father González was not discovered, which was something they were grateful for, but it left them wondering where he could be and fearing for his safety.

The next night Martínez was again wakened in the early hours. This time it was no blast that took him from his bed but a slight, urgent tapping, which stopped and started, stopped and started. The first thought that jumped involuntarily to the grocer's sleep-riddled mind was that Bernardo had returned and was hoping to elope with Elvira in the middle of the night.

He left the bed quietly. His wife was a sound sleeper and had heard nothing. He thought it best not to disturb her, for if what he had assumed should be correct, she would shout and scream so much that the whole village would know within ten minutes of the shame to which his daughter had sunk. Again came the sound, and he peered cautiously out of the open window. He caught a glimpse of a dark figure down below whose identity he couldn't decide, for he could see neither the face nor the build of the man. He seemed huddled up or cloaked like a shepherd in order to conceal himself.

'Who is it?' he hissed. 'What do you want? Show yourself before I come down to open the door.'

'Don Faustino,' the man replied faintly, attempting to look up, and the grocer realised with a start that it was Father González and that he must be badly injured.

He brought the priest in, who collapsed in his arms. By the glow of the lamp, Martínez could see that his face was swollen and bloody, and he was frightened as he held him, realizing for the first time what devils had been released already by this civil war which had only just begun. They were all surrounded by enemies that they couldn't even recognise, perhaps a next-door neighbour or one's best friend. Faustino had believed the whole district to be staunchly on the side of the rebels, but someone had burnt the church, and someone had beaten Father González. He half carried, and half dragged the priest into the living room and, leaving him for a few minutes inert on the floor, hurried to let down all the blinds facing the square so that no one should know he was there.

The priest stayed in the grocer's care for four months, a month of which was spent in his own house. They cared for him as best they could, treating his injuries themselves and having no recourse to Dr de Rosas, not wishing for anyone outside the family to be aware of his whereabouts, fearing reprisals, fearing the unknown enemy.

When he was strong enough to be questioned, Father González told of how he had been dragged from his mule and set upon by three men as he arrived on the outskirts of Peña Alta. They must have knocked him senseless, for when he came round he found himself in a barn, his hands behind his back and tied to his feet, surrounded by most of the male population, who surveyed him with spite and profanity. He was able to notice an odd face here and there out of place among the rest, someone scared but afraid to speak a word in his favour for fear of suffering the same fate.

They abused him cruelly, at first mocking him and the God he represented, later trying to frighten him into renouncing his beliefs before, urged on by drunkenness and the priest's obdurate silence, beginning an assault on his body. He was kicked, hung upside down from the rafters and beaten before, tiring of their sport, they cut him down, untied him and went away, leaving him to fare as best he could.

If anyone saw him crawling and stumbling the hot and barren miles back to Quintera, they were either indifferent or afraid to help him, and he came like a wounded dog instinctively searching its home, hardly aware of the distance or the sun, hardly aware that he was still alive and that this torture was not the first punishment of purgatory for sins unconfessed and not paid for.

He rested in Faustino's house and slowly recovered while everyone else wondered what had become of him and presumed him dead. Only the grocer's wife, Fidel, and Elvira knew of his presence in the house. Not even his eldest son was informed, not even Vicente in the casino next door. The fewer who knew, the fewer tongues could wag. Nothing was done about the priest's attackers, for all that their names were taken and written down, for it would mean revealing his whereabouts, and the grocer was afraid, uncertain of the strength of the 'other side.'

The time would come for justice to be done, and until then, it was best to keep the evidence a secret. He gave Fidel the list of names. They included the three original attackers and those who seemed to be the ringleaders in the crowd, and among them were men of both Quintera and Los Pinos as well as Peña Alta.

'Lock it up in the safe,' he said, pulling the key from his pocket. 'That's the best place for now. Bring back the key as soon as you've done so.'

Fidel took the folded paper, but before locking it away, he opened it and read it through. There were eight names and a few spaces below them the priest's signature, forced and hardly legible. Fidel saw that there was room for at least one more name and, forging his father's handwriting, at which he had become something of an expert, he added carefully, *Bernardo de Rosas Zabaco, Los Pinos.* Then he locked up the paper and took back the key to his father.

Faustino was telling the priest about the destruction of the church, and Father González wept. He was very weak for a long time, his nerves completely broken and his conscience suffering too, for he was afraid he had been a coward at the end, begging for mercy and denying everything he had dedicated his life to.

'You're too good to me,' he insisted, 'and I mustn't stay here. If anyone finds out, the retribution will be on your head, yours and your family. I can't let that happen. I must go.'

'Silence! Not a word! Do you suppose I can see you go from this house while ill and in danger? Don't mention it again unless you wish to offend us and the religion we've been brought up in. The house is yours for as long as you wish.'

The grocer was voluble in his insistence, and Fidel, listening to him, watching him smile and preen himself, thought with derision, 'You're an old fool, and I'll soon have you dancing another tune.'

II

The sheltering of the priest was not to be Faustino's only problem that summer. He received a telegram from his son in Madrid saying that he was putting his wife and child on a train to Aranda the next day as he feared for their safety, asking his father to go to meet them. He neither requested permission nor waited for it to be given, and the bitterest words for the man who read the letter which the daughter-in-law handed over to him as soon as she entered his house came at the end:

'I would have brought them myself were I free to do so. But every man here is needed to defend the city and I would rather die than see it in Nationalist hands.'

'One of my sons a Republican, a Red!' shouted Faustino at his wife as he finished the letter and tore it wildly to pieces. 'And he sends his wife to me for protection! What is the world coming to? Can this be a son of mine?'

Eugenia remained silent during this outburst and the many that followed. She went about preparing a room for the girl and her child and Faustino had no alternative but to accept them. But he was cold and unbending. Though she was tired and the child was crying, she had to endure a lecture outlining her position in the household, together with a warning that she was there on sufferance only and must voice no wild Republican sentiments before the neighbours and take no liberties. She nodded her head but remained silent. She never did speak much, and no one ever found out what she was really like or what she thought of the people she had to live among.

She was small, thin, with black hair, brown eyes and pale southern skin. She was pretty in an abstract kind of way. She took over all the sewing in the house, being a seamstress by trade, and hummed as she sewed, gay tunes mostly, although she was so silent apart from this that no one could really say she was happy. With Elvira, she forged a certain relationship, but it was only that of one young woman in need of another. There was no great confidence between them. She couldn't forget that Elvira was the grocer's daughter, while Elvira had problems of her own.

Once Elvira asked her, 'Why do you sing so much? Don't you miss Gustavo?'

She replied with an old proverb, 'When an Andaluza sings, she has something stuck in her throat,' and Elvira was silenced.

After that, if she hadn't been so immersed in her own problems, she might have been able to pity the little Andalusian girl too and her equally silent son who was as fair as his father, as blond as the summer corn, though his eyes were dark and big like a fawn's.

She was kept unaware of the presence of Father González, which was not too difficult as he was transferred before her arrival to the store-room above the shop. Martínez felt it too risky to keep the priest in the house while his daughter-in-law was there. Who knew what contacts she might have with the Reds?

'She's ruined Gustavo,' he insisted to his wife. 'It was probably she who persuaded him to communism with tales of poverty and injustice in the south. And why to goodness is she always singing? It's very irritating.'

'I suppose it helps her to pass the time,' suggested Eugenia timidly, afraid to defend the girl more than that.

Even when she learned that Gustavo was dead, she continued singing. She was like one of those little southern birds imprisoned in a wooden cage that sing even while they pine. When the war was over, she went back to Madrid.

'She'll probably end up on the streets and her son a beggar,' said Martínez, angry because he had offered to keep his grandson, and she would not have it.

III

In October, Eugenia, pale-faced and fearful, confessed to her husband that she was positive that Elvira was pregnant. Martínez couldn't believe it. From the day she returned from Burgos, she had never in any way given him to believe that she still entertained thoughts of Bernardo, let alone any feeling for him, and as far as he was aware, she hadn't even seen him since before she went to Burgos. He hadn't noticed any particular change in her figure either.

'Have you asked her about it?' he said, incredulous.

'No, but I know.'

'How can you be sure, woman? I've seen nothing. She's thinner, if anything, not fatter. It's not possible. You know she's not seen that man since you found those letters.'

'I'm sure because I've borne ten children and know the signs.'

'Then how, where, with whom? For God's sake, woman, think of what you are saying!'

Eugenia grew paler, and the grocer knew that she had kept a secret from him, for she was afraid to look into his eyes and meet his gimlet stare.

'I want the truth,' he insisted. 'I've got to know how it happened when to my knowledge, she's had no association with any man in the last eight months. What are you hiding?'

'It must have been after the bull caping,' began his wife timidly. She hadn't the courage to mention all the other occasions; this once was bad enough.

'But you were watching her the whole evening.'

'I was. I was. But . . . ' She trailed off, nervously wringing her hands. 'What will become of her? How could she do such a thing? What disgrace!' she wailed again and again until Martinez coldly snapped, 'What happened after I left you with her?' Once his wife began in this vein, he would never get to the bottom of it.

'She was dancing in the plaza, like everyone else, mostly with that Señor Segundo. I was watching her all the time. I swear by the Virgin Most Blessed I was watching her, and she never spoke to that young man. I don't think he even stayed for long.'

All this in a rush, anxious to quit the blame from her own shoulders and place it firmly where it belonged. If she were hurt and angry, it was because Elvira had put her into an impossible situation. 'How could she do such a thing?' she moaned again, terrified of her husband's reaction.

'If you were watching her as you say, then nothing could have happened.'

Martinez was coldly precise, but beneath his calm exterior, his heart was almost bursting with rage at his daughter's defiance and lack of respect for him.

Half incoherent with fear, she rushed to defend herself. 'Well, you see, I was talking to Ysa Urea. She'd had her first grandson only a week earlier, and she had the little thing with her. Such a sweetheart, and just like the father, and she let me hold him for a while. While I was nursing him, everyone came to have a peep because he was crying. He was hungry, and I had such an urge to put him to my breast but—'

'Woman, will you get on with it! All these details aren't important. I suppose you're trying to tell me that you forgot all about your own daughter while caring for the child of some other woman who should have been caring for it herself.'

'No, no. It wasn't like that. I didn't forget her. I only took my eyes off her for five minutes, no more, I swear, but when I looked again, she was gone. I couldn't see her.'

'And why have you left it until now to tell me? When did she come back?'

'Not for the rest of the evening.'

'How long was that?'

'A couple of hours. I looked everywhere for her, and in the end, I came home. She was indoors, sitting at the table. She said she'd felt sick and had a headache, so she came home. She said she saw me enjoying myself and didn't want to bother me.'

'And you believed her?'

'Well—'

'You didn't believe her, but you did nothing?'

'What could I do?'

'Why didn't you tell me? Why leave it till now?'

'I knew you'd be angry.' Before he could interject, she sought to exonerate herself with coaxing words. 'You had so many worries already, what with one thing and another, and the meetings with the mayor and all this war business. I didn't want to worry you unnecessarily.'

'It hasn't proved to be unnecessary, has it?'

'There was nothing we could do. If she'd met the man, she'd met him, and it couldn't be changed. But perhaps she really did have a headache. How was I to know?'

'You didn't notice anything?' sarcastically. 'She looked no different?'

'She was a little flushed, but that might have been from the dancing, from the headache.'

'Or something else.'

'I wasn't to know,' she moaned. 'Oh God, what will become of her? What shall we do?'

'I'll throw the hussy out, that's what I'll do. She's defied me and defied me, and I'll have no more of it. Out she goes, and that's the end of it.'

Eugenia stared at her husband, saw the veins almost bulging from his head as he fought to control his passion. No one had ever defied him as Elvira had done, or so mocked him, and his pride was unbearably wounded. She knew he would never forgive her, and knowing that it would be unwise to plead for her at that moment, she left him alone, relieved that he hadn't hit her.

Elvira couldn't believe it when her father told her to go, and for the first time in her life, she realised the depths of his malice; she had played with fire too long in defying him, and now the flames were about to scorch her. She was dumbfounded and gazed at him as if unable to comprehend the finality of his words. For once, she had no quick retort to sting him to greater anger.

She said at last, quietly and incredulously, 'But where shall I go?

'To the man responsible for your condition.'

'I don't know where he is.'

'Run away and left you?'

Martínez was triumphant now in the face of his daughter's crestfallen attitude. Perhaps she would beg forgiveness, and he would see her crawl to him at last.

'Didn't we tell you that's what would happen? All men like him are the same. They get what they want, and then they don't want it any more.'

Elvira grew sullen under his rantings, her brows drawn fiercely. She flung back the hair which drifted across her face, glared defiantly at her father and retorted:,'He hasn't run away from me. He loves me.'

Faustino hit her across the mouth with the back of his hand.

'Loves you!' he almost screamed. 'Loves you so much that he leaves you like this and disappears,' and twice more, he hit her until, at last, she put up her arms to shield her face.

She blinked away the tears that had come involuntarily to her eyes, and the blood she tasted made her reckless. She had never hated her father so much as in that moment, and she would have sacrificed herself to Bernardo, had he been the devil himself, if only to escape this power-crazed lunatic who called himself her father and had never offered her an ounce of understanding or affection in all her life.

All this she told him, adding with deep scorn, 'Who are you to talk of love? What do you know of love? You've never loved anyone in your life. Ask my mother, ask any of your children, so who are you to decide whether Bernardo loves me or not?'

'But at least I've supported you all for a lifetime, worked myself to the bone for you all. What's that man going to do for you now that you've a child of his on the way?'

'He doesn't know about it. He was going to write and—'

'When?' snapped Faustino, his passionate rage on the wane and a coldness overtaking him that was more dangerous and more implacable than the other.

Elvira hesitated. But there was nothing to lose now by confessing all, and she said slowly, dully, 'He was going to write to me in August, just before my birthday. We'd arranged that he would go to Madrid first. His brother has a job for him there. He was going to find us somewhere to live and then send for me. We were going to be married.'

'But the letter never came. I wonder why?'

Did he think that she had never wondered, that every day had not been a torture to her, especially since Gustavo's wife had come away from Madrid as it was now dangerous to live there?

'The war,' she faltered. 'The war has changed everything. Maybe he has to fight. Maybe he wrote, and the letter got lost.'

'And maybe he didn't write at all.'

'I don't believe it. He loves me, and he's going to marry me.'

'Then you'd better hurry to him before it's too late. But I don't think you'll find him waiting for you. Why should he? He's had all he wants already, and there are plenty of whores in Madrid without him having to send for you.'

Elvira's whole face contorted itself into one of intense hatred. She flung herself at her father, hardly aware that she did so, ready to claw his face.

'I hate you!' she screamed. 'It's all your fault.'

The grocer, astonished, flung her aside with a heavy blow, and she tumbled to the floor, weeping. 'It's all your fault,' she reiterated. 'Why wouldn't you let us get married?'

'My judgement of his character was well-founded, and if you'd listened to me, you'd have had reason to be grateful now. One day you'll realise that, but then it will be too late. I'll hear no more arguments nor suffer you to touch me again. I'll not have neighbours staring at me and whispering behind my back. You can leave this house before your shame is generally known. There'll be no whores or bastards in this family, and that's my last word.'

He strode from the room, mopping his face with a handkerchief, trembling but satisfied by the sobs that burst uncontrollably from Elvira. Though shaken by the violence of his daughter's reaction, no pity stirred him, and he had no intention of jeopardising his good name because of her wilful foolishness. There was already talk of deposing the mayor, for there was a good deal of uncertainty as to where his true sympathies lay, and it was the opportunity that he had been waiting for.

Later that day, he broke his angry silence to tell Elvira, 'I'll give you the money for your fare to Madrid and a little to see you through until you get settled somewhere, but more I will not do.'

He had decided that it wouldn't give a good impression if people were to discover that he had turned her out with nothing.

'I'll manage by myself,' she returned scornfully. 'If you can't give me any understanding or sympathy, I certainly don't want your money. You look after the priest and Gustavo's wife. They'll cost you enough without spending anything on me. It's a good idea to throw me out now that you've three extra mouths to feed.'

Elvira went the next morning without speaking to her father again. She took a suitcase with a few possessions, and he didn't know if she had any money or not.

IV

If Martínez had any qualms about his daughter's well-being when she set out on her own for Madrid, they were soon smothered by other fears which touched him far nearer home. About a month after Elvira had taken her to leave, a rough-looking stranger came to visit him. He said that a certain person had advised him that the grocer was sheltering the priest and that if he didn't immediately turn him out, he would suffer for it.

'I don't know what you're talking about,' blustered Martìnez. 'I haven't seen the priest since the day he went to visit a dying man in Peña Alta and never returned.'

'He's in your shop, upstairs in the storeroom. He's to be out of there tomorrow or by Thursday that stable of mules you've got will be done for. And if that doesn't persuade you, we'll burn down the casino. Be a sensible man, Don Faustino. We don't want to harm you, but we don't like traitors either.'

What was he to do? Until some legitimate law and order were restored, it was dangerous to meddle with these violent men. The civil guards had disappeared. Had they been murdered, or had they thrown in their lot with the Reds? Nothing more had happened since the church was set ablaze, and as most of the young and able-bodied men had been conscripted by the Nationalist army, it had been agreed that retaliation should be left to the authorities, whoever they might be.

He said nothing to Father González at first, hardly believing in the threats he'd received. He was given only a day to decide and chose to stick by his promise to the priest. On Thursday, he went to the stable and found every mule hamstrung, six of them, the finest beasts in the village, which he had rented out to small farmers who couldn't afford to keep a beast of their own. Dangling from a nail in the wall was a sheet torn from a missal, and written across it was just two words, 'Casino tomorrow.'

In the face of such financial loss, Faustino's heroic spirit deserted him. He went to Father González and told him that he would have to go. He explained what had happened, and the priest understood. He cut short Faustino's embarrassed explanations.

'I was on the point of taking leave of your hospitality in any case. I feel it my duty, now I'm well enough, to report to my superiors and arrange for another priest to be sent here in my place.'

'You're a noble man.' Faustino spoke with unction, anxious to see the priest gone. 'At least change out of your soutane,' he begged him. 'I'll get you some old clothes and a beret. You can pass as a labourer, and no one will molest you.'

'No,' said Father González. 'I shall go as I am. I've been a coward long enough. When I leave here, I've done with hiding. Give me some food. That and the missal will suffice.'

'It's bitter weather, Father. I wish you'd take my advice. There's no shame attached to disguising yourself.'

'I shall reach my destination,' insisted the priest calmly. 'Bring me some food, and tonight I can let myself out. I only hope no retribution will fall upon you.'

Martinez privately thought that six hamstrung mules were retribution enough. He wanted no more, but it was with misgivings that he let Father González go for it had abruptly turned bitterly cold, and still he was not strong. But the fear of losing his business and perhaps his life swamped his fear for the priest. He had his family to think of, and he had already done his duty. It was up to someone else now to help him and Martínez, following the priest, decided to trust him to God.

His body was found a fortnight later by a shepherd from Los Pinos, only a couple of miles beyond the monastery. The temperature had plummeted after the priest left Quintera, and it would seem that it was the cold that killed him. There were no fresh wounds on him, and the missal was clutched against him, frozen into his hands, one of which was also clinging to a rosary. None of the food that Faustino had given him had been touched, and the grocer had to think that Father González had planned it like this and that in death, he had reached the destination he was seeking.

The discovery of the priest after his long absence led to much speculation, and eventually, the grocer decided to let his son Faustino into the secret. The miller felt as strongly as his father against the regime. He had wanted to enlist and was impatient to join the Nationalist forces, as had done many of his contemporaries already, restrained only because he was needed to run the mill and keep the fields, there being no family member to replace him. Without a word to his father, the younger Faustino went to Peña Alta to find the ruffians and accuse them publicly of the priest's death, but the grocer learned soon enough that his son had been meddling, for he was found one morning beside his own mill, shot through the head.

That same winter, a mixed company of Nationalist soldiers and Legionnaires arrived in the district to rout out Reds and anarchists. The village of Peña Alta was almost completely destroyed, the houses blasted wall from wall, the livestock commandeered, the vegetable plots trampled. The few men who didn't die defending their women from rape or their poor dwellings from plunder, mostly lads and ancients, were put against a wall and shot along with two anarchists who had been staying there. The women of Los Pinos and Quintera didn't stir out of their houses that day, and the few labourers made themselves inconspicuous. The righteous wore a smug expression, thinking on the destruction of Peña Alta not many miles away, and the fearful were silent.

On the night that the captain was fêted in the grocer's house, Martínez brought from the safe the paper that the priest had signed, condemning the men whose names were there written. The captain read silently through the list and had a sergeant called for.

'Check to see if any of the men listed here are still in the district. If so, bring them here.'

Faustino tentatively interrupted. 'I think you'll find there are none here now. Most of them absconded soon after the event. They could be anywhere.'

'If that is so, I'll have the list sent on to headquarters for reference, should any of them fall into our hands. Now, how about some more wine?'

Fidel joined in the conversation which followed the meal, applauding the captain for the swift action of the morning. Privately, it had relieved him considerably when every man in Peña Alta was shot without any questions asked. It might have come out that Fidel was behind the hounding of the priest from his father's shop in revenge for the slighting manner in which Father González had always treated him; that Fidel had hamstrung his father's mules, and that Fidel had encouraged the murder of the brother who had relentlessly bullied and humiliated him all his life.

A case of cognac and a good meal was enough to persuade the captain that the mayor should be relieved of his position and the grocer became the new mayor in recognition of the part that both he and his eldest son had played in resisting the enemy and protecting the priest. The captain had been willing to have the mayor executed, but Faustino was genuinely shocked by the suggestion.

'No more blood, Captain!' he exclaimed. 'The man's a fool, but he's not dangerous. I don't want his death on my conscience. He's finished, anyway.'

The sense of magnanimity that flooded him at that moment was something he savoured for the rest of his life. The satisfaction in the power that money and position had brought to him over the years was superseded by the realisation that he now held a man's life in his hands and could use that knowledge to his benefit if ever he needed to. He made sure that the mayor knew that he had saved him.

PART FIVE

The train which carried Bernardo away from Aranda in the afternoon, crossing the endless Castilian plateau with alternate rush and slothfulness, swept him to a far bigger place at nightfall. He was bewildered by the transition when he stepped down on to the platform and, like a sheep, followed those who knew the way to the exit. There was no one to meet him, and he felt utterly lost. The size of everything, the noise of everything, was beyond his experience, and he wasn't even sure how he found himself inside a taxi, being asked where he wanted to go.

This state of bewilderment was not to leave Bernardo all the time he was in Madrid. Everything seemed suddenly to move too quickly. His actions were now beyond his control. Events took charge. It was as if on leaving the village, some hidden hand had suddenly plucked him out of the world he knew and thrown him down on a heap of scurrying chaos. He had arrived in Madrid at the beginning of July, and it was not only his own bewilderment he felt but the general restlessness of the whole population. Fearful expectancy was in the air, a revolutionary excitement which spread from the lowest to the highest, the oppressive summer heat adding to the temperature of the people.

Arturo immediately rushed him about from one place to another, introducing him to friends and associates in endless bars and taverns and small, crowded flats, mostly in the poorer districts. The bars were always full of smoke, perspiring bodies and noise; the streets at night were crowded with neighbours who screamed out their opinions one to another, reluctant to return indoors. Radios blared as if in competition, and people raised their voices rather than turn down the volume. There was never any silence, and for a man used to the slow pace of the village, where even the mules were rarely obliged to break into a trot, it was very stressful. The few questions he had been able to ask his brother remained unanswered. He was only expected to follow where the other led, and so he followed, not knowing what else to do. All the people he met welcomed and accepted him without reserve because he was Arturo's brother, "one of us." It did not take him very long to figure out that it was all disturbingly political.

The only times of tranquillity were in the hours that he spent with Paquita and the children when Arturo didn't require or demand his company or even return home. She talked to him about his family and Elvira, who all now seemed suddenly a long way away, much farther than the train journey. He longed for Elvira as he had never longed for her, lonely and sick at heart, completely lost and wishing he had never left her or the village. It was too soon for him to be able to comprehend the city mentality, its rush and noise, its lack of space, and also this sense of dread and expectancy which pervaded everything and which he could feel over and above all that was alien to him.

His first reaction was that he could not possibly live here for long or bring Elvira to such a place; to one of those tiny, airless flats reached by dark staircases, with a vista of crowded streets or endless roof-tops, and even Paquita's ample home, with its balconies that overlooked an elegant street, seemed restricted and too artificial to put him at ease. He was tempted to return to Los Pinos, to let destiny carry them where it would, rather than have to face and conquer the uncertainty that confronted him here.

His brother seemed to be on friendly terms with half the population of Madrid and intent on introducing Bernardo to everyone he knew. One day, in yet another overcrowded bar, he was given an impressive-looking document that informed him that he was now affiliated to one of the many trade unions. He was doubtful about accepting it; where he came from, anyone who had even the slightest connection with a union was likely to receive an unfriendly visit from the civil guards; but Arturo insisted and said that it was necessary for his own protection. Men without union cards were already being marked out for censure, or worse.

'You'll never get work anywhere without one,' he warned him, 'and I shan't be able to help you if you get into trouble. If you get arrested, that card will save you.'

'Save me! And why should I get arrested?'

'Just take my word for it. You'll soon understand.'

Bernardo was by no means sure that he wanted to get involved with his brother's activities, still not certain whether he might be a socialist, a communist, an anarchist, a republican or affiliated to one of half a dozen other parties of whose existence he had been only vaguely aware until now, and who seemed to hate each other as much as they hated fascists and monarchists and anyone on the right. He doubted whether he would soon understand and was greatly disillusioned, having put all his faith in his brother's promises, but now he could see that anything outside his political activities was immaterial to him. People as separate individuals didn't matter to Arturo, not even his wife and children. He seemed hardly to care about himself, driven by utopian ideals with the zeal that had always possessed him since childhood. Until now, he had led Bernardo with assurances of a future for him. Now it appeared there was no future at all unless he subjected himself to Arturo's demands and be rewarded with an income sufficient for home-making, or there was a void into which he could fall unheeded.

For a while, he saw nothing of him and passed restless hours with Paquita and the children, not caring to spend much time on the streets where the milling crowds could be scattered by unreasoning violence at any moment. His only consolation, apart from the children, was in the books on the shelves whose authors he'd had no opportunity to discover, but thoughts of Elvira constantly distracted him. How must she be feeling without him? Did she ache for him as much as he ached for her? How would she react when she learned that their plans might be overturned by events beyond their control?

Even while he struggled to make some sense of this alien existence and come to some decision, chaos broke out in reality with the murder of a lieutenant of the Assault Guards whose fellow officers shot Calvo Sotelo three days later in reprisal; the soon-to-be-declared state of war, followed by the citizens' assault on the barracks of the Civil Guard and its ensuing massacre, while the weak government tried to negotiate with the rebels, afraid of arming the people. Arturo was delighted by all these events and expected his brother to share his enthusiasm.

The very day after war was declared, a plane swept low over the city, scattering bombs in the streets and squares where children played and disappearing with the same rapidity with which it had it come. Roused to bitter anger, the retaliation was on churches and schools, which were now burning in various places, while priests and nuns begged for mercy in vain.

How could Elvira be brought to this Madrid where stroke and retaliation lurked in every street? What could he tell her in a letter, and would there even be a reliable postal service to deliver it? He longed to pour out his heart to her on paper but, afraid that her father might intercept any mail and not wanting to alert him to their plan, he held back, hoping that within a few more days, he'd at least have somewhere for them to live and perhaps a wage of some kind to pay for it.

Arturo returned from wherever he had been to tell Bernardo to make up his mind. Did he want a job or not? This brother of his was always slow!

'Are you staying or leaving?' he demanded. 'There's no end of work, and I need some help. Most of the fellows are a lot of peasants. They'd do better if they were digging trenches instead of trying to play at politics. But at least you can read and write and understand plain statements.'

'Thank you!'

'Well, you know what I mean. I haven't time for wrapping things up.'

'But what am I supposed to do?'

'Just keep your ears and eyes open and your mouth shut. That's all that's necessary for now. You'll soon learn. By the way, I was talking to a friend who knows of a vacant flat. Maybe tonight, there'll be time to go and see it. But put in a day's work with me first.'

Then he was gone again, almost as hurriedly as he'd come, leaving Bernardo with the address of his office and the choice of pleasing himself.

He went. The office was in a tall back street block near the royal palace. There were two tough-looking men at the door who roughly demanded to see his union card but showed more respect when they discovered he was Arturo's brother. And when he had climbed three flights and reached the office itself, he had to repeat the process with two more guards who were even more security-conscious than the others. The door opened onto a hall with oil paintings, a chandelier and two solid chairs in which sat two of the 'peasants' to whom Arturo had referred. They eyed Bernardo with suspicion but said nothing. One was cleaning his teeth with a grubby stick, the other smoked cheap foul-smelling tobacco. They would have looked more at home in a tavern.

When he asked for his brother, the one with the toothpick led him through a large room in which a number of silent, listless-looking people of various ages seemed to be waiting for something, to another where he, at last, found Arturo sitting on the only chair at a large table leafing through an untidy pile of papers. Waving a handful at Bernardo as he came in, 'You see what I mean,' he greeted him. 'I need someone to go through this stuff intelligently and save me time.' And to the other man, he said, 'Leave him here, Remy. He's harmless.'

When he had gone, he explained, 'That's my watchdog. He quite loves me and would break the neck of anyone who tried to harm me.'

'He certainly keeps his teeth in good condition for biting, anyway.'

Arturo laughed, then looking directly at his brother, he said, 'You've arrived in time to see how the workers' tribunal functions. Come and stand beside me and make yourself look important. But keep your mouth shut.'

The morning passed rapidly. It didn't take Bernardo long to realise that the people he had seen in the outer room were suspects picked up from the street or forcibly dragged from their homes to be interrogated, then released or condemned according to the evidence. The majority of them had been denounced by neighbours and were accused either of fascist activities or sympathies, these ranging from a youth, holding a bloody handkerchief to his nose, who was accused of instigating riots and declaiming against the government, to an old man whose only obvious offence was that his wife and daughter were fanatical church-goers and he himself donated large sums to his parish church.

Arturo called in two assistants to help him judge the cases. One was Remy's companion, who smoked throughout the whole morning and nearly choked everyone, and the other a nervous-looking youngster who seemed only anxious to agree with Arturo's every opinion even though he was supposed to defend the accused. Bernardo stood silent as ordered, listening, watching, incredulous. Most of the evidence jotted down almost illegibly on the papers on the desk was so cursory that no kind of conviction could be a just one. Only the youth with the broken nose had definite evidence against him in the form of a membership card of the Falange; that and his behaviour, which was to reply to every question with a curse.

When he had been taken away, Arturo turned to Bernardo and said, 'You see, he could have been useful to us. But Remy has an annoying way of smelling out the rats and getting at them first. He only antagonizes them. With a bit of smooth-talking, he might have told us quite a lot. He's only a kid, after all. That's what I want you for. Talk to them. Make them feel confident. Smile at them or quote a bit of poetry—a gentle interrogation before I see them. You write down what they say. We discuss it. You can even defend them if you like. It would save me a lot of work. You understand?'

Bernardo nodded. 'I understand perfectly.'

There was a pause during which Arturo realised that his brother was burning with an anger he could hardly control.

'And the ones found guilty, what do you do with them?' he asked.

'What does it matter to you? You've only got to interrogate them and write down what they say.'

'I'd still like to know,' insisted Bernardo.

Arturo controlled his own rising temper with difficulty. Bernardo's last-minute obstructiveness was something he hadn't anticipated, and he was contemptuous of his naivety at such a time as this. But instead of giving way to anger, he laughed derisively.

'Your innocence amuses me,' he replied at last with sarcasm. 'I sometimes wonder if you live in this world, although I suppose your head is still floating around in the village. She must be quite something, that girl, if she blinds you so much to what's going on around you.'

Then before the other could reply, he added abruptly, 'Come with me tonight. You can let your own eyes answer your question.'

At about three in the morning, the two brothers crossed the half-deserted streets to reach a district that, until now, Bernardo had not visited. They went down to the river, to a place of slums and gipsy-inhabited shanties, overshadowed by the long, low building of the city's slaughterhouse. The river banks were wide stretches of grass, with a few trees, where people picnicked in better times, where fairs were held, and where decrepit donkeys and mules grazed.

There were a lot of people about, shadowy among the trees, more than was normal for that hour of the night. Arturo and Bernardo joined them, and there was an air of general anticipation in the waiting as a lorry drew up, and some ten or twelve people were ordered down from it. Bernardo recognised some of them. They were lined up among the trees, and then the driver of the lorry and his companion pulled out revolvers and shot them one by one through the back of the head. It was all done so smoothly, with so little fuss, that it hardly seemed true. But when Bernardo and Arturo joined with the spectators to look at them, they were all most certainly dead.

II

The two brothers walked back through the streets in silence. They were as complete strangers to one another, although Arturo was acutely aware of the turmoil in his brother's stomach if not in his heart. He had stood impatiently a little way off from him until he had stopped vomiting but said not a word because there was nothing to say.

He broke the silence at last. 'Where shall we go? Home or to the office?'

'The office.'

There was only one guard at the door, and he was half asleep. He murmured a greeting as they went up and then dozed off again. Remy was snoring in his chair at the entrance. Had he no home of his own? He was immediately alert when the two men arrived, hovering around like a dog awaiting commands from its master.

'It's all right, Remy. Go back to sleep. There's nothing doing. But don't let anyone else in,' Arturo calmed him.

Bernardo had already gone through to the office, and as Arturo entered, he turned on him savagely, throwing all his weight into a blow that sent the other sprawling across the room.

'I don't even know what to call you!' he cried. The most appropriate profanity had died on his lips because they shared the same mother.

Remy came charging in with ferocious readiness to defend Arturo, but that he, on the floor and with blood oozing down his cheek, checked him imperatively.

'Get out and mind your own business. This has nothing to do with you.'

He looked bewildered for a moment and stared sullenly at Bernardo before, after a long moment, he obeyed.

When he had gone, Arturo said: 'Well, shall I stay down here, or do you allow me to get up? Don't hit me again. I'm in no condition to defend myself.'

But he didn't attempt to move, watching carefully the heaving body, the clenched fists and scorn-filled eyes of the other. This was a brother he did not know, and he was cautious.

'You've deceived me, you—' Again, he checked himself, dashing a hand wildly through his hair. 'You've deceived me from the beginning. You take me for a fool. A peasant who can read and write and understand plain statements. That's all I am to you—'

'You're not going to bring that up!' broke in Arturo, dragging himself to his feet and pulling out a handkerchief to stem the blood now running into his collar.

'What a bastard you are!'

'I'm sorry. I shouldn't have done it. I might have guessed you'd take it badly. Still the kid that cries at a pig-sticking!'

Bernardo moved to hit him again, and he backed away with raised hands, putting the desk between them.

'No, no! Once is enough. But you wanted to know, and it was the most explicit way of telling you.'

'Telling me that my brother is a murderer! That the man who set out to do good in the world, who was given the education to do so, mixes with thugs and blackmails men into being executioners for fear of being on the wrong end of the revolver!'

'But they were fascists, every one of them, enemies of Spain and the Republic. Do you suppose that the fascists are not doing exactly the same, somewhere else?'

'That old man—'

'He confessed to hiding a priest in his house. You heard him.'

'Is that a capital crime?'

There was a long silence as they stared at each other, the one unrepentant, the other still sick with shock and incredulity.

'What are you going to do?' Arturo asked at last.

'I'm going.'

'Where to?'

'I don't know. Anywhere as long as it's away from here. To the village, probably.'

'Don't be a fool. You'd never get through. You'd be caught, taken for a fascist and shot. If you don't work with me, you'll have to join the militia or—well, I don't know what else. You can't just run away. We're under attack!'

'You can be sure I don't want any work that you can offer me.'

'All right, all right. Do as you please. But if you join the militia, you'll not see your girl again for . . . ' He shrugged. 'Who knows how long? Not until the war ends, anyway, and you certainly won't be able to think about marrying her.'

Bernardo was silent. Overcome by shock and exhaustion, his rage was gone. He turned his back on his brother, clutching his head as if trying to stop it from bursting.

'Listen!' demanded Arturo, struggling to contain his own anger. 'When I asked you to come here, I genuinely wanted to help you. If you'd have come sooner, I could have found you a place to live and a decent job, and by now, you'd have been more or less settled. But you had to leave it and leave it and land in Madrid just a couple of weeks before war breaks out! What do you expect me to be able to do for you?'

'I don't know, but . . . ' He lifted his hands despairingly. 'But not this.'

They were silent for a while and could hear Remy moving about on the other side of the door, listening clumsily.

Eventually, Arturo broke the silence.

'We're in the process of organising a professional armed force, properly trained by experienced officers who've remained faithful. The 5th Regiment. It's a great project and desperately needed if we're to save Madrid and the nation. You could teach men how to use arms and look after them.'

His brother's scornful response to that proposal needed no words, and the distance between them grew wider and deeper. He suppressed a growing desire just to be rid of him, used to being obeyed without question, not resisted by someone with a will as implacable as his own. He had misread his brother's lazy, easygoing character, perhaps because he knew him so little, and that in itself annoyed him. He rarely made mistakes about men and had a bruised and still bleeding cheek in consequence.

Bernardo was about to turn away and leave the office when Arturo came up with another suggestion. "How about going to Toledo?'

'Toledo? Why should I go there?' He made no pretence of disguising his suspicion of anything Arturo might propose, realising now, and perhaps too late, how deeply he was involved in the Communist Party and the authority he wielded within it.

'Because a comrade there has just been transferred here. He's brought his wife and left a furnished flat behind. It would be just right for you and your girl if you can get her here.'

'Do you expect me to trust you again?'

'No, I suppose not. But it's a pity. It's ideal if you want to keep your hands clean. Administration. Food supplies, safe-conducts, that kind of thing, basic stuff but important. And a place to go home to at the end of the day.'

Bernardo said nothing, but wearily let him talk.

'Of course, Toledo is in a bit of a mess at the moment. But as soon as the fascists are routed out, things will settle down there, and you could get married straight away.'

'And if they don't get routed out?'

'Don't talk like a fool. They haven't a chance. They're stuck in the Alcázar, and it's only a matter of time before they surrender. If they don't surrender, they'll die of hunger, and the result's the same.'

A new idea suddenly occurred to him.

'It couldn't be that I've mistaken your political sympathies, I suppose? That you're in favour of the monarchists or a Spain controlled from Berlin?'

'No, but neither do I care for a Spain controlled from Moscow.'

'Well, you've got to choose between one and the other. Now that you're here the latter would be the most sensible course, don't you think? You don't have to be a communist to defend the Republic, after all. A love of freedom is enough.'

'Freedom! Since when was there any freedom in Spain? Don't say the last few years have been freedom unless you wish to choose it as a more respectable name for anarchy.'

'The people aren't prepared for freedom yet and don't know how to respond. The dam has burst. The water must flow and take us where it will.'

'It's blood that's flowing, not water.'

'Yes, but when the war is over, things will be different, the old hierarchy swept away.' He spoke with a passion that chilled Bernardo's heart.

'And how many people must be eliminated meanwhile?' he said.

'Just enough to clear up the mess. Do you suppose the revolution in France would have succeeded without the help of the public prosecutor and the guillotine?'

Bernardo sighed. Until now, he had steered clear of politics, with all its trickery and corruption and misplaced ideals. It hadn't been too difficult in a small village where each man minded his own business and no one starved. He realised that he had been dreaming, accepting only what he saw on the surface without troubling himself with deeper waters. He'd had enough problems of his own without thinking more than superficially about the bigger problem that faced the whole country. If only he could take a few paces backwards through time, just a few weeks would be enough, back to the forgotten little house with Elvira and untouched by the rest of the world's agitation.

Arturo could read his brother's thoughts easily; they were written so plainly on his too-open face.

He said: 'I don't suppose I shall ever read as much poetry as you do, but I do recall something I once read. How did it go? You must know it. *"Last night I dreamed I heard God shouting, Be quick!*

Awake! to me. Then it was God who slept, and I was calling, Wake up, to him. Wake up!"'

At last, Bernardo said: 'So what should I do? You and people like you seem to have taken charge while God sleeps, so tell me what I should do.'

'You still want to get away?'

'Yes.'

'Then go to Toledo. I promise you, no tricks. You can talk to the fellow who's coming here. He'll tell you about the work and give you the key to the flat.'

III

If Bernardo had been able to know Toledo before the war, he might have been agreeably surprised by all that he found there. Then it had enjoyed the air of a sleepy country town while antiquity seeped from the very cobbles. The houses were charming, with southern-style patios filled with greenery and decorated tiles; the streets were as narrow as any he had ever encountered in Burgos. There were so many pleasant discoveries to be made in that city which hinted of the Orient and exotic dreams, blended with a sinister reminder of the Jewish metalworkers who had fled or died in those streets some four hundred years earlier; so many unexpected corners, small squares and picturesque alleys, all overlooking the blood-coloured earth with its countless olive trees and the wide, serene river that meandered through flat meadows and suddenly poured tumultuously over treacherous falls.

August had come when he went to Toledo, the month that had promised to fulfil his dreams. There was Elvira expecting a letter from him, the letter—it wouldn't even matter if her father found it first—and he didn't know what to write. He had the flat, small but big enough for two; he had a position that paid him as much as he could expect to earn and which excluded him from military service for the time being at least; he had the countryside within reach of his eyes. From Elvira's point of view, it would be ideal and yet . . . now that it was time to write the letter, he didn't know what to tell her.

The sleepy town hadn't been silent for a long time. The main square was wrecked; the cathedral—which he felt he knew because of the book by Blásco Ibañez that he had read, and which he had looked forward to seeing with his own eyes—had been crudely violated; the great fortress, the Alcázar, besieged on all sides, was being daily demolished by a variety of means.

This battering down of the obviously impregnable Arab fortress that overlooked the river disturbed Bernardo deeply. It represented so clearly vengeance for the sake of vengeance, government-encouraged stupidity when least they could afford to be stupid, for wounded self-esteem. How could he bring Elvira to a place where stubborn pride and unbending vengeance ruled, where hearts instead of heads held sway? Surely the poet was right. God was sleeping, and no amount of blood-strangled cries could reach His slumbering ears.

Bernardo had been kept too busy to do much thinking, and the continuous bombardment of the Alcazar gave him and everyone else almost endless headaches, making both working and living conditions difficult and nerve-wracking. Only one thing among all the doubts and chaos seemed quite clear, that under no circumstances was Elvira to attempt to leave the village. It was certain that most of the road south from Burgos would be thick with the movements of both armies, and a woman travelling alone in such circumstances would be exposed to many dangers. But he couldn't bear the thought of her impatient waiting and wondering, knowing that she would be expecting him to do something, even though the war had intervened to wreck their plans.

An idea had been forming slowly, but as its outcome could not be clearly foreseen, and neither could he discuss it with anyone, he hesitated. So much was at stake. The only certainty was that a wrong decision would be fatal.

For all that Arturo had been optimistic about the outcome of the battle for Toledo, Bernardo was not so sure. If things were to go badly and by some miracle the Alcazar were to be relieved, he would be at a loose end again. If he wanted to keep clear of politics, he would have to go to the battlefront, and there, his separation from Elvira would be complete until the war ended. Arturo had suggested the new Republican regiment, but Bernardo was considering the advantages of enlisting with the Nationalists.

If he could somehow get past the front lines, he could request a reincorporation to his regiment and thus hope for a quick and safe transfer back to Burgos. The fact that he volunteered should help to prove his loyalty should this be doubted. Once established, he could request a couple of days' leave to see his family before being sent on active service, which would at least give him the opportunity to see Elvira once more and not leave her in doubt as to his intentions. The biggest disadvantage was that his request to be transferred to his unit in Burgos might be ignored, but it was a risk he would have to take.

At last, he wrote, words coming slowly, often interrupted by the unnatural thunder that shook the town.

'Have patience a little while longer. It is too dangerous for you to think of coming here. I shall try to get to Burgos and come to see you. But don't think of leaving Quintera. Trust me. I shall do my utmost to be with you soon, one way or another.'

Even as he finished the letter with many words of love, he doubted that it would reach her, but he had promised to write, and more he could not do. Were she not to receive it, Bernardo knew that she would have much to endure and perhaps for longer than either of them could imagine.

IV

By the end of September, Bernardo had lost the flat and the job and was in danger of losing his life. The Republicans had wasted too much time over the Alcázar instead of concentrating their energies elsewhere, and all they achieved was to lose Toledo completely while making martyrs and heroes of the men, women and children who had defied them. It was every man for himself as the Nationalists overran the city, and Bernardo found himself tagging along with his office companions, a fugitive with no more than the clothes he wore and the money in his pockets to get him by.

His only idea now was to put into operation the plan he had been forming against the events that had occurred, but it was too risky to do so at once. First, he must separate from his companions without arousing their suspicions and then make for other Nationalist-held territory. To volunteer his services to the conquering army in Toledo was too dangerous. Any man who hadn't actually been inside the Alcázar during the last few months would have difficulty in proving his loyalty, and it was likely that his offer would be met with a bullet rather than open arms.

The Guadarrama would be the best place to make for, with only Republican territory to cross until the front lines were reached. It wasn't too far away, and much of it had been in Nationalist hands long enough for them not to be too trigger-happy when he presented himself. But his plan had to be abandoned, for, at every checkpoint, they had so much difficulty in proving their identities without safe-conducts that he knew he would never get to the front lines safely. So he returned to Madrid and, unwillingly, to his brother's house.

To his relief, Arturo wasn't there. Paquita had seen almost nothing of him and said that he'd talked about going to Valencia on his last occasion at home.

'And what are you going to do?' she asked him when a few days had passed, and he had lost the nervous exhaustion with which he had arrived.

'I don't know,' Bernardo answered at last.

For all he trusted her, he couldn't tell her his plans. He knew that she was wholeheartedly in favour of the Republic and would try to stop him. She would consider him a traitor, regardless of his personal reasons for wishing to get to Burgos, and he valued her good opinion too much to lose it unnecessarily. He had already realized that she knew nothing about Arturo's present activities. In fact, it seemed to Bernardo, now that he knew her better from having spent so much time with her, that his brother, in spite of his libertarian philosophy, treated his wife in the same traditional way as any ignorant peasant. He had no respect for her intelligence or cultural background. She was there to serve him, not to share his interests unless it suited him. She read his books and the newspapers but interpreted what she read in the light of his convictions. She knew he was a communist but didn't know how deep was his commitment to the cause and how far it took him. How could he disillusion her?

At that moment, a rackety car came crawling along the avenue, a loudspeaker attached to its roof and posters flapping from its doors. A man was shouting out propaganda persistently.

'What's he saying?' said Paquita. 'I can never understand those loudspeakers.'

Bernardo leaned over a balcony and listened more carefully.

'The usual stuff,' he called back. 'They want more men for the militia. If the Nationalists aren't held back—'

He stopped, an idea suddenly striking him.

'Paquita! I'm off.'

He was already returning indoors.

'What do you mean? Where are you going?' She followed him to the door, startled and uncomprehending.

'You heard him. They need men.'

'But you can't go like this, so suddenly.'

'Why not? There's nothing to keep me here. Tomorrow, with a bit of luck, I'll be in Guadarrama.'

The door was open now, and Paquita laid a restraining hand on him.

'Are you sure you know what you're doing? You haven't thought about it for a minute.'

'You're mistaken. I've been thinking about it ever since I went to Toledo.'

He suddenly took pity on her bewildered, solitary state. How could his brother neglect her so, and neither realise nor care what she suffered without him?

'You've been very good to me, Paquita, and I don't want to hurt you. But I must go. Don't worry about Arturo. You can be sure he knows how to look after himself.'

He embraced her and gave her a slight kiss on the forehead, and then he was gone, running down the stairs, in too much of a hurry even to say goodbye to the children who were in another room.

V

As a volunteer with military experience and a bona fide union card, Bernardo was issued with a rifle of doubtful qualities, but no ammunition, a blue boiler-suit and a beret—the current militia uniform—and soon found himself on the way to the Guadarrama among a truck-load of others who were anarchists in the main. The men in the long line of north-bound vehicles whole-heartedly sang Republican songs and shouted inspiring slogans back and forth, determined to push the advancing Nationalists right back to the Pyrenees, and what they lacked in equipment and preparation mattered little while spirits were high.

They were soon in the battle area, and from what he saw, Bernardo quickly judged that Madrid would soon be another Alcázar. It didn't take him long to recognize the inadequacy of this volunteer army with its lack of order, discipline or united purpose, let alone the scarcity of equipment and ammunition. The will was there, the indomitable will of a people too long crushed by poverty and injustice and with nothing left to lose but their lives. But for all its valour, surely such an army couldn't win a war?

Among the political divisions in Madrid, a jungle law was enforced, and it was not only right-wingers that died in Republican hands. In Toledo, stubborn pride had ruled and crashed. Only the fighters seemed to know what they were doing, but passionate determination and headstrong courage, unsupported by adequate arms and training, was an insufficient defence against an equally determined but disciplined and well-armed opposition. It was the same in war as it had been in peace. Five years of chaos had brought about this final disorder, and no one knew how to correct it.

As a youth, Bernardo had welcomed the Republic. From childhood onwards, he had absorbed his father's views of justice for the common man, as well as from much of his reading, and agreed in his heart with republican ideals. But he had no interest in politics, his imagination captive to histories of long ago and to the poetry which stirred his deepest feelings. His time in the army when, through the clerical work he was assigned to, he was obliged to turn a blind eye to the frauds that seemed endemic, had only made that imaginary world more attractive to him. The corruption he either became aware of or was made party to against his will sickened and disillusioned him. He had his own world to go home to once he had served his time and, like one who has escaped drowning in a stagnant pool, he altogether distanced himself from the political agitation that was in the air, trusting none of its advocates, and soon to be totally absorbed by his love for Elvira.

Circumstances had brutally forced him out of that world. His brother had only spoken truth when he told him he would have to face reality, make a choice, and he was now unhappily convinced that the continuation of the present government would cause the country's downfall into a different but inescapable tyranny. He could not know what kind of order the Nationalists might impose, should they win, but at least there might be stability as opposed to the political infighting that had led to the plunge into the present catastrophe.

Yet even as he watched night and day for the chance to defect, he felt he was betraying these men with whom he shared trench-digging, danger and hunger as well as often useless weapons. He had rubbed shoulders with such companions in the many bars of Madrid, cocky, good-natured fellows with a street slang he could hardly understand at times. They had been caught up in this insanity, just as he had, but never having experienced want and repression, having always been a free man, he couldn't share their enthusiasm for killing and dying or their hatred for their fellow countrymen. It was always the poor who paid for the politicians' follies, and they extravagantly threw away their lives for a cause that promised them Freedom. Each one was a Don Quijote or a Sancho Panza, their hopes and dreams often frozen in their staring, lifeless eyes. How easy it would be to catch their faith and share their fated glory, that of his brother's Spain.

The only reality in all Bernardo's thinking, the only sane and clean thing in his life, was Elvira, and for her sake alone, he must get out of this morass as soon as he could, before his ongoing inner conflict rather than the chances of war destroyed him. Unable yet to come to terms with the obligation to kill men with whom he had no quarrel, whatever their political convictions, he convinced himself that once he was able to see her again, to hold her and love her, he would regain purpose and balance and no more be swept helplessly along by the winds of circumstance.

On a moonless night, he found the opportunity he needed, slipping into a thick, foggy darkness that blanketed the rough terrain and gave him good cover. He kept as close to the ground as he could, stumbling often among the slippery rocks, every moment expecting to hear a shout or a shot from one side or the other. But the fog protected him even while it made his progress difficult and unsteady. He doffed his militia identity while still at some distance from the line he was making for and debated within himself how to approach without getting shot on sight. Sheer boldness was all he could think of, so, with heart racing and muttering the Rosary to drown his fear and bolster his courage, he covered the final stretch at a steady walk and with his hands on his head. He could see no one but became aware of sounds and movements somewhere within the fog. Almost at the same moment he heard a staccato, 'Halt! Who lives?' and froze.

'One who wishes to join the Nationalists,' he shouted back with forced confidence. 'I haven't been able to get here before.'

A figure loomed from the fog, bayonetted rifle at the ready.

'Don't try to be funny. We'll soon find the truth of the matter. Keep your hands up and march.'

He was taken before the captain on duty and allowed to explain his actions, a mixture of invention and truth. His Castilian accent and his now much-bedraggled suit gave some veracity to his account, but the captain's initial distrust showed no sign of diminishing as, with outstretched hand, he snapped, 'Papers!'

Bernardo rummaged inside his jacket and produced the military record that his father, with more foresight than he could have realised, had advised him to take to Madrid together with proof of his identity. The captain perused both documents carefully for several long minutes. If he didn't accept them, there would be no future for Bernardo to worry about. The guard with the bayonet was uncomfortably close behind him. In the silence, Bernardo suddenly thought of his union card. What had he done with it? A second of panic hit him as just as suddenly he remembered he had left it in the abandoned boiler-suit.

The captain looked up sharply, as if with animal instinct aware of his fear, his eyes coldly scrutinising. However, 'They seem in order,' he said at last, almost with a note of regret in his voice. 'But you'll spend the night in detention. Tomorrow there'll be time to consider your request.'

The next morning he had to repeat his story to another officer, and his papers were again carefully examined. He was asked to recall the names of various officers and describe them and Bernardo was in luck, for he remembered one who proved to be the brother-in-law of the man interrogating him, and the atmosphere changed.

Within three days, he was in Burgos and reporting to his old barracks. He felt a certain apprehension similar to when he had first been called to military service and the unknown, but this was worse, worse even than when he had joined the militia in Madrid, knowing how high the casualties were. Fear then had been countered by a sense of urgency to reach Burgos by the quickest possible means, to get home to Elvira and let her know that she wasn't forgotten.

Confident that he would be with her within a day or two, the inner conflict had receded. His mind was less disturbed even while his heart and body longed for her. Together they could discuss and face the prospect of an indefinite separation and all that the war implied before he surrendered himself fully to the demands of a different loyalty. This was his apprehension now as he received a uniform and all the paraphernalia of an infantryman - the realisation that he too was launching himself into a cause, against his brother, against Paquita, against many a good companion of recent months, even perhaps against natural justice. The apprehension was for his integrity. He believed he had made the only possible choice, but supposing he was wrong?

VI

Good luck had followed Bernardo, but now it suddenly changed. It changed first of all when he requested leave to return to Los Pinos to see his family, and the request was ignored. Refresher training came first, and meanwhile, he was confined to barracks. Then there was a call to immediate active service, and he found himself with only one free day beforehand, which was as good as none at all. He decided to go to see Sole and at least leave a letter with her for Elvira, but it was with heavy heart that he crossed the familiar streets, remembering all his broken promises, wondering how she would be able to accept the first bit of news he could send her.

It was a Sunday. The shop was shut, so when Bernardo knocked, Paco opened the door. He reminded Bernardo instantly of a younger version of Elvira's father, and the sudden dislike he felt was mutual.

'Well, what do you want?'

Bernardo hardly realised that he had been staring and that his feelings showed. 'Is the señora at home?'

'Who wants to know? I'm the husband.'

'I'm from Quintera. Your wife knows me. I'd be grateful if you'd let me have a word with her. It's important.'

Begrudgingly Paco opened the door a little wider to let him pass. He left him in the room, which brought back many memories to Bernardo while he waited, but the consternation that he saw in Sole's face as she recognised him drove all thoughts from his head.

'What's happened to Elvira?' he cried. 'Something's happened, hasn't it?'

Paco was beside her, inquisitive, indignant as he began to realise Bernardo's identity, but Sole was too anxious to preserve appearances. She was obviously embarrassed and even struggling with fear and shame.

'I don't know how to tell you.'

She wrung her hands and looked pleadingly at Paco, but he stared stonily at Bernardo and was unaware of her gaze.

'She's gone,' she confessed at last.

'Gone! What do you mean?' Further hesitance was more than he could bear. 'For the love of God, Sole, what are you trying to tell me?'

Then Paco took over. There was intense dislike in his tone and gaze, together with a certain satisfaction at Bernardo's agitation.

'I suppose you're the young man who's responsible for my sister-in-law's condition? A fine time to come looking for her, I must say. She went to Madrid some two months ago in search of you.'

The words were a physical blow. Sole saw Bernardo reel under them. He was speechless for a moment and suddenly very pale.

'She came here first,' Sole rushed to explain. 'We couldn't keep her. She had your brother's address. She wanted to go. We gave her money and—'

'How could you let her go?' cried Bernardo to Paco, ignoring Sole as if she didn't exist. 'Have you no idea at all of the conditions between Burgos and Madrid? God!'

He turned about the room in anguish, hands clutched to his head. A chair got in his way, and he kicked it violently, whirling on Paco again.

'How could you let her go?' he cried again. 'What kind of a person are you? Are you mad or inhuman?'

Another thought struck him, which stopped his movements abruptly. The look he directed at Paco made the latter shrink back.

'You spoke of her condition,' he said, breathing heavily. 'Are you telling me that she's pregnant?'

He had grown closer as he spoke, his fists clenching, and Sole suddenly thrust herself between the two men.

'There was nothing we could do. You must believe me, Bernardo. Things are very bad here. She couldn't stay.'

She was pleading with him, her hands on his chest. He looked at her fully, understanding her so well. She was even prepared to physically protect her miserable husband. Her silly interference calmed him, and he moved away, back to the door. Sole ran after him.

'What are you going to do?' she cried, holding him at the door.

'What can I do?'

Paco pushed Sole aside and slammed the door. He could hear him shouting at her as he started down the stairs. He collapsed in the middle of the flight with a groan and sat with his head in his hands for an interminable length of time, unaware of those who now and again brushed past him and the early gathering darkness of the afternoon. The concierge peered out of his cubbyhole from time to time but was too much impressed by his immobility to disturb him. When he eventually continued down the stairs, he still didn't know what to do. The letter he had meant to leave for Elvira was still in his pocket.

He wandered the streets for a while and then entered an almost empty bar and sat down after ordering coffee and cognac, desperately needing to clear his head. If only he could contact Elvira or, in some way, be sure she had actually reached the capital and was safe! His recent experiences denied him the comfort of hope, and he could only imagine her being caught up among refugees in a strange town or village, without money or friends and soon with the added burden of a baby. Who would care for her or have the compassion to understand and forgive her condition? Suppose she were to die through lack of attention? And could she ever forgive him for the suffering he must be causing her? If he could believe her to be safely in Madrid, he would worry less, knowing that Paquita would do her best for her. But the belief that she could ever reach such a distant destination would not come, and he was haunted by the predicament in which he had involuntarily left her, cursing both heaven and himself for their misfortunes. He had to do something!

Finally, only one idea occurred to him. His brother had so many contacts, so many avenues of communication that if anyone could make sure she was safe, he could. He himself would soon be at the front that was pushing implacably towards Madrid. He was aware of the shady characters, black-market dealers probably, who came and went with immunity, as well occasional deserters. Perhaps he could get a message to Arturo through one or the other of these if chance favoured him. It was a risky undertaking, but these days every hour was risky. It was the present way of life, as if Death itself rose and set like the sun and moon, capriciously choosing its victims.

When the barman brought him a second coffee and cognac, Bernardo asked for writing paper and, while his lad ran off to buy a couple of sheets and envelopes from the nearest kiosk, he pressed his weary mind to consider what to write to his brother in a covering letter to Elvira without compromising himself should it fall into the wrong hands. Eventually, he tore one sheet in two and pencilled a brief sentence on each—for Arturo,

'I believe Elvira went to Madrid. Find her and give her this.'

And on the other half sheet . . . What could he write to this girl who was tearing him apart? Words of love tumbled over one another in his head, paralysing his will. What could he promise her? What hope could he give her? Would anything he wrote even reach her? At last, feeling certain that Madrid must fall, he wrote,

'My heart and my soul, don't lose hope. We shall be together very soon, I promise.'

He used no names but hers. However, he had to put an address on the envelope and, after much hesitation, directed it to Arturo's office. There were several other businesses in the same building, but the guards on the street would know where to deliver it. On the second sheet, he wrote to Paquita in the hope that the postal services might still be functioning, asking her to help Elvira if she arrived there.

When he got up to go, the barman, having observed his distress, didn't charge him but wished him luck and God's protection at the front. Bernardo forced a smile as he thanked him, but there was still no peace in his heart or mind.

VII

There was to be no peace for him from that time on. Although he was not immediately involved in any front-line activity, he could find no way of passing on his message. Frustration was paramount. Only his conviction that Madrid must fall soon and that he might even be among those who marched into the city helped restrain his fears and longings, and the one book of poetry he had managed to hold onto throughout all his changes of fortune gave him some consolation. This was Machado's "Fields of Castilla," whose descriptions of the earth that was in his blood reminded him of home, of all that meant everything to him—and more real than his actual surroundings.

The first offensive action he was hurled into, to take control of the Madrid to Corunna road, was so ferocious that there were no thoughts about anything beyond surviving the carnage. Hardly any advantage was gained, very little if counted in the many thousands of casualties, but the enemy was pushed back for the moment. In the brief respite, he remembered the letter protected within the pages of his book while wondering if he would even survive long enough to pass it on. He was too weary to think coherently about anything except holding Elvira in his arms once more.

It seemed as though they had hardly finished dealing with the dead and wounded before a fresh assault was ordered regardless of the freezing fog that shrouded everything. The infernal slaughter was renewed for another week until, with thousands more dead and wounded, both armies had fought to a standstill and, with no advantage to either side in spite of Russian tanks and German bombers, the battle ceased. Madrid was saved from the northwest advance for the moment.

Bernardo was still alive and unwounded, at least outwardly. Along with many of the survivors, he was in a state of severe mental and physical fatigue and with the cessation of hostilities, his anxiety about Elvira returned with full force. Suppose she had been in one of those towns or villages which had been so heavily shelled and bombed and overrun by fear-crazed men? Suppose she might be among the civilian corpses lying somewhere in the rubble?

He struggled to keep the terrible thought of that possibility at bay as he had no way of finding out. Gruesome images constantly invaded his mind and would not be dispelled. At such moments he even thought of defecting so as to search for her himself. In saner ones, he clung to the hope that, wherever she might be, his brother would instigate a search for her once he received his note. And he became obsessively determined to find some way of getting it delivered. Now that the lines were quiet, surely a chance must come.

At last, it did when he found himself one of the front line patrollers throughout the night. He was performing this duty for the third time that week when he became aware of a figure trying to struggle through the defences some fifty feet ahead of him. With a loud, 'Halt!' he ran to detain to him, recalling even as he did so his own defection not so long ago. The soldier had begun making a gap in the wire but had dropped the cutters. Searching for them in the darkness, he had got himself firmly entangled and was beginning to panic.

'Where do you think you're off to, friend?' Bernardo asked him.

'For God's sake, let me go. Don't stop me. I won't be stopped now whatever you do.'

'You've not made an exactly brilliant attempt to get away. I think I should stop you for your own good.'

'No, I'll not stay here a minute longer. Kill me if you like, but I won't fight any longer for you fascists. If I could have been in Madrid when the war started, I'd have been on the other side of this wire from the very beginning.'

'Don't make so much noise,' Bernardo warned him. His hysterical utterances were loud enough to stir the whole camp.

While the fellow had been talking, Bernardo realised that here was the opportunity he was looking for, and he hurriedly found the letter and pushed it into the other man's hands.

'Look. I'll let you go with one condition, that as soon as you're safe, you take this letter to the address on the envelope and make sure that it reaches Arturo de Rosas Zabaco. You'll remember the name? It's very important that he gets it, so don't fail. I'm risking as much as you are.'

The man nodded, repeating the name as if reciting the Rosary so as to keep it in mind and perhaps to help calm his nerves, for he was very jittery, while Bernardo, having found the cutters, set him free.

'Why don't you come with me if you're one of us?' he urged him as he straightened himself up.

'You're mistaken. But I have relatives in Madrid who need to know where I am. Now get going, and for the love of God, man, don't be so careless.'

But even as he spoke, there was a shout behind them, and another sentry came running, Bernardo's companion on the patrol. The deserter took fright and ran in a mindless fashion, making himself an easy target.

'Stop him, man!' cried the sentry and, seeing him make no effort to do so, lifted his own rifle and fired. The fugitive stopped with a short gasp and sprawled in the snow to move no more.

'Let's go and get him,' said the sentry, eyeing Bernardo with distrust and suspicion, noticing the wire cutter which he still held.

Heedless of caution, for he must retrieve the letter before the other found it, Bernardo ran to reach the body first. The other was close behind him, and he called out, 'Wait, man. Are you mad?' but he didn't want to shoot him, too, especially as he knew him, for someone would have to explain the events he had witnessed.

Instead, he took his rifle by the barrel and swung it at Bernardo's legs, hoping to trip him up and so reach the dead man first. It hadn't taken him more than a moment to realise that the race between them was for this. There was a crack of butt against bone, and Bernardo fell to his knees with a sharp cry. Through a whirling, blackening mist of pain, he saw the other reach the body, push it with his foot and then, his attention caught by something close to the dead man's hand, reach down to pick up the letter which the deserter hadn't even had time to put in his pocket.

VIII

Bernardo was in so much pain when he was dragged here and there for questioning that the seriousness of his situation was meaningless. He mainly muttered about Elvira and wanting to know where she was, and eventually, he was judged not fit enough for interrogation regarding the letter that had put his life in jeopardy, as well as saving him from immediate execution. He was sent handcuffed to the Burgos garrison and thrown into a cell where he sat in a corner, exhausted, floating in and out of consciousness. It was now morning, but he had no idea of the time. He was roused from a semi-comatose state a few hours later by footsteps, voices, the noise of the door being unlocked, and being jerked to his feet by a pair of guards. Once more, he was half carried, half dragged, this time to a small office with a big window. The sky was grey, heavy with snow that was yet to fall. There was not even a whisper of sunlight.

The commander sitting behind the desk was a veteran of the Moroccan wars, old wounds keeping him from active duty. His penetrating glance at once took in the crippled state of the prisoner held up before him. Military discipline demanded that he stand to attention in the presence of an officer, but as this was clearly impossible, the commander's first words were, 'Bring a chair,' and when this was done, Bernardo was ordered to sit. This gave him some physical relief, but the unnatural situation added to his already overwhelming sense of disadvantage and helplessness—exhausted, handcuffed, and in relentless pain.

He had reached the limit of his endurance, yet he knew he had to find stamina from somewhere and that obdurate trait in his otherwise easy-going nature, and which he so rarely exercised, subconsciously came to his aid. His thoughts were interrupted by the first words directed to him by the commander, signalling to the defenceless man that the interrogation was about to commence.

'Bernardo de Rosas Zabaco, late of Los Pinos and lately of Madrid?'

This was read from a report on the desk, and then the man looked up, directly into Bernardo's eyes, the penetrating stare giving the sensation that he could read his mind. It wasn't a threatening look, it didn't need to be; in fact, there was something of the man's personality in it that reminded him of his brother. They were two of a kind, and without realising it, Bernardo shook his head to dispel the thought.

'That's correct, isn't it?' There was a hint of surprise to this apparent response but no aggression.

'Yes, sir!'

'And perhaps you would be kind enough to tell me what took you to Madrid and what brought you back here.'

Bernardo slowly and carefully explained, taking refuge in short sentences, for he was finding it hard to concentrate. He had gone there to look for work. He wanted to start a new life. Find somewhere to live. Get married. No, he had no family there, no connections. That's why he took the first job that came his way. He had very little money. The war had forced him to change his plans.

'You were trapped on the wrong side of the fence?' suggested his interrogator to help him along.

'Yes, sir.'

'And you patriotically chose to return to your regiment, apparently at great risk to yourself, according to the information I have here? That was a dangerous thing to do.'

Bernardo said nothing, and he wasn't ready for the next question.

'What would you have done if you'd been conscripted?'

After a long pause, he answered, 'Sir, I don't know. It didn't happen.'

'I have to take your word for that, don't I?'

The line of questioning was straightforward so far until he suddenly demanded with a sharp change of voice, 'Who were you writing to?'

He waved the envelope as he spoke and almost theatrically pulled out the contents, scanning them as if he hadn't seen them before.

'To someone who knows your girlfriend, Elvira.' It was a statement, not a question, and without waiting for any response, he took the envelope again and snapped, 'We are aware of this address in Madrid. Our sources tell us that a Red or anarchist syndicate operates from there. Which is it, and why did you send it there and to an unnamed individual? Explain.'

'Sir, I don't care about politics. All I wanted was a job. It was the only address I had, sir.' Even as he spoke the last few words, Bernardo knew he was lost, and the man's next question confirmed it.

'Who gave you that address?'

'A man in a bar, sir.'

'And you went there, and they gave you a job, just like that?' After a long pause, he added, 'It's a fine tale you spin, but surely you don't expect me to believe it?'

'No, sir.'

'Then why not think of something better? Why make things unnecessarily difficult?'

Bernardo said nothing. The effort to think clearly, let alone inventively, was almost beyond him.

'I suggest,' his interrogator easily proposed, 'that you were sent to Burgos to make contact with someone here, a military infiltrator perhaps, and that this message is a code you'd arranged with your people in Madrid.'

'Sir, I've told you the truth.'

'Tell me again in more detail.'

The story sounded even thinner the second time round, and before he'd finished, the commander broke in with, 'The deserter you helped, tell me about him. How did you know him?'

'Sir, I didn't know him.'

'You had the wire cutters. You were helping him. Do you deny it?'

'No, sir. He was entangled in the wire when I caught him. I set him free.'

'Why didn't you arrest him?'

'Sir, he agreed to take the letter to Madrid for me if I let him go.'

'Such a risk to pass on a few words of love! The man was a Red. You must have known that. It was your duty to arrest him. He was your contact, wasn't he?'

'Sir, I didn't know him, and I'm not interested in politics. I just wanted someone to find my girl and make sure she's safe.'

'Then you must have given him a name, someone to pass the letter on to, someone who knows you. I want that name.'

'Sir, I only gave him the letter.'

'I see.' He paused for a few moments before confidently adding, 'But you did have a name.'

It wasn't a question, so Bernardo said nothing. What was the use of denying it?

'"Don't lose hope. We shall be together very soon, I promise,"' the commandant quoted, then asked, 'Together where? Madrid?'

The affirmative response raised the next question. 'And how was that going to come about?'

'Sir, when I wrote those words, I thought we were going to take Madrid, and the war would be over. And I might be there.'

The commandant's expression visibly hardened at the memory of that recent defeat when so many good men lost their lives in most bloody conflict. No one had expected that result, and he couldn't help but believe the prisoner's answer.

But the sudden alteration of the man's countenance at this reply unexpectedly reminded Bernardo of the morning when he had seen Arturo impassively condemn men to death, and the face before him dissolved into that of his brother. He shut his eyes, hardly in his right senses at that moment, as a flashback of the executions he had witnessed at Arturo's side burst in on him again. In spite of all he had gone through, all he had witnessed since, its impact was as vivid as at first.

The officer noticed his distress and decided to change tactics.

A long silence followed while he returned to the report on his desk, thoughtfully scrutinising its several pages. When he looked up, it was with an expression less severe, his tone encouraging confidence.

'Look, soldier, your past military record is a good one. Perhaps your story is true. We've all lost our heads over a girl at some time or another, and we don't always think straight on the battlefield. You've come through a very rough time. Perhaps you have just been excessively stupid. We can be lenient.'

He gave him time to let the words sink in and then returned briskly to the attack. 'You say you went to Madrid in July and returned to Burgos to present yourself to the regiment in November. What took you so long? What were you doing in all those months?'

Bernardo repeated his story, but his listener wasn't satisfied.

'Were you in Madrid the whole time?' he asked, and when the other affirmed this, again demanded, 'What were you doing?'

'Sir, I worked in an office checking receipts, authorizing food tokens, things like that.'

'You worked in an office authorizing food tokens while the rest of Madrid was under siege, needing every able-bodied man it could get? Surely you don't think I'm going to believe you? Your story is less likely every minute.'

'Sir, they needed someone who could read and write and understand plain statements.'

His brother's words had sprung out of their own accord. He instantly regretted them, but they hung in the air while the commander decided what to make of them.

'Yes,' he finally said, 'I'm sure they could use an intelligent man like you.' An age seemed to pass before he spoke again.

'You worked for a union, most probably a communist union. They must have trusted you. You must have been a Party member. You must have had a card. Who vouched for you? Give me his name.'

This was tricky. He wouldn't be believed if he said he didn't have a card. But if he said he didn't remember his sponsor, he would be admitting his membership of the Party. The commander broke in on his deliberations.

'Let's have the truth now, soldier. It will save you a lot of trouble. If you wanted to get out of the Red zone, why didn't you return sooner?'

The words slid over Bernardo. If he hadn't been so numbed with fatigue, he might have been able to make his story more convincing, but the disturbance in his mind, together with the endless throbbing of his smashed ankle, had the greater hold over him.

His interrogator realized this.

'That injury needs to be looked at. I'll see what can be done. It's hard to resist severe pain.'

Bernardo's heart beat faster as a medical orderly was sent for. Concern for him at this point was not to be trusted, and surely a threat was implied? While he waited, the interrogation went on, beginning with a repetition of the last question, again and again, interspersed with two others, 'What were you doing' and 'Who did you work for?'

Bernardo stuck to what he'd already said. He was clear-headed enough to remember not to mention Toledo and his time with the militia, but beyond that, he was losing grasp of his mind.

And so he stopped responding because his only other option was the truth.

The commander recognised this and changed tactics again, relaxing into a more participatory tone.

'You must realise, Rosas, that your actions have been far too reprehensible for me to be able to believe a word of anything you say. You could be shot for dereliction of duty and would have been by now if it were not for this intriguing pair of messages that were so important to you.'

When this elicited no response, he added, 'Can anyone verify your story?

'Sir, there's my girlfriend's sister and brother-in-law. It was they who told me she went to Madrid. She's expecting a child. I need to know if she's safe, if she got there. That's why I wrote. I was desperate. I wanted, I need to know.'

The commander made a note of the address, and at that moment, an orderly with a medical bag entered the room and was told to examine the prisoner's ankle. Pain exploded round him while boot and sock were roughly and with difficulty removed from the swollen foot. Bernardo clenched his hands to the seat of the chair to keep himself from crying out and jumping in agony, hardly aware of the guards who were ordered to hold him still.

The commander's voice, harshly piercing through the havoc he was struggling with, helped recall him to his senses.

'I want the names of your associates in Madrid and Burgos, the meaning of the message you tried to send, the name of the person you addressed it to and anything else of interest. What was happening in Madrid in the months you were there, anyway? I know. Do you?'

The questions came one after another, and Bernardo hardly knew what he answered as he panted out words between waves of pain. His head swam, and he felt sick. But the pressure was relentless.

'Where else have you been apart from Madrid? There's a lot more you can tell me, and I want to know it all.'

The first violence of shock having receded, Bernardo realized he had to regather his senses if he were not to babble like an idiot. He determined to say no more. Restrained by the two guards, the handcuffs chafing his wrists, the orderly standing by, waiting for the next order, he stared back at the commander. There was no accusation in his stare, more a recognition that he was reaping the result of his actions and had no expectation of mercy. What would a veteran of Africa know about mercy, any more than the pig-sticker at the annual slaughter?

The commander was momentarily disconcerted, more accustomed to savage glares of hatred than resignation, but brusquely responded, 'Look, soldier, I dislike all this as much as you do. I'm not a sadist, but I have a job to do, and you are making it unnecessarily difficult. If you've nothing to hide, give me the information I want, and all this can be over very quickly. You can have that injury properly attended to. The medic on duty today used to stitch up bull-ring nags. He's not very sensitive, as you can see. Where were you between July and November?'

The question hung in the air. It was not going to be answered.

The commander sighed heavily and made a last appeal to reason.

'I admire your loyalty, Rosas, but it's misguided. Give me some names, tell me where you've been, and it might just be possible to save you from a firing squad. I shall get what I want, one way or another, make no mistake. It's up to you.'

Bernardo obdurately shook his head. 'Sir, I have nothing more to say,' he respectfully replied, and the commandant, with a sharp, 'Get on with it,' to the medic, began looking through the papers on his desk.

IX

They were walking hand in hand along a riverbank, only this time there was no need to hurry, no need for secrecy, and they were happy, laughing about silly, unimportant things. Then suddenly, everything was different. Elvira was lying on the ground, groaning, clutching at her stomach. She was having the baby and calling for him to help her, to stop the pain. He stood by helplessly, not knowing what to do, and the doctor stood smugly beside him, watching her with calm disinterest, letting her writhe and groan. 'You're a doctor,' he cried. 'You must help her. Do something.' But he just watched, unmoved. He leaned down to gather Elvira in his arms, unable to bear her agony any longer, and as he held her, blood suddenly spurted from her head, and a great red patch grew on his shirt. He was horrified, and Elvira began to laugh at his startled face. 'What a fool you are,' she taunted him. 'You shouldn't have trusted me,' and then it was Arturo's face and his body that he held so close. He flung him away with a cry of rage and woke up, panting, bathed in perspiration.

He didn't know where he was and lay struggling with his memory as he took in the small windowless room with an electric light burning. He supposed it was some kind of cell but didn't remember being brought there. How long had he been there? He didn't know that either. His last clear recollection was the interrogator's icy expression, reminiscent of his brother's, framed by the big window and the depressing sky. As greater clarity returned to him, so did the pain, the never-to-end throbbing which rose from his foot and seemed to fill his whole body, the only relief from which was a sharper, more agonising pain which the slightest movement instigated.

He sat up slowly, feeling dizzy and sick, and saw to his surprise that his foot and ankle were bandaged. Memory returned along with a wave of nausea, and he marvelled at the orderly's ability to inflict such agony with every turn of a bandage. He stared down at the now intensified injury for a long while, a sense of helplessness swelling with the realisation of his desperate situation. What a fool he had been!

He recalled the commander shouting something about locking him up until he was ready to speak and wondered how long they would keep him in this basic cell which was hardly more than a box. What would happen to him? Would he be dragged out and shot? Would he be interrogated again? He dreaded the latter more than the former just then, having lived for months with death as a constant and almost casual reality, supposing that a second interrogation would be more severe. Had he known of the notice that was chalked on the other side of the door, he might have dreaded the future more. One word, "Incomunicado," which meant solitary confinement for an indefinite period. It was a severe punishment cell.

When Bernardo had been locked up for several days, the strain began to tell. The light was never switched off, and longed-for sleep evaded him, except for brief intervals of total exhaustion and until pain or nightmares brought him to himself again. He lost all track of time, the unchanging prison ration of beans or lentils, bread and a mug of water delivered almost silently through a hatch giving no indication of morning, noon or night.

The cold was extreme, but his good army greatcoat which he had been wearing when arrested, had been taken from him, as well as his few possessions, and he spent most of the time huddled on the straw mattress under the one dirty blanket provided, his body aching from lack of exercise as well as the injury which kept him from taking more than the few necessary jarring hops across the cell to the latrine.

He composed long love letters to Elvira in his mind and relived, again and again, the few blissful hours they had spent together in that paradise of their own making. But when he slept, his endless dreams of her became intermingled with nightmares involving his brother and the recent bloody assaults he had survived until eventually, he was almost afraid to close his eyes for the terrors that crowded his overwrought imagination.

Once, he was jerked into a terrified wakefulness by a burst of screams. Whether real or imaginary, these screams catapulted him back to the day when they were to extend the front as far as a small town believed to have been abandoned by the enemy. A couple of tanks led the advance along the main thoroughfare, already blasted by a previous bombardment. The road was strewn with wreckage, making it hard for the infantry column to follow the tanks in an orderly fashion. Without warning, the second tank received a direct hit from a hidden source, and moments later, men began to struggle out from the turret as if from the pit of hell, screaming, shrieking, monstrous apparitions amid roaring tongues of fire. The surviving infantrymen scattered in every direction, leaving the tank drivers writhing in their agony as they ran to escape the machine-gun fire that burst from the church tower above them, fresh cries filling the choking air adding to the fiendish chorus as men fell all around them. He was one of the few survivors of the ambush, which until now he had blocked out of his mind.

He rocked back and forth in anguish, covering his head with the blanket and his arms, trying not to hear, but the shrieks were in his head, and the writhing, burning creatures who no longer looked like men refused to be banished from his sight. He shouted and swore at them, but they would neither go away nor be silent. He thought he was going mad. He sobbed and sobbed and eventually fell into exhausted sleep.

In an effort to escape these torments, he took to reciting aloud, again and again, all the poetry that he could bring to mind until it became a meaningless and often muddled repetition, to which he added the liturgy of the mass and any other prayers he could think of, and even the crude soldiers' ditties that had stuck in his mind, anything and everything that could keep him sane. Several times he dreamt that a child was crying, sobbing slowly, shudderingly, desolately, and he wandered along an endless corridor of mutilated bodies needing to find it. They were both lost. Eventually, he saw it sitting on the floor, its back towards him, and as he ran to gather it into his arms, it vanished, but still he could hear the doleful sound.

He set himself the task of going through his favourite *Don Quijote*, chapter by chapter, but in spite of his determined effort, he kept losing his way, sinking into a semi-conscious world, vacillating between a sleep that brought nightmares and a wakefulness that induced desperation. Loyola himself couldn't have imagined a more perfect hell, where all eternity was in one hour and the hour never-ending.

Weeks went by in this fashion, and when the cell door was finally unlocked, two guards ordering him to his feet, he wasn't sure if this was just another dream, especially when he was taken to a washroom where they sat him in a chair, and one of them cut off his beard, gave him a fairly reasonable shave and allowed him to wash his face. The cold water roused him. This wasn't a dream, at least he didn't think so, but he couldn't be sure, finding it hard to adapt to the abrupt change of circumstances.

He was given a walking stick and warned not to attempt anything unwise, although they knew he was incapable of any kind of insurrection, every slow footstep costing him dearly. Throughout the whole process, hardly a word was spoken, and Bernardo only realized where he was being taken when they stopped at the door with the commander's name on it.

Back in the same small room with the big window and the humiliating chair, he avidly examined the sky. The pale March sunshine seemed to fill his heart as it filled the room, choking him. It was almost more than he could bear as he struggled to catch up with reality. Meanwhile, the commander busied himself with paperwork as if unaware of his presence until finally, he asked, without even raising his head while scribbling yet another signature at the foot of a page, 'You're from Los Pinos, aren't you?'

'Yes, sir.

'Do you remember the priest there?'

Now the interrogator looked up, taking in every detail of the prisoner's wretched condition, hardly improved by the recent shave which he had ordered, hoping thereby to raise the man's expectations, perhaps lower his guard, if he was not already completely broken.

'The priest?'

Bernardo couldn't think beyond the question, not understanding the sense of it. But the commander was patient, aware that his mind was probably in as wretched a state as the rest of him.

'That's it, the priest, Father González. You know what happened to him, don't you?'

Bernardo shook his head. 'No, sir.'

'You don't remember?' He made a show of disbelief as he waited for a reply.

Bernardo was finding it hard to get his thoughts together. The mention of the priest's name confused him, and he didn't know what to say. Finally, he replied, 'Sir, he was well when I left the village.'

'And when was that?'

When? The memory came to him of Elvira's distress when he told her he was definitely going to Madrid, that it wouldn't be long before they could always be together, and her bitter accusation, 'It's eight Saturdays long!' How she had pleaded for him to take her with him, reckless in her passion! Eight Saturdays. A lot more than eight had passed. How many, how many? He clutched his head in anguish, recalling the taste of her tears as he had kissed them away.

Someone shouted his name. 'Rosas!' and he dropped his hands, recalled to the present.

'When did you leave the village?'

'It was summer. Before the war. Eight weeks. Eight weeks, sir!'

'And where did you go?'

'To Madrid. You know that already, sir.' The fog in his mind was receding as he forced himself to remember where he was.

The interrogator patiently shook his head. 'No, Rosas. I only know what you've told me. Have you any proof that you went to the capital and not somewhere else first, to Peña Alta, for example?'

'Peña Alta!'

Bernardo's incomprehension was too genuine to be doubted. The commander, however, produced the now somewhat tatty piece of paper which contained the list of names confirmed by Father González, guarded by Faustino and eventually finding a place on a desk in this military prison. He read out the first five names.

'You know them?'

'They're from Peña Alta, sir, not friends or neighbours. I don't know them.'

'And these three?' The other names followed.

'The last two are from my village, sir, so I know them. But not as friends.'

'These men were responsible for the persecution of Father González, which led to his eventual death last November. We are trying to trace them and, to date, have had the pleasure of executing a couple of them. There's one more name on the list. Your own.'

He handed the paper to Bernardo and allowed him to look at it. He remembered the grocer's handwriting and was perplexed. Even had Martínez been prepared to concoct false charges against him, he couldn't imagine Father González being party to it, and yet he had signed the paper.

'Sir, there must be some mistake. I had nothing to do with it.'

'You were not in Peña Alta—or somewhere nearby—last July?'

Even as he put the question, he knew he had received an honest answer but intended to exploit his advantage as Bernardo replied, 'Sir, I was in Madrid.'

'With a group of Reds or anarchists whose names you are unwilling to disclose.'

When this elicited no response, he said, 'Would it help you to know that we checked the address you gave us, the grocer fellow? He denied all knowledge of you, although he admits that he has a sister-in-law by the name of Elvira. But you didn't call on him as you stated.'

He waited for a reaction, but there was none that he could notice.

Finally, Bernardo replied, 'He doesn't like me. He's a—' He stopped in time, remembering where he was. He had been about to say, 'Fascist pig!'

The momentary sardonic expression he saw in the commander's eyes made him wonder if he could read his mind. It made him almost human. For one ironic second, they connected as one man to another.

But then the implacable interrogation went on. 'If you tell me about your associates in Madrid, it would be proof enough that you were not in Peña Alta beating up the priest.'

'Sir, I've never beaten up anyone.'

'So, give me the names I want, and I'll believe you.' After another silence, the commander clicked his tongue, sighed and then, in a persuasive tone, said, 'You're making things very hard for yourself, Rosas. I believe you. I like you. You're the kind of soldier we want. Give me the names, and you can get properly cleaned up, be transferred to the medical wing, and it might even be possible to deal leniently with the dereliction of duty charge. Think about it. Just a few names. We'll have them sooner or later anyway.'

Bernardo returned his persuasive stare momentarily. He knew he was beaten. He knew there was no way out for him. The thought of being clean and getting his injury dealt with was a cruel temptation, and perhaps keeping silent was senseless. But almost against his own will, and in a rush of desperate determination, he finally replied, 'I don't know any names. Sir! I can't give you any names. Sir! I don't know any names. Sir!'

The commander knew men and knew he was lying. But he also knew from the explosive response that at this point he would get no further.

'It seems that two months solitary has taught you nothing, Rosas. Or perhaps you prefer to be alone?' and calling for the guards, he snapped out the order, 'Take him back.'

Panic hit Bernardo as he realized that the interrogation was over, and he would be returned to the living death of pain-filled isolation, that separate planet populated only by nightmares and silence. He wanted to cry like a small boy and beg for mercy but trapped in his obduracy, he regained control of himself and struggled to his feet. As he did so, the commander said, 'You can have more time to think it over, but not much.'

The guards returned him to the cell. At the door, he held back, but the realisation of the futility of his action made him lose heart, and he dragged himself in, staring at the door as once more it was locked and he was left alone.

There were three more weeks of the same treadmill to be endured: worry, dread, desperation, until all thoughts and dreams, either sleeping or waking, became merged into one blurred state of unreality, and he was no longer sure as to which was which. When would it end, how would it end? Had it ended already, and was this purgatory? He twisted and turned, shivered and sweated, lay silent and still or groaned and muttered aloud, seldom rising from the planks which were his bed, his worsening neglected injury an ongoing hell.

When the cell door was opened again, Bernardo thought he was dreaming. The warders' impatient voices and the stick they again put into his hand brought him back to reality, and he limped for a third time to that small room with the big window, and now framed by a brilliant, cloud-streaked April sky. This time there was a subordinate officer in the room with the commander. The two guards were ordered to remain beside him, but Bernardo was impervious to anything except the dread, the terror of being put back again into solitary confinement once the interrogation was over.

Being released from that characterless cell, hearing voices, seeing faces, realising that he was still in a living world made the return to isolation something unendurable. Any amount of physical torture would be nothing in comparison if that was what these changes portended. At least with that, he could hope for oblivion.

'Well, Rosas, aren't you interested to know why you're here? You have a visitor.'

Bernardo's heart leapt wildly for a second. Elvira! But of course, that couldn't be possible. He had been brought out for further interrogation, and this was another effort to wear him down.

'Don't you want to know who your visitor is?'

Bernardo looked at him. His expression was a plea not to be taunted.

'Your mother.'

It was almost as unbelievable as if he had said 'Elvira.'

Bernardo had hardly thought of his mother in the last year. That lonely woman in Los Pinos, grieving for him, praying for him, was half-forgotten, and he was hit by a conflict of emotions almost more than he could bear! He hadn't given any thought to his neglected appearance up to now but knew that it would pain her deeply and add to his own hell. And yet every instinct now cried out for her, as they cried out for Elvira. He wanted the comfort of her love so much, and yet—how could he bear what this visit would do to her, to both of them?

Again it seemed as though the commander could read his thoughts.

'Your mother won't be very happy to see you as you are. I expect you'd like to get cleaned up first?' he suggested.

'Yes, sir.'

'Very well. Guards!'

They stepped forward to help him out of the chair, but, 'One moment!' halted them.

'I still want those names, Rosas. That's the price of a shower and a change of clothes. What do you say?'

Bernardo bit back the oath that almost escaped him for fear that he would be denied seeing his mother, not even sure now that this visit wasn't a lie. He was at breaking point, and his interrogator knew it. What he did not know was that for his mother's sake, Bernardo would not betray his brother. Only for her sake. Not for anything else.

He slowly shook his bowed head, defeated but silent.

The commander snapped an order. Following his own train of thoughts, the words didn't sink in until the guards pulled him to his feet, and one helped to steady him while the other removed the chair. The second officer also stood up with a document in his hands and commanded him to stand to attention. The impossible order required immediate response, and his effort to obey while every part of him was utterly shattered had no effect on the officer who began in a firm voice, 'Bernardo de Rosas Zabaco . . . ' The rest of the many words just drifted over him, and he only realized the man had stopped speaking when one of the guards was allowed to grab his arm to keep him on his feet.

The commander saw that he had taken in nothing of the sentence which had just been read out, so with a few staccato words, he explained it to him.

'Today is the 16th of April. You can tell your mother that on the first of May, you are to be executed.'

He waved to the guards to take Bernardo away, and outside the door, they gave him back the walking stick with impassive faces. He struggled along several corridors between them as if back in his dream, despairingly seeking the lost child, numb to physical pain, unaware that the sobs that haunted him were his own as a different, harder pain swelled within him. He stopped automatically when the guards halted and waited for them to unlock the door. He had forgotten that it wasn't *the* door until he dragged himself through it.

X

The doctor had died only two weeks before Dionisia received a letter from the prison authorities in Burgos, informing her of Bernardo's imprisonment and giving her permission to see him for twenty minutes on the 16th of April. Soon after Bernardo had left Los Pinos, his father suffered the first of a series of strokes which in the beginning left him partially paralysed and eventually, and very suddenly, killed him. He had always worked too hard and drunk too much wine, and the combination was eventually too much for him. Being himself the doctor, there was no one to call when he was ill. When he died, she realised that she was very fond of him.

So she travelled to Burgos with a heavy heart, feeling lost and without the courage she knew she would need in order to face what lay ahead. In the prison, she was shown into a tiny, dirty room that had no furniture whatsoever and no window. An electric light hung on a long cord from the high ceiling, its bulb speckled with fly dirt. She remembered every detail. She was left on her own, the door was locked, and inside herself, she was already crying to think that her Bernardo should be locked in such a grim place, for what reason she couldn't imagine.

She heard sounds in the corridor, an impatient voice and the jangling of keys, which emphasized the nightmare quality of her distress. In a moment, the door was unlocked, a guard walked in, said abruptly, 'In here,' and the son she had last seen so strong and determined as he walked away from home in his smart suit to make a new life for himself with Elvira limped clumsily into the room, not able to disguise the cost of the effort. There was a second guard behind him, and they stayed in the room, one on each side of the door, their silent presence adding to the nightmare sense of unreality already gripping her heart.

'My son!' was her anguished cry as she moved towards him, arms outstretched. Was this her lovely boy, so gaunt, so dirty, so pale beneath a rough beard, his once merry eyes so hollow and pain-darkened?

For a moment, he seemed not to recognise her. He stared and said nothing, then just one word, 'Mother!' as he let go of the stick that held him up and fell to his knees at her feet, thrusting his head into her skirt. He clung to her as if he were a young child again. She had to be strong for him, so she withheld her terrible desire to weep as she saw his broad shoulders bowed before her, shaking with the sobs that were wrenched out of him.

'Don't cry, my heart, don't cry. It's all right now,' she crooned, stroking his head, instinctively using every mother's words to comfort a hurt or frightened child.

They appeared to help, for he stopped sobbing, but when he tried to get up, he was overwhelmed by the effort. All his strength was gone. Seeing his plight and his mother's distress, the two guards pulled him to his feet with good-natured if rough encouragement while Dionisia, watching helplessly, felt as if her very womb was being torn out.

After a few moments, when it looked as though he was trying to get his thoughts together, he said, 'Mother, they're going to kill me.'

She was afraid to let the words sink in and thrust them away. 'What have you done to your foot?' was her reply.

'It's broken.'

'Haven't they seen to it? How did it happen?'

'That doesn't matter now. It was my own fault.'

There was a long pause before either of them spoke again. There was so much to say and yet no words or time for anything that mattered. Neither of them knew where to begin.

At last he spoke. 'Mother, what do you know about Elvira? I'm going crazy wondering about her. I haven't seen her since I left home.'

'She left Quintera . . . When was it? Months ago. I supposed she'd gone to Burgos—or to you.'

'She's expecting a child. Did you know?'

'I know nothing. You've never written to me, neither has Arturo. There was only the letter . . . the one saying I could see you here,' and she felt a new stab of pain in her already wounded heart, a stab of jealousy almost.

She had come to him, but he was thinking only of Elvira. He was still in love with her. After all he had suffered, after being so long apart, he thought only of her, and she realised that if he cared about dying, it was because it would take him away from her before he should ever have a chance to see her again.

'She went to Madrid,' he told her, 'but I don't know if she arrived safely. If only I could know about her . . . It's the not knowing that's so bad.'

At that moment, one of the guards coughed gruffly, came forward and said, 'Time's up. The prisoner must return to the cells now.'

'But . . . but we can't have had twenty minutes. I was told twenty minutes. Please, allow us just a little more time,' Dionisia begged him.

'You can say goodbye, that's all.'

Mother and son looked at each other. Bernardo was calm now, as if his original outburst hadn't occurred.

'Look after Elvira if she comes to you. Tell her that I would have married her properly, even in a church if she'd wanted, and that I love her still.'

'I'll tell her,' she promised, hardly able to speak for the anguish that constricted her throat.

'And believe me, Mother, I've done nothing bad. Tell Elvira that, too. Tell her I've done nothing bad.'

She could only nod her head.

He made an effort to smile in his old way as he said, 'I'll be all right, Mother. Don't worry about me,' and he didn't see how that smile smote her heart as he kissed her on both cheeks and clumsily hugged her for the last time.

'I'm sorry for all the pain I've caused you,' he added. 'And Father, too. I hope you'll both forgive me and remember that I love you.'

'I'll tell him,' she forced out in barely more than a whisper. She hadn't the courage to tell him that his father was dead. He had too much pain to bear already.

When he had limped away, and she was alone once more, the little room no longer seemed empty. She supposed that it was only really within herself, but it felt as though it were full of the anguish they had both endured there.

Afterwards, Bernardo wasn't taken back to his previous isolation but to a communal cell, originally intended for some twelve prisoners and inhabited by nearly twice that number. It stank of sweat, filth, suffering and bad language, but to Bernardo, dreading renewed isolation, it was the next best thing to heaven. The prisoners made room for him, welcoming him with outstretched arms of assistance even while they cursed him for adding to their discomfort, and in their profane and defiant company, he began to feel he was in the real world again, no more drowning in nightmares. They asked him questions, he listened to their misfortunes, and for the first time in many months, he could talk about Elvira and have a sympathetic audience. He called her his wife.

The youngest among them was a lad of sixteen who had been caught stealing army provisions. He had been thrown into the cell and seemingly forgotten, and these hardened soldiers alternately teased and comforted him according to their mood. When he learned that Bernardo had seen his mother, he was envious.

'Don't be,' advised Bernardo. 'The day that yours comes to see you, it may be the last time you set eyes on her.'

In its own way, this real world was as unreal as the other, only made bearable by the fact of not being alone in it. This mixed bag of prisoners, whether professional soldiers, conscripts or victims of circumstance, were all half intoxicated by every dark emotion where some longed for death as much as they feared it, when each new day became a mocking carnival of imaginary hopes, either for release or revenge or debauchery and where the most dreaded thing was silence, a silence which resounded with pain and despair.

When they discovered that Bernardo was a storyteller and a reciter of poetry, even the roughest among them listened with child-like fascination, while the long-remembered words and tales helped to restore his balance of mind as he shared them. He was quickly nicknamed 'The Poet,' and the bored guards would sometimes exchange a cigarette for a poem.

A couple of days before the end of the month, Bernardo persuaded one of them to bring him some paper and a pencil. He wrote a letter to Elvira, addressed to his parents, and gave it to the priest the following evening when he came to confess him and two other men who were to face the firing squad with him. The priest promised to send it on. That night in the cell, nobody slept. Once the boy began screaming for his mother, suddenly hysterical, but was calmed between them. Now and again, a deep sob escaped him as he leaned against one of his comforters who had put a fatherly arm round him in their small space on the floor. Then it was quiet once more, an alert, restless kind of quiet which kept even the guards awake.

Bernardo, who had fallen into a feverish state, found himself searching again for the lost child whose face he never saw. Elvira floated in and out of this shadowy realm, growing clearer as he struggled to hold on to her. One of Becquer´s short rhymes suddenly came into his head—*'For a glance, a world; for a smile, a heaven; for a kiss . . . I don't know what I would give you for a kiss!'*

It was still chilly when the three condemned men were called out to the place of execution. Bernardo was helped to his feet, but few words of farewell were spoken, hardly any looks were exchanged, while a handshake and one or two claps on the shoulder were the maximum expressions of feeling. The boy was shivering, and Bernardo gave him his jacket. There was a discussion among the guards and officers as to how he could be marched with any dignity to the place of execution, and finally, they allowed his two companions to help him, and the escort got underway, Bernardo with an arm round each of their shoulders.

The sun had been in the sky too short a time to disperse all the shadows and warm the cold grey yard where the firing squad stood in formation opposite a solitary stool beside which the priest was waiting to dispense the last rites as soon as the condemned men were in line, Bernardo sitting on the stool between them. Once all the formalities had been dealt with, he asked to be allowed to die on his feet, and this request was granted.

XI

Only a mother who has lost her son as Dionisia lost hers can know what she had to endure during that last fortnight. She took a cheap room in a boarding-house near the prison, hoping that by her nearness to him, she might somehow be able to help. She went every day to the garrison, begging to see Bernardo again or to be allowed to talk to someone in authority with whom she could plead for her son, but to no avail. She never even passed through the gates until, on the twelfth day, she sold the earrings she wore and used the money for a bribe. The sentry at the gate agreed to send for the prison chaplain.

The priest was a man of some forty years, and he seemed kind enough. At least he was willing to listen to her, and in those moments, she badly needed someone to talk to. But he told her when she had explained, 'I'm extremely sorry, but there's nothing I can do. Your son has been found guilty of more than one serious offence and must therefore pay the penalty.'

'But what has he done? When was he tried?'

'A military court passed sentence based on written evidence.'

'What written evidence? Please tell me.'

The priest was hesitant in his reply. 'There was the matter of the priest in your village.'

'But he had nothing to do with that. He was in Madrid at the time. Everyone knows he was there. Surely my son must have made that clear? Who could have said he was in Los Pinos when Father González was persecuted? It isn't true.'

Her insistence died away in hopelessness. The priest already knew. She saw it in his face. There was a long silence between them while she digested this fact. At last, the priest spoke, uncomfortably.

'Señora, I don't try to pretend that I like the times we're living through. We are dealing with a revolution that must be stopped at all costs. Your son has unhappily become one of its victims. Do you know how many innocent people have been murdered by the republicans, priests and nuns particularly?'

She shook her head. She knew hardly anything about the war, either what caused it or what they were all fighting about. She hadn't even known that Bernardo had enlisted on the Nationalist side.

'My son could never hurt anyone,' insisted Dionisia. 'You must believe me.'

'I do believe you. I've spoken to him, and it's given me a chance to judge his character. I believe in his innocence in that matter and also in his loyalty to the Nationalist cause. You can be proud of him as a soldier even though one of the charges was dereliction of duty. He might have received a more lenient sentence on that count if he hadn't refused to explain his actions which then implicated him regarding the priest.'

He paused and sighed, raising his hands in a deprecatory gesture as he continued, 'There's nothing I can do to help him except hear his confession and perform the last rites.'

He changed the subject abruptly. 'You probably know that he's exceedingly worried about his girl. If I can assure him that you will do everything to help her if she comes to you, I'm sure his mind will be much at rest.'

Dionisia promised.

'I wish I could help him,' added the priest. 'Sincerely I do. All I can say is that he's more fortunate than those victims of the other side who aren't even allowed a priest before they die. Your son will receive all the final sacraments.'

'Won't I be able to see him just once more? Just for five minutes?'

'I'm afraid not.'

He walked with her back to the gates, and as she crossed the yard, the thought that Bernardo was so near to her and yet unaware of her presence there, trying to help him, was a bitter one. The priest advised her to go home.

'There's nothing you can hope to achieve by remaining here,' he said, but she had to stay because she had nothing to go home for. If only Pedro had lived a little longer! If only she could have had his strength to help her. She needed him so much now, more than she had ever needed him in all their life together.

She didn't go to the garrison again and spent most of the time praying in the great cathedral. She was there early on the morning of the execution. She was afraid that she might hear the sound of the rifle fire if she stayed in her room and the only small comfort she could find was there in the shadows of the solid Gothic pillars. The same day she went back to Los Pinos, feeling as though she was going to die too.

But sorrow doesn't kill people, and Dionisia reminded herself that she had another son who might one day need her. Whether he was alive or not, what he was doing, where he was, she had no idea, but she clung to her belief that God couldn't take both her sons from her. He couldn't be so deaf to her supplications.

She had a letter from the priest in Burgos soon after returning to Los Pinos to tell her where Bernardo was buried and that possibly she would be able to claim his body when the war ended. 'He received absolution,' he wrote, 'and died bravely.' He also enclosed a letter for Elvira, which Dionisia, with difficulty, resisted the temptation to open and read. She kept it with the old photo and a few of the toys that Bernardo had made, the only mementoes of him that she had, apart from memories.

After that there was nothing, only days following nights and nights following days, when sometimes she couldn't believe that what had happened was true. Sometimes she'd fall asleep and dream of that little room in the prison, and she'd see her son's face again as it was then, bearded and haggard and afraid. She'd hear him cry, 'Mother, they're going to kill me,' and she'd wake sobbing but relieved—relieved until she remembered that it wasn't a nightmare but reality.

PART SIX

It was only a few weeks after Bernardo had rushed out of Paquita's flat to join the militia that Elvira arrived there, wretched, exhausted and hardly able to believe that there was no further travelling to do, no more unknown fears to be faced. It was the blackest experience she had ever undergone, sick with fear and hunger, finding herself one of a crowd of refugees going in the same direction to escape the advancing army. How could Paco have refused to take her in? How could Sole have remained silent and not pleaded for her? They had given her money and some food from the shop, but they had shut the door in her face.

In Arturo's home, she thought she was safe at last. Paquita's welcome as she struggled with astonishment was genuine, and the children stared with excited curiosity. The flat was big and comfortable. Paquita was all kindness, even though they had never met before, her dark eyes concerned and filled with sympathy as Elvira told her tale. She prepared a hot bath for her, looked her out some pretty underwear, invited her to help herself to the perfumes in the bathroom and found her a dress which more or less fitted.

'Tomorrow, we'll sort out some clothes for you,' she said. 'Don't worry about a thing.'

It was a wonderful change for the beaten, discouraged girl, drained of all her energy and filled with many fears, to be generously taken charge of after so much rejection.

'Why are you so kind? You don't even know me.'

'But I do know you! When Bernardo was here, he never stopped talking about you. You're the sun, the moon and the stars. He was always—'

'Where is he now?'

Elvira's heart had beaten faster at the sound of Bernardo's name, and she broke in hastily, longing for her doubts to be smoothed away, for until now, Paquita hadn't given her the opportunity to mention him.

Paquita replied carefully. 'I don't know exactly. But you mustn't worry. He joined the militia only a few weeks ago. He was here in this flat. If only you'd come a bit earlier, you would have found him.'

'Couldn't I go to him? Can't I find him?'

Paquita smiled at Elvira's impatience. 'You're only here a couple of hours, and already you want to leave?'

'I'm sorry, but . . . you understand. I must see him. I can't rest till I've seen him. Tell me about him. Why didn't he write to me as promised? Is he well?'

Paquita was silent under the frightened, insistent gaze of this young girl, so much in love. She envied Elvira. She had envied her ever since Bernardo had come to stay and made it obvious to everyone how much he loved the girl he had left in Quintera. She had wanted Arturo to love her like that, but she had known from the beginning of their association that he never would. Arturo wasn't a man to love anybody, and yet he had a way of attracting and winning people's affection while giving them nothing in return. He had a charismatic quality along with his good looks, which devastated Paquita when she was twenty and still kept her clinging to him, although she knew he was heartless. If she hadn't loved him so intensely, she would have hated him for the times he had hurt her and gone out of the house to leave her weeping and remorseful.

She knew that he had married her because she was of the society in which he wanted to make a niche for himself. Through her family, he could meet the people he wanted to know, learn the ins and outs of social entertaining of which he had been ignorant when he came from Los Pinos. While in the village, she had thought to learn more of her husband through his parents and his brother and when she realised that Bernardo was all that Arturo could have been, merry and thoughtful and capable of passionate love, she was still more wounded and had to envy the simple village girl who could command such devotion while she, educated, well-groomed, socially far superior, should get nothing for the love she expended.

Bernardo's coming to Madrid had made her realise how little Arturo contributed to the family he had created, that he saw in her nothing more than an introduction to people he wanted to know and a woman to satisfy his physical needs. He was hardly aware even that he had four children, and their noisy chatter molested him on the few occasions that he stayed home. The boys hardly knew what it was to have a father, except for their occasional frozen encounters when Arturo was at home, when they had to talk quietly and be careful not to plant sticky fingers on his clothes. But their uncle Bernardo from 'the village' was something different.

Arturito still remembered him from the visit they had made the year earlier, and Bernardo was the boy's firm favourite. He would sit on his uncle's knees and beg for story after story, listening avidly to Bernardo's tales, although Paquita felt sure he could never understand even half of them. They were often as abstract as they were beautiful. But Arturito didn't seem to mind. He was enchanted by words, as was his uncle, and seeing them together, Paquita had to notice even the physical likeness between them.

'Please don't keep anything from me,' said Elvira anxiously, afraid of Paquita's long silence and lost gazing upon her.

'He's in the sierra with the militia.'

'Fighting!' She almost screamed out the word. 'And if he gets killed?'

Paquita said nothing, and Elvira knew that the idea had occurred to her also.

Warm from the bath, relaxing in the borrowed clothes and perfume, Elvira suddenly realised that the comfort to be offered her in this home would be no more than physical. Here she had hoped to resolve her doubts and start life anew with Bernardo, but here she had reached a dead end. There was still no Bernardo, and there was still insecurity, people helpless as she was, even afraid as she was.

She began to cry. She hadn't cried since she had left home with one small suitcase which, shortly afterwards, someone stole. She hadn't cried at Sole's house for pride; she hadn't cried on discovering that the trains were for troops, not civilians, or all along the road to Madrid with its many halts and diversions, because tears were a luxury she couldn't afford. Fear mastered everything until that became a luxury too. Once the city was reached, in a haze of exhaustion she was brought by some refugee agency to the address Bernardo had given her and collapsed into Paquita's care. But the generous welcome had raised her hopes too high, and now they were dashed more thoroughly than ever before.

Paquita didn't try to comfort her with false hopes and promises. She remained unspeaking until Elvira cried herself into silence, which took quite a long time, for she was weeping out all the hatred, violence and fear that had filled her ever since her father and then Paco had turned her away. Her black hair fell across her face and hid it from Paquita's unflinching gaze. She watched the clenching hands, the thin, long-nailed fingers which dug convulsively into her palms as Elvira sobbed and occasionally beat on her knees with closed fists until the fury was spent and she grew calm.

Paquita said, 'The only thing we can do is wait for Arturo to come home and see if he can get a message to him.' Even as she suggested this, she knew it would be fruitless, but she had to say something to comfort the exhausted girl.

'But when's he coming? And won't that take ages?'

'It's all we can do, and now you must get some sleep. You can't afford to be ill.'

Elvira weakly obeyed and, although she had thought on getting into the strange but comfortable bed that sleep would never come to her, Paquita had to wake her forcefully some twelve hours later.

'Arturo's here,' she said. 'Do you want to talk to him?'

Not even her desperation to find Bernardo would persuade Elvira to that. How could she face him, an unmarried woman carrying his brother's child?

'You ask for me,' she begged, 'and then tell me what he says.'

Paquita broke the news about Elvira's arrival. Arturo was too exhausted to show much interest and was only irritated when she began asking him if there was any way of contacting Bernardo or at least finding out where he was.

'I've no idea where he is or what he's doing. He should have stayed home, and so should she. You know more about him than I do. Didn't he come here after Toledo? Perhaps he's got himself killed at the front. There's nothing I can do. Go to the hospitals or the Red Cross. They might tell you something. I need some sleep.' He threw himself down on the bed, fully clothed, and within minutes was as if unconscious.

Elvira had overheard the conversation, listening at the bedroom door, which hadn't been fully closed, so Paquita didn't need to find soft words for her.

'Don't let it get you down,' she said. 'You've got through a lot already. You can surely find the courage to face this too. He'll come back just as soon as he can. You know he will.'

'And if he doesn't?'

'He will. He will. And when he finds you here, the whole of Madrid won't be big enough to celebrate in.'

II

The two women, the four children and the maid lived a sterile kind of life in the flat accompanied by a growing realisation that the hard times had hardly yet begun. There was bombing, there was shelling, there was murder in the streets, and each day it was more difficult to find fresh food, even those who had the money to pay for it. The government had deserted the capital, leaving it to fall into the hands of the rebels, and only the road to Valencia and the coast was still open.

Arturo turned up unexpectedly with half a sack of rice, another of oranges and some money, telling them that the Syndicate was issuing food tokens if they needed them and that he had arranged for his government salary to be paid to Paquita while there was still a functioning system. He stayed only a few hours, but Elvira kept out of his way, unable to overcome the shame of her condition. In her brief encounter with him, she couldn't connect this cold stranger with Bernardo and hurriedly collected up the children and took them for a walk, noticing Paquita's grateful glance as she smothered them in scarves. By the time they returned, Arturo had gone. There was only the rice, the oranges and the money to show he had been there at all.

Paquita told her he had advised her to join the women and children who were leaving Madrid daily in lorry-loads, but although the two women discussed it, they dismissed the proposal, Elvira because she was blindly hoping for Bernardo to come, Paquita because she couldn't bear the idea of the communal life of a refugee camp. She was very much a city woman, fastidious in many ways, and she still remembered how much it had cost her not to offend Arturo's relations by recoiling too obviously from sharing a common dish at the table, and being obliged by necessity to use the stable at the back of the house, sometimes occupied by a mule. A refugee camp would surely be even worse. She knew better than to expect Arturo to be around to resettle his family and make sure they had adequate accommodation and living conditions. And what would happen to her lovely home if she abandoned it?

Her home and her children were her life. She clung to them because she couldn't cling to Arturo. Neither she nor Elvira really believed that anything could happen to them. It happened to other people in other districts, but so far, their district had remained untouched.

Madrid was surrounded. From a tall building, you could see the enemy positions; the Casa del Campo—that wild, unending stretch of public countryside which before had been the private hunting grounds of the King—was manned by the rebels; everything to the north was threatened by the Nationalists. The shells from the cannons came right into the city streets, blew people to pieces, set houses on fire, even stray bullets cracked windows and killed the unlucky passer-by, but one grew used to it if not directly in the line of fire. Every now and again, a German bomber added to the death and destruction.

One wintry morning Paquita and Elvira decided to take the children out for a while. It had been rainy and miserable for more than a week, and the boys were tired of being pent up indoors. They were driving everyone crazy with their squabbles, so the minute a little sun began to creep over the rooftops, Paquita said, 'Come on. Out we go, quickly before we lose it again.'

They scrambled into coats and boots and scarves and flung themselves down the stairs. The two women had to laugh even while they scolded. The little maid, a twelve-year-old orphan whom Paquita had taken in six months earlier, stayed behind to tidy up the home.

'We won't be long,' Paquita told her. 'Only an hour or so.'

While they were out, the air raid siren sounded, and suddenly hell seemed to erupt all about them. Someone bundled them roughly into a dark doorway; one of the boys fell over and began screaming; there was a confusion of thunder, fire and shaking ground. They saw a fat woman come running for their doorway, her eyes bulging with fear. Then there was another explosion, a cloud of distemper fell on their heads and into their eyes, and when the dust of the doorway had cleared, they saw the building in front of them a heap of rubble and the fat woman had disappeared.

Elvira began to shake. All the children were screaming except Arturito, who clung to his mother and took in everything with his grave, grey eyes but didn't make a sound. Only Paquita seemed unmoved, but she was frozen into immobility, unable to understand how the fat woman had disappeared without a trace and trying to imagine how it would have been had she been crossing the road with her children at that moment. They had crossed it, almost in the same spot, only a few moments earlier.

'We must get back home as soon as we can. Pili will be frightened on her own. This is dangerous!' she exclaimed.

The inane remark set Elvira off into peals of laughter, mingled with hiccoughs. Some stranger who was also sheltering in the doorway with them demanded roughly, 'Stop it,' and she did. It seemed that the raid was over, for a heavy silence had fallen over the street while dust spiralled chokingly in all directions.

Paquita and Elvira half dragged and half carried the children home. As they turned into their avenue, they saw that it, too, had been hit. The first sight to greet them was the blood-swamped body of a twelve-year-old boy, still clutching a toy rifle in his hands. The children stared curiously. They knew him.

'It's Miguel,' said Arturito. He didn't seem to realise that he was dead.

Three properties had been hit, and one of them was Paquita's. There was only half a house, buried under the fallen upper storeys. No flames, only clouds of dust still settling. People who had been sheltering downstairs were clambering out through the blasted windows which gave on to the street. The door was hidden behind fallen masonry. Paquita's flat and the little maid had disappeared.

They spent the winter in the homes of different Party members, a week here, a few days there, a month somewhere else. No one could put them up indefinitely, for most of them were already sheltering others in the same plight or whose flats were too small to offer permanent housing to four growing children and another to come.

Paquita's parents had returned to their native Galicia a year earlier, anticipating the coming crisis. Her father had been disillusioned by his son-in-law, perhaps unwilling to recognise his political tendencies until it became impossible to ignore them, even more discomforted by and unwilling to admit that Arturo had taken advantage of his spontaneous nature. The cold deception practised by his son-in-law wounded him deeply. Paquita fiercely defended her husband's principles, however little she understood where they were leading, opening a bitter chasm between them that couldn't be crossed. Rodrigo took advantage of the offer of an excellent position in Galicia and rented out the family home on a long lease, while other contacts had also left Madrid before the conflict turned to war, fearing for their lives. She had no real friends she could ask, for they had either abandoned Madrid like her parents or were in hiding and had to rely on help from the Syndicate.

Then someone told them of an empty flat which belonged to a middle-aged couple who had fled from Madrid at the outbreak of the war.

'The concierge's wife is a special friend of mine. Tell her I sent you, and she'll let you have the place. It's a crime that rooms should be left empty when others have nowhere to go.'

The street was one that led into Lavapies, a poor quarter of Madrid. There was a big ancient door opening on to a passage under the first-floor rooms, which went through to the courtyard. At the end of the passage was a rickety, worn staircase leading up to the galleries onto which gave the doors of all the flats. There were five storeys of them, all equally tiny, with two rooms and a kitchen space between the two with an oven. One small window and the door served for ventilation.

From the courtyard, it looked quite picturesque. Washing lines were strung from one side to the other, and clothes of all colours hung dripping. Birds sang in tiny cages outside the doors; greenery clustered the barred windows and brought a note of colour to the ochre walls, the brown doors and the black railings. With the sun shining down, a square of bright blue sky above the dusty red of the tiled roofs, one caught a sense of liveliness, a sense of homeliness. It was a community cut off from the drab street outside. So Elvira and Paquita were not totally dismayed at first sight but, as they followed the caretaker across the courtyard and carefully climbed the stairs, which were dark and broken, their hearts began to shrink.

On each landing, by the stairs, there was a communal sink for laundry with one cold water tap and a hole-in-the-floor lavatory which served for the occupants of the whole storey, and they soon discovered that the cleaning and laundry rota was the source of many quarrels which the concierge refereed when she felt like it.

'Here it is,' sighed the woman as they reached the fifth floor and passed two-thirds of the way round the gallery, watched by curious eyes, before stopping eventually at one of the brown doors. She produced a key and opened up the flat. Paquita and Elvira followed her in. Even without furniture, it seemed terribly tiny. The rooms were some twelve feet square.

'The people who lived here have gone to their village till the war's over. Capitalist cowards! So you're welcome to stay here till they come back if they ever dare to,' the concierge informed them. She was shrewdly taking stock of them with the practised eye of all her kind, making it clear with her expressions rather than her words that they needed to keep in her good books, whatever their circumstances.

She looked questioningly at Elvira's swollen body, having noticed no wedding ring, and aware that free love was now promoted, though it wasn't going to work out free for this young woman. Not that she cared.

'You don't mind children, do you?' Paquita was almost afraid to voice the words.

'How many are there?'

'Well . . . four at the moment.'

'If you can manage here with four children, you're welcome. I've known what it is to have children and nowhere to go.'

She was not unkindly. There were times when she thought the bombs were going to fall on top of her, and being left completely bereft of a home, as these people had, excited her interest as well as her business sense.

'If there's anything you want or that I can get for you?'

'We must buy some things,' agreed Paquita. 'Mattresses, sheets and things.'

She didn't suggest beds, for the money she counted on might have to last them for a long time. Also, there was too little room. The Señora Emilia opened her hand while saying, 'Leave it with me,' and Paquita found herself putting money into it after Elvira engaged in some haggling on her behalf. She was not her father's daughter for nothing, increasing her standing in the caretaker's assessment of them both.

Once everything was installed in the two rooms, a single mattress for the children, a double for themselves, a few plates, pots and pans and all the children, the hearts of the two women sank into mutual depression. If they were to suffer nothing worse than this, they could consider themselves lucky, but both knew that worse was to come. Two babies were expected now, Elvira's in March and Paquita's at the end of July, the legacy of Arturo's last visit. Babies cost money, food costs money, fuel costs money, and neither Arturo nor Bernardo knew of their plight.

The children also were sadly bewildered by their change of fortune. Arturito was having nightmares, seeing again in his imagination the torn Miguel with his wooden rifle, and when he woke screaming, he would, through his sobs, beg for Bernardo to come to him and hardly allow his mother to console him. The other children were too young to have been greatly affected by anything they had seen, but they sensed the tense atmosphere and were more fractious than previously because of it. They complained that they had no toys and argued constantly about having to sleep together, used to their own little beds.

'Where's Pili?' the little one would ask. Pedrito, only two, had spent more time in Pili's arms than any of the others, and he missed her greatly.

'She's gone away, darling,' Paquita would tell him, and once Arturito added quietly, 'She's dead like Miguel.'

No one had told him that, but he had guessed it.

Another time he asked, 'Is Papa dead, too, and Uncle Bernardo?'

'Of course not, my angel. Why should you think that?'

'Because they don't come. Why don't they come?'

'They're busy. One day they'll come. Perhaps tomorrow.'

Arturito solemnly shook his head. 'They're dead, Mama. I know they are. Don't you know?'

Paquita shook her head, blinking from her eyes the tears that only the children were capable of drawing from her now. Arturito had been merry like Bernardo, but now he was so serious, thinking and talking about death as if it were the most natural thing in the world. She had lost all contact with her husband, and many a night, she dreamed that he had been killed, although, in her waking hours, she positively refuted the idea. But why did he never come? Was he still even in Madrid?

She called on the few acquaintances of Arturo that she knew, but they seemed cut off from each other, wrapped up in their own worries, thinking of food, wondering if Madrid would fall or how much the populace could endure without surrendering and again, thinking of food. She left her new address with them, but if Arturo were still in Madrid, no one seemed to know or care.

'You'll have to do what we're all doing,' she was told. 'Hang on and hope for the best.'

Elvira longed for her lover who never came, sustaining herself with the belief that one day he would come, that somehow he would find a way to return to Madrid soon and marry her. She read all the casualty lists, visited the hospitals, joined the queues for information at the Red Cross while she still had the energy, and her face grew thinner, the shadows under her eyes making them darker still. In the early days, she had even desperately asked every militiaman she saw if they knew Bernardo until, disheartened by every shake of the head and frightened by the hungry propositions with which some of them crudely responded, she kept away from them.

Her father had called her a whore, and seeing so many of these women on the streets, she at times foolishly and weakly feared that Bernardo didn't come because he had lost interest in her, hardly knowing which was worse, that he couldn't come or wouldn't. Who would support her child? How would she live? If it were not for Paquita, she might have already ended up on the street, for she had arrived in Madrid with nothing but the clothes she had set out in when her father disowned her.

III

It was difficult for Elvira to recall, after the nightmare period she passed in Madrid, how much she had loved Bernardo and what had caused her to throw caution to the winds that early summer, which seemed so long ago. There were so few memories to make Bernardo real to her. Looking back, it seemed that they must have still been children in their innocence when they would stroll together through the fields laughing about silly things, sit to watch a slow-moving stream or the aerobatic display of the swallows as they caught their supper on the wing then swiftly flew homeward before the gathering dusk overtook them, when Bernardo would recite poetry or make up stories about ants or lizards and time would stand still; a darker memory of the time in Burgos when he had coldly deserted her; their passionate reunion; and that last evening when she was sheltered so closely in his arms, and he had whispered in the shadows of the abandoned ruin, 'We're one now. No one can ever change that, no matter what comes,' and she had thought that all paradise was in that moment.

In spite of every adversity, she clung to the belief that somehow she and Bernardo would be reunited. It was all she lived for; this hell was only endurable if she could believe that one day there would be an end to it. She would sometimes dream that he took her into his arms and made love to her, and she would cry with relief, her worries floating away at the feel of his caressing lips, only to be overwhelmed with a sense of loss when she awoke.

But the memory and imagination of such bliss could in no way compete with the reality of the hardly endurable nightmare of the baby's birth. There was no money to spend on a professional midwife, but one of the neighbours, a middle-aged woman who had assisted at many births, promised to help, and Paquita knew enough from her own experience to reassure Elvira that everything would be as clean as they could make it. But having a baby on a mattress on the floor, trying to stifle cries because the children were asleep in the next room, was something beyond Elvira's imagination. The woman was common and not even clean. She was friendly enough, but Elvira was horrified and whispered to Paquita, 'Don't let her touch me or the baby. You hold the baby when it's born. Please.'

It was a long and difficult birth. Elvira was narrow-hipped, and the baby didn't come easily. She was also weak from malnutrition and hardly had the energy to resist the long hours that gradually wore down her courage and patience.

'Will it never end?' she moaned to Paquita, perspiring although the night was cold. 'I can't bear it much longer.'

'It will end, and you must bear it. There's nothing else to do. Try not to think about it. Put your mind on something else.'

'Oh God, that's impossible.'

'Think of Bernardo,' she urged. 'Think of the things you've done together. Think of anything but the pain when it comes.'

Elvira tried, but her mind was empty. She couldn't even see Bernardo's face clearly. There was a vague shadow of a smile, but the eyes she saw dissolved into Arturito's eyes, perplexed and introverted. As the pain gripped her again, she tried desperately to think of some conversation they had shared, one of his tales; she searched in her mind for Bernardo's voice but couldn't remember it, and then everything was blurred and unbearable, and she muttered and gasped and cried out and almost broke the bones of Paquita's hands, so fiercely did she hold them. Nothing was real beyond the crescendo of pain in whose grip she writhed until suddenly, almost without her realising it—so delirious was she at the end—everything stopped, and the baby was bawling.

'It's a girl,' Paquita informed her, and she washed it gently, wrapping it in an old clean towel before placing it in Elvira's arms.

With exhausted, wondering eyes, Elvira stared at the screwed-up scarlet face and shock of raven-black hair, which seemed more abundant than the face itself. In her wildest dreams, she could never have imagined her first experience of motherhood would be like this.

'It's a tiny thing,' said the woman who acted as midwife. 'Smaller than any I've had. You'll have to be careful if you want it to live.'

Paquita was more worried about Elvira herself, so pale, so pinched and thin and worn was she.

'I wanted a boy,' whispered Elvira. 'I was going to call him Bernardo.'

'You can call her Bernardina. I think you're lucky having a girl. Four boys are too much for any woman. If mine's a boy, we'll do a swap. What do you think?'

The little creature squalled incessantly until, desperately hungry, it found its mother's breast and sucked itself to sleep, not finding what it sought. Elvira, holding it close, wept and wept, thinking of Bernardo and what their love had produced. She longed for him with unbearable intensity, and the baby's unsatisfied hunger was somehow akin to her own. She needed him as much as his child needed milk, but they both cried in vain.

Eventually, she fell into a dreamless slumber from which she didn't awake until the afternoon. Paquita, meanwhile, had remained unsleeping. She watched the girl and the newborn child and imagined herself in their place. She didn't mind the birth. It was something she was used to, and it held no terrors for her. But she thought of their present resources and was afraid. Better almost for the child to be born lifeless than have to struggle in a starving world. By the time her child was born, the war would have been in progress for a year. If already they were in such desperate circumstances, what would be awaiting them if the war didn't end soon and neither Arturo nor Bernardo came to relieve them?

IV

The war continued for another two years, and Madrid stayed under siege all that time, weakening constantly but unbreakable in its pride. It became an island in the middle of conquered Spain and only the people who lived there during that period knew how they survived winter cold, sickness and the unending daily hunger, when potato peelings were a luxury and wilted vegetables something to queue and barter for, and only low-grade lentils mixed with sweepings on offer. When supper was more and more frequently a cup of hot water before bed for the adults and breakfast a cup of chicory for them all with a mouthful of bread, the over-riding necessity of both women was to provide enough for one main meal each day, a task which might take hours. A queue would begin before dawn, and they took it in turns to arrive early as there was no point in waiting unless they could be somewhere near its head. There was a place that issued free milk to toddlers, but it was of poor quality, already watered. At home, it had to be watered down more to make it go round so that its alimental value was next to nothing by the time the children drank it. They were entitled to a weekly tin of condensed milk which had to be carefully rationed and often caused tears and howls of dismay when it was all gone.

Their main diet was a kind of stew made up of whatever could be obtained - an onion, a potato, a doubtful fish head, a tomato, more rarely a small piece of meat which might once have been someone's pet, a few wild herbs, and the inevitable lentils. By now, this was the basic dish for most of the population. It was known as Saint Antony's soup, for he was the patron of lost and stolen things. Prayer to him might lead the supplicant to something edible. Elvira's reminder to the children when she left them for her daily search was, 'Pray to Saint Antony if you want to eat today.'

Once Arturito replied, 'Why doesn't he help you to find some nice food like we used to eat?' and she snapped back, 'Just be thankful for anything he gives us,' rebuking him for echoing her own thoughts.

When one day Paquita triumphantly returned with a big bag of maggot-ridden locust beans, Elvira, watching the children eagerly chewing away at them, remembered how locust beans had been fodder for her father's mules. She remembered too when she had defiantly told him she would be happy to live on chick-peas with Bernardo, and his mocking response, 'You? Live on chickpeas!' What wouldn't she give now for a bowl of them, stewed with salted pork, or even without the pork! She could see them, smell them, almost taste them. The real thing would have been ecstasy indeed!

When Barcelona fell to the Nationalists, everyone knew that the war was lost. Madrid's half-starved population still resisted for several months, however, fearful of the break-through of Franco's forces and the horrors that might result, while at the same time longing for an end to the ongoing misery of every day. No one anticipated the city's terrible and shameful betrayal into Nationalist hands through a Republican military coup led by Colonel Casado, who deluded himself and his followers that Franco would be grateful and make terms. Socialists and anarchists formed an alliance to wipe out the communists in savage warfare without rendition, while the Nationalist army held back and let them kill one another until they could march in and demand unconditional surrender without firing a single shot.

The Republican dream ended in chaos, merciless betrayals and massacres, while the sense of togetherness that had brought the inhabitants through the worst of privations disintegrated into a climate of suspicion and fear on one side and triumphalism on the other.

Elvira and Paquita had every reason to be panic-stricken. Even though Arturo's salary had lost value month by month as prices soared, they had still been able to pay the rent, eat at least one meal a day and buy fuel. Overnight even this security vanished. Only desperation drove Paquita to make her usual visit to the Syndicate, needing to find out if any kind of assistance might still be available and where she could turn if not. Elvira waited anxiously for her return, not wanting to wander the streets for fear of . . . everything, when even comrades of war were now killing one another. The hours went by, but Paquita didn't return. She dished up a bread soup flavoured with an onion but had no appetite, her stomach clenched with dread. Vainly she tried to fight off the "what ifs" that insisted on pushing through her defences, especially the 'what if Paquita never came back?'

She did come back but not till the next morning, exhausted and traumatised, having been arrested and dragged off to a police station where she was thrust into a cell crowded with women like herself, all waiting to be interrogated as to the whereabouts of their men who were on a wanted list. She wasn't physically abused, but the verbal violence of the interrogation was more than enough to devastate her. She was put back in the cell in the expectation of a second round of questioning, where she passed the night without having been offered either food or water since the time of her arrest.

Weak, exhausted and terrified, she was called out again in the morning and told to wait in the corridor outside the interrogation room. The wait was a long one, and she sat on the floor, overcome with dizziness. She looked up when she heard footsteps coming towards her and, to her astonishment, recognised an acquaintance of her father's who had dined at the family home on more than one occasion in the past.

'I don't know if he was more astonished than I was,' she told Elvira after she had recovered sufficiently from her ordeal to talk about it. 'He was obviously extremely embarrassed and ashamed. He marched into that room, slamming the door, and the next thing there was a lot of shouting. Then he came out, helped me up and brought me home.'

She burst into tears at this point. Then recovering herself exclaimed, 'Oh, Elvira, it was like a miracle. I might still be in prison but for him!'

All the children were listening to this story, crowding round, deeply impressed as well as bewildered by it all. Elvira sent them off to play on the gallery so that Paquita could get some sleep and then reluctantly set off late on the daily round, refusing to think of anything but the immediate needs, for no miracle was going to feed them.

In this, Elvira was mistaken. Paquita's rescuer came to her assistance again. He was a recent widower and needed someone he could trust to look after his four children. His live-in domestic couldn't manage them, but her presence assured the respectability of the situation. He could guarantee some basic rations for her family along with a small salary, and her Sundays would be free. He would also be able to protect her from any further trouble connected with her husband.

It was an offer that put both women in a quandary. Elvira would become totally responsible for all the children while Paquita would hardly see them except for a few snatched hours once a week. She felt the incongruity of the situation deeply; the war was stripping away even what remained of her self-respect for, gratitude aside, once she had recovered from the initial humiliation, she had been profoundly embarrassed at being found on the floor in the corridor of a police station, and now she was being offered the job of a nurse-maid!

Then there was the man himself. He was roughly her father's age, well-dressed, and had apparently been able to move fearlessly and authoritatively from one political band to another. This Don Marino was playing a very dangerous game. Was he a double agent, and what would happen if he should be denounced or discovered by either band? With the city collapsing about them, threatening even the precarious stability they had managed to maintain until now, all sorts of frightening scenarios presented themselves to the two women as they struggled to decide whether or not Paquita should accept his proposal. The reality of their situation decided the issue for them, and within just a few days, Elvira found herself alone with six children totally in her care.

If only she had never come to Madrid! If only Bernardo had never loved her and made her love him in return! If only they had never . . . and yet, there was Bernardina, the seal of their love, with cruel innocence reminding her of a lost and irredeemable past, but in whom she could find none of her father's carefree nature and affection. Surely she was being punished for her wickedness. That's what her father would say, and perhaps he was right. All those who had despised, desecrated and burned the churches—where were they now? Dead, imprisoned, hunted down like dangerous animals.

Was Bernardo among them? She couldn't bear the weight of such thoughts, but neither could she escape them.

Bernardina was just two years old when Madrid was handed over to Franco, a small, thin, pallid and almost speechless child with straggly dark hair and big grey eyes. In her bony face, there seemed to be nothing more than eyes and mouth. This latter was too large to make her beautiful, and she was a little featherless bird in appearance, crushed by life's circumstances. But if Elvira saw her child a weakling, Paquita's was worse. Her first daughter, Rosario, was a poor little scrap, hardly able to stand for all that she was only a few months younger than her cousin. Arturito had a strong affection for these two little girls and defended them from his rough and careless brothers. For Elvira, it was painful to see how her daughter would cling to the boy who was so much like her father in every way, looking to him for comfort and help, preferring to sit on his lap rather than her mother's. No wonder, really, as she had so little time for, or experience of, mothering.

Even when the war was over, there was no relief from hunger. All the refugees that had flooded Madrid at the beginning returned unwillingly to their villages. Their fields had been long neglected, and much work had to be done to restore them to their former production and, meanwhile, there was nothing to eat. The city was crammed with these, with soldiers of the new regime, with affluent visitors who came to see the war-ravaged and humbled city, and whatever food now came to Madrid was for those who could afford to pay black market prices and for those poor who could prove themselves devout Catholics and Nationalists. The families of those who had supported the previous government were allowed to continue starving, and when Elvira suggested applying for the charity food, Paquita violently opposed her.

'What of Arturo and Bernardo?' she demanded. 'They wouldn't want us to humble ourselves.'

'Then they should have helped us,' argued Elvira, who was haunted by the face of her own child and her own hunger.

'If they've been killed or imprisoned, they wouldn't want us to accept charity from their enemies.'

'But, for the children? What have children got to do with war and politics? They have to be fed.'

'And do you think a regime that can let children starve because their parents happen to be undesirable is a regime to support—because that's what you'll be doing if you accept their charity. They should provide food to all children, regardless of their parents' political beliefs. Not say, "Food for Jaimito because his father was a Nationalist soldier, and Pepito can starve because his father's a communist." Arturo was and, if he lives, is a communist, and if there's no food for his children because of it, then they'll have to continue as they are. We've managed until now, and we'll continue managing. Things will get better soon, you'll see.'

Elvira wasn't convinced. She was more practical than Paquita, as well as caring nothing about politics, only glad that the killing had stopped and the war was over, and the parish priest had offered assistance if she were to become a regular member of the Church and be able to prove that she had no connection with the Republicans.

'The first thing they'll want to see is your marriage licence,' returned Paquita scornfully as Elvira enthused over the idea.

'I'll say I've lost it.'

'They won't believe that. They'll ask for all the details and check before they'll allow you a morsel of bread or a mouthful of soup. You try it, and you'll see.'

Elvira was silent. She knew Paquita was right. It wasn't so easy to deceive the Church, and so the only way to obtain food was by paying for it, exorbitant prices and poor quality. Don Marino's rations arrived sporadically. He had seven mouths in his household to satisfy, and Paquita sometimes brought home only meagre rations of rice or beans or a couple of eggs. The concierge did some black market dealing, and she persuaded Elvira to distribute the goods to her scattered customers, her own legs not up to the weary task. Elvira knew she would face a harsh penalty if caught, but she was willing to risk anything to feed the children. She was paid in olive oil and tins of sardines and was rewarded by a new light in their eyes. But the long distances, the heavy loads, the constant tension took its toll, and she was often too weary to care what the boys were up to and left the little ones more and more under Arturito's supervision.

And then one Sunday afternoon, a small package came, delivered by a stranger who stayed only for a few minutes and left before they could ask his name. The children were lying on their tumbled mattress in their underwear, which was shabby and much darned. They were all in the bewildered state of being half awake and half asleep, and only Arturito was aware that something unusual was happening, something he felt to be portentous. He had risen at the sound of the man's voice in the other room, but the hurried words, the mixed reactions and high tension he could sense in both women made him cautious and kept him silent. He went back to the mattress, deeply puzzled, unnoticed by them.

Elvira watched as Paquita cut the string that tightly bound the newspaper-wrapped package. There was a wad of banknotes in new money and a letter. Neither woman spoke. Both were trembling. Paquita handed the money to Elvira and stared at the folded sheet of paper, the letter she had longed for, the letter that would relieve her agony and yet which she now hardly dared open. Watching her, Elvira felt a strong stab of jealousy. Why was there still no letter for her? But perhaps, just perhaps, there would be news of Bernardo and, unable to remain silent, she demanded, 'Read it, Paquita! Read it! I can't bear any more.'

She read silently. It didn't take her long. She shut her eyes and sharply drew in her breath, seeming to stagger for a moment until the breath then rushed out in a howl of pain. The letter dropped as she threw herself face down on the mattress and clung to it, spasms shaking her whole body from which terrible sounds were wrenched. Then as suddenly she sat up and stared at Elvira with a look that frightened her, there was such violence in it.

'Elvira!' Even her voice was frightening. It was completely without emotion, deathlike. "Until today, I would have told you that

I still love Arturo. Now I tell you that I hate him. I hate him. I shall never forgive him as long as I live. I shall hate him till I die.'

She threw herself down again, moaning over and over, 'I hate him, I hate him,' and then came a torrent of lamentation which turned into deep sobs that somehow began to bring calm.

Elvira was shocked into a kind of paralysis in the presence of so much anguish. She was still holding the money, money they desperately needed, but which at that moment meant nothing to either of them. She put it on the table and knelt to pull Paquita into her arms. The letter lay temptingly close, but she was afraid to pick it up.

At that point, the children trooped into the room, led by Arturito. His thin face was unusually alive, and he was too excited to take in the women's distress. As Paquita turned to them, hurriedly wiping away the tears with her hands, he triumphantly shouted, 'That was Papa, wasn't it? Why has he gone so soon?'

'No, it wasn't Papa.'

'But—'

Paquita stopped him sharply. 'That was another man who came to tell us that Papa is dead.'

'But, Mama, it was him. I know it was him.'

His insistence pierced her to the depths. He couldn't even remember what his father looked like, and the pain of it was too much for her. She slapped his mouth.

'Your father is dead and that's the end of it.'

The boy's eyes filled with tears, and he rushed from the room. Elvira followed him, and the rest stayed staring at their mother, uncomprehending, for now she was weeping again with deep groans, her face pressed to her knees.

Hours later, she handed the letter to Elvira. 'Read it,' she said. 'I want you to read it. If you don't read it, I can't believe it's real.' She was in a state of frigid calm. 'Read it out loud,' she insisted as Elvira hesitated at the first word.

"*Paquita, Believe me when I tell you that I haven't been able to come to you, even after I heard what happened to the flat. And I still can't come. All I can do is write these few words to tell you that I'm leaving the country. If they arrest me I'm a dead man. If I manage to stay alive perhaps we can get together again one day but who knows how far off that day might be. I suggest you go to my family unless your own parents will have you back now I'm out of your life. It may be impossible for me to return for many years, if ever, so I'm willing to free you from our marriage vows. I was never a good husband anyway. Decide your own future, as must I. All I can do for you now is give you what money I can spare, not much I'm sorry to say. The messenger is faithful so I know you will get it. Forget me if you can. I have associates where I'm going who will set me on my feet and we shall carry on the fight. Long live the Republic! Your husband, Arturo.*"

After a long silence, Paquita said, 'Not a single word of love, not a word about the children. He doesn't even know about Rosario. And how long has he known this address and not sent anyone till now? He cares about nothing but the Cause, the Party, his damned politics! Oh, Elvira, what a fool I've been! The years I've wasted on him, all the time knowing in my heart that he has never loved me.'

Elvira was longing to burst out with her own pain, 'And what about Bernardo?' for she had hoped for just a moment when the packet arrived that she might learn something about him from his brother. She bit her tongue and stayed silent even though she was frightened. Suppose Bernardo had never really loved her? Suppose he was like his brother and had forgotten her?

The very next day, Paquita sold her wedding ring and wept half the night because of it.

V

In summertime, the heat in the little flat was unbearable. It was on the top storey under the roof, and the sun beat down from early morning so that by mid-day, the heat from above them was like a charcoal-filled iron, flattening the inhabitants like sheets. The two rooms became an oven, sticky, smelly and impossible to keep in order, and the children spent the best part of the day and night in the street. They were turning into a band of urchins, unruly, heedless of discipline, with the coarse customs and language of the street.

Paquita continued working for Don Marino and saw little of her family. She worked like an unthinking machine all week and, on Sundays, let herself drop. The children begged for attention in vain, and to Elvira's dismay, they always behaved worse when she was there. If they went for a walk, they quarrelled so much as to who should hold her hand, or be near her, or first in everything, that the evenings became unbearable to her, and she usually boxed all their ears and drove them, wailing, home again.

Only Arturito remained silently above the squabbling, impervious to his mother's attempts to give him affection. She was glad that he looked like Bernardo and that the other boys took after her. Only Rosario had her father's features, and it gave Paquita no pleasure to look at her. Elvira never knew what torture she suffered mentally, trying to drive Arturo's callous abandonment from her mind, unable to understand that the man she had loved to distraction should care so little about her and the children. Every time she thought of him, which was often, she wanted to scream and tear the offending memory from her head. She began to suffer violent headaches and couldn't sleep.

As the months passed, one much the same as another with their fortunes neither worsening nor improving, the two women began to dread the approaching winter. It was difficult enough now to obtain fuel and oil. When winter came, it would be almost impossible again. Money was scarce, and the children needed jerseys and boots. They continued playing in the street. They didn't want to be at home, cooped up in the tiny rooms, and escaped whenever Elvira stopped watching them for a moment. She was horrified to discover them one day playing with the cockroaches rather than killing them, throwing them at the girls to make them scream, and dropping them over the gallery railings, hoping they might fall on someone's head!

School was impossible, costing money they couldn't spare, and in the free schools, they weren't accepted as Arturo had allowed none of them to be baptised. This hadn't been a problem under the Republic, but the church was adamant. Besides, neither woman could escape the fact that Arturito was needed at home. The smaller children looked to him almost as they might have looked to a father had there been one. They obeyed him with less reluctance than the adults; they went to him with their problems. He was willing to stand hours in a queue for a tin of condensed milk for the infants and was quite an expert at scavenging among the rubble for bits of overlooked wood or anything combustible, bringing it home with pride. Fuel was as scarce as food, and anything that would burn was treasure.

They all caught colds, their runny noses adding to their generally poverty-stricken appearance. Rosario cut her hand on a broken bottle; Pedrito split his eyebrow falling down the stairs; Arturito scandalized the neighbours by doing a balancing act on the railings which surrounded the gallery, and Rodrigo, the second eldest, began to suffer from his ears keeping them all awake sometimes with howls that couldn't be quieted. On the long, dark winter nights when there was insufficient fuel to keep the stove burning, Elvira would huddle them all around her on the big mattress under the blankets, keeping one another warm, while she entertained them with stories till they all fell asleep, She told them about Don Quijote and Sancho Panza, and the wicked brothers who murdered their father and threw his body in a deep, deep lake which was ever after haunted, and Bequer's beautiful and mysterious princesses, and Bernardo's own tales about lizards and birds, and sometimes she would fall silent without realizing it, overwhelmed by memories, unwillingly brought back to the present by a complaining chorus, demanding more.

'Mama never tells us stories,' stated Rodrigo one night.

'That's because she's not here,' Arturito defended her. 'She would if she was,' and from the tone of his voice, they knew the matter was settled.

Elvira was worried about Arturito. She cared a lot for the boy who reminded her so much of Bernardo, and she realized more than did Paquita that he wasn't well. He never complained, but the shadows beneath his eyes grew darker. His cheeks were hollow and, more than any of the others, the bones stuck out on his thin body. He had been coughing on and off for a long time, for so long in fact that no one took much notice of his cough, except to be irritated by it.

'He ought to see a doctor,' Elvira told Paquita one Sunday.

'Doctors cost money. He'll be all right. It's only a cough. They've all got them.' Paquita was too exhausted to care.

Another problem arose when the housekeeper came to tell them they would have to find somewhere else to live by the following spring as the rightful tenants of the flat had written to say they would be returning then.

'You can go back to the village, Elvira. You should have gone before.'

'And what about you? I can't leave you alone here with no one to help you. We've been through too much together for that.'

'Oh, I shall sort something out. You go to Los Pinos. You'll find out about Bernardo there. Staying here, you'll never learn anything. If he could, he would have contacted you somehow. You know he would.'

Elvira didn't reply. She knew Paquita was right, that to discover Bernardo's whereabouts, she must return home. But she was unwilling to go, afraid that there would be confirmed the fear that weighed down her heart.

'You come too,' she urged. 'We could go together, and it would be wonderful for the children.'

Paquita shook her head. 'No. I couldn't live in one of those little villages, Elvira. I'm a city-dweller. I hate the country, the flies, the ants, all the inconveniences. You're used to them. You don't know how miserable it is for someone like me.'

'But what will you do?'

'I'll contact my parents in Galicia. They'll do something for the children, but I'd rather be independent. I have my job with Don Marino. But it's different for you. You have family there and Bernardo's parents. They'll look after you, I'm sure of it.'

Elvira made a face. 'In Quintera, they'll hate me. I can never go home. And I hardly know Bernardo's parents. And everyone in Los Pinos will talk about me. I can't bear it.'

'But who's to know you're not married? You tell everyone you are married, and if you do find Bernardo, you'll get married. Don't you see? It's the only thing you can do.'

Hard though it was to accept, she knew that Paquita was right. She had to go back, however bitter and humiliating it might be. She knew that things couldn't continue as they were. This was no life for Bernardina, a street urchin, always hungry, dirty and condemned to ignorance. At least in the village, there would be food in plenty, clean air and a roof over their heads, even if . . . She refused to think any further than that. Surviving each day in Madrid was more than enough to keep her mind occupied and her feelings suppressed, although Paquita's 'if you do find Bernardo' was a constant shadowy thorn. She must find him. She must. How often the noiseless tears came now at the end of each weary day, heart heaving with pain as she lay in the dark with the sleeping children sprawled around her, not wanting to wake them!

That winter, they had to spend money on a doctor for Arturo and also for Rosario. The little girl's cut hand had grown worse without anyone being aware of it until suddenly one day she was in a high fever, delirious, and then Elvira noticed how swollen was the wound, with a blue vein running all the way up to the armpit which was also swollen and hot. The doctor said there was nothing he could do. It was too late. And in response to their shocked pleas and protests said, 'Look for another doctor if you like, but he'll tell you the same.'

'What can we do for her? There must be something,' they both cried.

'Aspirin for the fever, hot compresses for the swelling, and keep the wound clean. But it's not enough. She's very sick.'

He examined Arturito's chest with a stethoscope and with his fingers.

'This boy needs the air of the sierra and plenty of good food. I can prescribe some medicine if you like, but it won't do him much good.'

Paquita urged Elvira to get away to Burgos the following spring and to take Arturito with her as well as her own child.

'He'll get better in the village. I know he will. Arturo was right. I should have left him there four years ago when first he suggested it.'

'You couldn't have known then what would happen.'

'But I did. Arturo knew there would be bad times ahead, and he wanted me to leave the children with his parents. But I was selfish and wouldn't have it. I couldn't bear to be parted from them.' She laughed ironically. 'And now I am parted from them. I see them for a few hours of the week, and two of them are sick, and I can't be with them.'

The responsibility for the two sick children weighed heavily with Elvira. She'd already nursed them through measles and chickenpox and half a dozen minor complaints, but both these things were more serious.

Rosario died so suddenly that it was unbelievable. She was tossing and sweating at Elvira's side during the night, and then she lay still. Elvira fell asleep, no longer disturbed by the restless movements, but an hour later, she was awake again, the unnatural stillness of the child playing upon her subconscious mind until it woke her. But it was too late. The little body was already losing its heat, and the eyes stared unseeingly when Elvira lit the candle.

VI

Rosario was given a pauper's funeral, and the only flowers came from Paquita's employer. He also gave her three days' leave from work to arrange things and get over the shock, but three centuries wouldn't have been enough for the weary, unbelieving mother.

'She never stood a chance from the beginning. I've neglected her. I didn't even know she'd cut her hand, let alone that the poison had crept through her whole body.'

'It was my fault, not yours. I was looking after her, not you,' insisted Elvira.

'But I should have been caring for her. She was my daughter, my only little girl. I know you do your best, Elvira. Don't think I'm trying to blame you. On the contrary, if the children are as well as they are, it's thanks to you. I've hardly looked at them closely since I started work. I've just let things slide. I don't know what's the matter with me these days. All through the war, I did my best but, now that there's a chance for things to get better, I don't seem to care any more.'

In her three days at home, she kept the other children near her, undressed them at night, washed their faces and hands, and carefully examined their bony bodies and any cuts or bruises. She looked for a long time at Arturito until he was shivering with cold and begged to be allowed to get into bed.

'Are you all right, my heart?'

'Yes, Mama. Don't worry about me,' and, taking confidence in her unusual solicitousness and the old endearment which she hadn't used for a long time, he added, 'Mama, why don't you stay at home with us any more?'

'Because I can't, my son. I have to work to earn money.'

'Mama, when we have some money, can I go to school? I used to go to school, do you remember?'

'I remember, and I promise you when we have some money, and when we don't need you to help with the little ones any more, I'll send you to school. If you like, tomorrow I'll buy you a writing book and you can copy the letters. Would you like that?'

Arturito nodded happily and tucked himself down beside Rodrigo, who was already asleep. Paquita stayed humming to him for a while until his eyes closed. Then she kissed his black curls and whispered, 'My poor little one.' He was only eight years old, and yet he carried so many responsibilities on his thin shoulders, rarely complaining and generally good-natured, so much like his uncle.

But she felt suddenly that a ray of light had pierced the heaviness of her spirit, for tonight was the first time that Arturito had been kind to her since she had told him that his father was dead and slapped him into accepting the lie. She told herself that she must pull herself together and stop living in the past and with her nightmares and think only of the future of her sons. And she tried to be more of a mother to them on the Sundays when she came home, helping Arturito and Rodrigo with their letters, telling stories to the others, fighting off her tiredness and depression.

The children were overjoyed by the change in her and behaved better. Elvira felt happier, too, for she had been burdened by a sense of guilt ever since Rosario died. But now it appeared that the little girl hadn't died in vain; the family had become more closely knit by the tragedy, and Paquita realised again that she had a family of her own to care for as well as that of Don Marino.

She had been putting aside a few pesetas each month from her wages to buy the children some toys for the festive season and on the 5th of January, while they were asleep, filled their shabby shoes with trashy odds and ends, bound to delight them. In Arturito's shoe, she put a little pencil box with some coloured pencils and an eraser, and he was overjoyed.

'I must go and show my friends,' he cried. 'I bet none of them has got a pencil box like mine.'

Elvira forbade him to go out. It was snowing slightly, and the wind tore bitterly along the streets. He didn't even have a jacket to wear, and his only decent jersey wasn't really thick enough for winter. But he sneaked out on his own with his pencil box, and when Paquita came home in the afternoon, free until the following morning, Elvira had to confess that she didn't know where Arturito had got to.

'He'll be back soon, I expect. He's gone to show his pencil box to his friends.'

But the boy wasn't back soon, and the streets were dark before he returned. When he did eventually come through the door, the two women were horrified, for he was soaking wet, shaking all over and deathly pale.

'Don't be cross, Mama,' he begged, cringing as she dragged him in and began tearing the frozen clothes off him.

'For God's sake, where have you been? What's happened to you? You deserve a good thrashing for this. Oh my God,' she groaned, 'if this doesn't kill him . . . '

Elvira brought a towel and blankets to wrap him in.

'It's not my fault, Mama, honestly. I went down to the river with my friends—'

'Who told you to go down to the river?' broke in Paquita savagely, raising her hand as if to hit him. She dropped it again. 'What's the use? It's already done. Go on, what happened?'

'Some other boys were there, and they pinched my pencil box. They wouldn't give it back. They said I was a coward because I wouldn't fight with them, but they were bigger than me, and my friends didn't want to help. I'm not a coward, am I, Mama?'

'You're a fool and an idiot and a good-for-nothing. I wish I'd never bought you the pencil box.'

'I said, "I'm not a coward," and they said, "Well prove it then. If you want your pencil box go and get it," and they threw it in the river. Then they ran away. I tried to get it with a stick but I couldn't and it was floating away, so . . . ' He hesitated.

'Go on.'

'I took my shoes off. I didn't want to get them wet and make you cross. But then I slipped on a stone and fell in. But,' he ended forlornly, 'I got my pencil box back anyway.'

'And have probably killed yourself into the bargain.'

'No, Mama, I'm all right. Just a bit cold.'

His teeth were chattering by now, but the iciness of his body went, and it began to burn, although he continued to say that he was cold. By eight in the evening, he was delirious. At ten, the doctor came to see him and said that he had pneumonia. At four in the morning, he died, gripping his mother's hand but calling weakly for Bernardo, as he had always done when he was dreaming and afraid.

The pencil box was burning slowly on the stove. Elvira had put it there to dry out when Arturito came home, and it had stayed there, forgotten, its new paint peeled and scarred, the pencils and eraser lost.

VII

Elvira managed to get a train ticket for Burgos in March of 1940, and she left Madrid with mixed feelings of regret, relief and a fear of what lay ahead. Now that she was escaping the nightmare years, she was almost reluctant, accustomed to them and not sure if something worse might not be awaiting her. Paquita—who had, at last, accepted her employer's reiterated proposal that she take up permanent residence with him as his 'wife'—had assured her that it was her only way of finding out about Bernardo, but she wasn't sure that she wanted to find out any more.

In her heart, she could not admit to the possibility that he might be dead, though reason told her it was the only likely answer to his unbroken silence. In Madrid, she could keep on hoping and be sustained by her hope. If she had to face the fact that he no longer existed, what would she do? What could she do?

Always when this thought had come to her, she had pushed it away. She would not let herself believe it. Surely she would have had a premonition? Surely if this hope within her never failed, it was because instinctively she knew there was reason to hope? It was as if by her very hoping and refusal to accept the possibility of his death, she would keep him alive, wherever he might be. It was a childish belief that had remained with her—if you didn't want a thing to happen, you mustn't imagine it happening, for some evil spirit might be watching and bring it about just because you were overconfident. 'Don't think about it, or it might come true!'

But occasionally, when her spirits were lower than usual, and everything was black and hopeless and without future, she could not help but wonder, 'What shall I do if he's dead? How can I live without him?'

True, she had been living without him ever since he first went away, and during that time, she had forcibly frozen her heart. But it was easier to freeze her heart than her body, and the yearning for his physical closeness was sometimes harder to bear than the hunger for food. She had told herself that she would not think of being without him but concentrate on the future when she would always be with him. When she saw other parents taking a small child for a walk between them, she would put Bernardo in the man's place and herself in the woman's. 'That'll be us,' she would tell herself and, for all Paquita's disillusion, she would not allow herself to think otherwise.

She had gone from Quintera with childish hopes, still hardly a woman for all that she was bearing a child. She had gone expecting to find Bernardo waiting for her, ready to shoulder her burdens, and she had steeled herself to wait, still hoping. She had seen buildings topple, she had seen people mutilated, and she had been forced to the lowest rungs of hunger and poverty. She was no longer a child when she took the train back to Burgos that spring.

Only one thing within her was the same when she returned, the belief that Bernardo would marry her, that he had to be there waiting for her because if he were not, it would be the end of her world. It was the only thing still childish about her, this lingering illusion, and it was this that kept the light from fading altogether from the dark eyes half sunken in the haggard face.

The child sat blankly on her lap, finding nothing in the bare Castilian landscape to attract her interest. The sun glared down from the cloud-scattered sky, and Elvira found herself thinking of the times she and Bernardo had watched the clouds together and either agreed or disagreed on what their shapes represented. She shut her eyes to dispel the image, and the man who sat opposite her solicitously asked if she wanted to change places with him, thinking that the light was bothering her.

He tried to amuse Bernardina, but she stared at him coldly and rebuffed all his efforts. She was a reserved child, suspicious of strangers, wary even with those she knew. She hardly spoke throughout the whole journey, for she was not one to share words. If she saw anything interesting, she would point rather than speak and wait for someone else to make a remark. She looked very much like her father, except that the laughter which had nearly always been mirrored in his eyes was absent from hers. She'd had little to laugh about so far and was unhappy now because she'd had to say goodbye to her little sweetheart, Santiago, to whom she had transferred her affection when Arturito was no more.

The light had disappeared when the train eventually drew into Burgos, and Elvira disliked the thought of having to beg charity from Sole. But she hadn't had the courage to take a direct route to Los Pinos, which would have saved her time and money. She needed a breathing space. Sole could tell her things she needed to know before going there. So much might have changed there, as everywhere else. She couldn't be certain that her sister would receive her but surely, for one night at least, she wouldn't be turned away. There was no hope of a train to Aranda, from where she could get the bus to complete her journey until the following morning, and she hadn't the money for a night in a boarding-house. Perhaps she would at least hear some news, and she carried the travel-sleepy child in her arms, anxious to confront whatever awaited her.

She kept pushing out of her mind the nightmare dread that haunted her. Suppose Bernardo had forgotten her? Suppose he was like his brother after all and had found another woman, perhaps even married her? Men were never faithful for long. If only she could tear such thoughts out of her head! Surely her sister would know.

Sole was all exclamations of amazement and delight when Elvira arrived. The child was a sun, an angel, beautiful and bright, all in one breath, and then she hurriedly introduced two more children, born since Elvira had last seen her. Paco was less agreeable, but at least he was polite and didn't turn her out as he had done before. He looked distastefully at Bernardina, by his expression already disowning her, but offered her a handful of biscuits, something she had never seen before and refused to accept from a stranger's hand.

Later, Paco went out, the children were put to bed, and Elvira and Sole sat down together in the kitchen as had been their custom and talked. It didn't take Sole long to realise that Elvira was unaware of Bernardo's fate, that a thing of common knowledge in Quintera and Los Pinos, and of such importance to her sister, remained unknown to her, and she hadn't the courage to enlighten her.

When Elvira at last forced herself to ask the unwilling question, 'Have you seen or heard anything of Bernardo?' Sole hedged. She couldn't look her sister in the face.

'You have, haven't you?' Elvira urged her. 'Tell me what you know. Don't hide it.'

'Tell me first what you know. Did you get married after all?'

Elvira shook her head. 'I haven't seen him since . . . since he left Los Pinos. So you see, I know nothing, and I must know. That's why I've come back. Someone in the village must know something. I'm going to his parents.'

'You're not going home?'

'Never. If I can't stay in Los Pinos, I shall come away again, but I'll never go back to Quintera as long as I live.'

There was a long and awkward silence.

'What do you know of him, Sole?' asked Elvira again.

Sole got up to stoke the stove and answered with eyes averted, 'He came here, you know.'

'Here! When?'

'A while ago. More than three years it must be.'

'But what was he doing here? The last I heard of him, he was in the sierra near Madrid.'

'He'd come to look for you. But, of course, you weren't here.'

'What else? Do go on. Tell me about him.'

'He was in uniform. He was going to the front the next day, which is why he came here. He didn't have time to go home. He was upset when he found out what had happened to you. Paco was furious, and he slammed out.'

'Oh!' Elvira's heart slumped. Nothing but ill-fortune had dogged their steps. 'And you've heard nothing more since then?'

Sole hesitated. 'It was dangerous, you see. He was a communist, after all.'

Elvira was taken aback. 'Why do you say that? How could he be a communist if he was in uniform and going to the front? He wouldn't have come here if he was a Red. I don't understand. Did he tell you he was a communist?'

'No, but afterwards . . . ' Sole began to quail at her sister's rising passion and stopped. But then her fierce demand, 'Tell me!' made her go on.

'Well, a while later, someone from the military police came to see Paco. He wanted to know if Bernardo had been here. He was in some kind of trouble. Paco had to say he didn't know him. Which is true in a way,' she rushed on defensively. 'He couldn't take any risks.'

'What risks, just answering a plain question? Why didn't he tell the truth? Or you? You know how much Bernardo means to me, far more than Paco can ever mean to you. If he was in trouble, why didn't you help him?'

Sole grew red and furious. 'You don't understand. You don't know what it was like then, informers everywhere looking for a chance to do you down. So you just be careful of what you say about my husband under this roof. If he couldn't help him, it's because he was thinking of me and the children. If Bernardo had ever thought of you, he wouldn't have got you into this mess in the first place.'

'Paco was thinking of his own skin, not yours. And if Bernardo came here, it was because he was trying to find me and putting himself in danger to do so.' She turned pale. 'What happened to him?'

Sole shook her head violently. 'I don't know. I don't know any more than what I've told you. Go and ask his mother. See if she'll put up with your storms and fancies. I can tell you that your own family's had enough.'

'I knew that four years ago, Sole. You don't need to remind me. I'm going to bed.'

She went to lie down with Bernardina in the same bed where she had struggled so many times with conflicting thoughts of the child's father before finally realizing that she loved him. But she didn't sleep. There could be no rest for her until she reached Los Pinos. She knew now that it was silly to hope any more, but her silly heart persisted in hoping. There was nothing else she could do until she knew for certain. Didn't she know already? No, still she didn't know. Until she heard the words, until some actual proof existed, she would believe nothing but make her heart sustain her until it could do so no more.

She and Sole hardly spoke the next morning. They both watched Bernardina gulp down a bowlful of milk and eat up the biscuits on the plate. Elvira wasn't hungry. A dread had caught at her stomach and was churning her to pieces. She swallowed her pride and asked her sister for some money. Sole gave it to her.

With the money, Elvira hired a taxi from Aranda to take her to Los Pinos. She couldn't bear the thought of travelling on the local bus, to have to answer questions and ignore mutterings, to be the focal point of all their eyes. It was reckless when she was penniless, but she would have rather walked all the miles to Los Pinos than take the bus. The taxi driver wasn't keen to carry her. Petrol was scarce, the road was bad, and the taxi was already falling to pieces. She had to be very persuasive for him to capitulate. She told him that Bernardina was sick, and the child's pinched, sad little face convinced him.

Elvira had steeled her heart to make this journey, or else she could not have borne it. As the familiar countryside appeared on either side of her, so many memories began flooding back to her from childhood onwards. They came to the watercourse on whose bank she and Bernardo had made love in another time, crossed it and were soon on the cart track that led to Los Pinos. There Elvira stopped the driver.

'This will do. I'll walk the rest.'

She wanted to come unobtrusively upon the doctor's house, hoping that no one would recognise her. It was silly to try to hide, she knew, but until she had seen Bernardo's parents, she didn't want to be accosted by anyone. While standing to watch the taxi shake away again with a cloud of dust under its wheels, Bernardina asked one of her rare questions.

'Where are we going, Mama?'

'To see your grandparents.'

'I've got grandparents?'

'Of course. All little children have grandparents.'

'Your mama and papa?'

'No. They're the parents of Papa.'

'And who's Papa?'

'You'll see. Soon you'll see. Now be quiet and don't ask any more questions.'

They came in silence to the village. There were few people around, for it was almost two o'clock and most of them were in their houses, eating. Those that did happen to be in the street stared curiously at Elvira and the child. They saw no necessity for disguising their wonder and began slowly to follow her, avidly interested.

She heard someone whisper, 'It's the shopkeeper's daughter, Bernardo's girl.'

'The child looks just like him,' remarked another.

Elvira greeted no one, ignoring the trickle of women and children not far behind, as she continued almost breathlessly to the doctor's home, battling to contain the profound longing and fearsome dread that was threatening to engulf her.

She had never been inside this house in spite of Bernardo's determination to take her there one day and properly introduce her to his parents as his bride-to-be.

'Your mother won't like me,' she had declared. 'She'll be jealous and not let me look after you.'

'Maybe you'll be the jealous one because she loves me more than you do,' he had laughed.

'Tell me what your house is like,' she had begged. 'Then I can pretend I've been there,' and he had happily set the scene as if telling one of his stories.

'Well, first of all, you must imagine you are a princess, a bride, a very beautiful one, and your husband—the prince, a very handsome one—brings you to his ancestral home, which has fallen on hard times because his relatives were always going off to war and all he had to offer her was the place where he was born and the love he'd always known there, which was kept in a chest waiting for her to open as soon as she steps through the door.'

Then, beginning at the threshold, he had described every room as a poet might describe them, as if there were some kind of magic or mystery about the ancient beams and the way the sun fell at different times of day or in different seasons. It was a very old house with big rooms and high ceilings, heavy oak doors and underfloor heating in the living area.

She had closed her eyes as she listened, imagining herself being conducted from one room to the next, with a pause to raise the carved lid of an old chest where bedding was kept, and another to make out her reflection in a tarnished wardrobe mirror, her hand in his until he brought her to the big bed he had shared with his brother when they were children, its thick mattress stuffed with wool from the family's sheep. There he had stopped before adding, 'And every night I dream of sharing it with you.' She had hit him playfully and run off, and when he caught her, they had struggled and laughed and passionately kissed.

She stood before the door with his child at her side though she had never shared his bed, shocked by the raw vividness of the unexpected memory, freshly filled with loathing for the father who had made it impossible. If only Bernardo could be there now, to open the door with the smile that expressed everything that was good about him and which had originally drawn her to him! If only he were there, this tiredness, this emptiness, this wretchedness that had deadened her for so long would fall away. If only he were there to take her to his bed!

At last, she stepped up to the door and twice lifted and dropped the heavy knocker. The women who followed her stood back in a tight group, waiting. Dionisia opened the door. She looked surprised, she looked bewildered. Elvira and the child went in, the door was closed, and the neighbours turned to gossip among themselves, buzzing with morbid speculations.

VIII

Dionisia was unable to fill in for Elvira the missing months of her son's life. She had believed him to be with Arturo in Madrid, and in the short time they had talked together in 1937, there had been no opportunity to ask questions. Elvira, with instinctive politeness, sat stiffly on the chair she was proffered, pulling Bernardina close to her side, her dark eyes painfully expectant, fixed on the woman's heavily lined face.

Dionisia curtly said: 'He's dead. Shot. Murdered.'

She found satisfaction in seeing the girl's pain as she uttered the staccato words, wanting her to share all her own suffering. But Elvira was stronger than she had imagined, and there were no hysterics, only a long, difficult moment while she struggled for breath, and then the question, 'How? Tell me everything. I must know.'

Dionisia told her about the letter and the prison and Bernardo's pain. She was weaker than the girl, for the sobs escaped her as she remembered while Elvira remained stonily erect and silent. Dionisia told Elvira everything that afternoon, wiping tears that came to her eyes while she spoke, holding her hand to her mouth at times as if unwilling to let the words escape and, with them, her terrible memories. When she had finished, she took the little Bernardina onto her lap, held her crushingly close and rocked slowly back and forth with her as if to allay the pain that filled her.

She smothered the silent, bewildered child with a hundred kisses, smudged the pallid cheeks with her tears, and repeatedly passed a hand through the lank black hair. She was muttering, 'My little daughter,' again and again, but she was thinking, 'My son.'

Elvira watched her. She, too, would have liked to rock back and forth in her agony, but in front of this unforgiving, broken-hearted woman, she could not do so.

Instead, she said, 'I'd like to see the letter, please.'

Her voice was frigid. She didn't mean it to be so, but only in this way, by not giving way to her pain, could she endure to stay in this house without screaming. The very walls seemed to crush her; her whole being was in one long contraction of despairing agony, and she forced herself to stay erect and still on the chair she had been offered as if it were her only safe anchorage in a world that had finally collapsed about her. She had held on for so long, through four years of delayed hope and starvation, that it didn't seem possible that at the last minute, everything could disintegrate so swiftly with but a few words and leave her grasping at a chair for salvation.

Dionisia found the letter and gave it to her.

'My beloved: I write without knowing when these words will reach you. Perhaps they never will, although I have faith in that one day you will return to the village even though I can never be there with you as I have often dreamed. I persuaded one of the guards to let me have this paper, but it's only one sheet, so all I've been wanting to say to you since we were last together must remain forever unsaid, all except that I have never stopped loving you for

a single moment. It is difficult to write. So many thoughts are in my head, so many feelings are in my heart that I don't know where to start or how even to find space for them. Don't feel bitter, don't hate me or even love me too much. Just remember the things we did together and the dreams we had and keep the memory untarnished by whatever may have happened afterwards. I know I must have caused you much suffering but, believe me, I did try to come to you as soon as I could. But it was too late. You'd already gone in search of me, and in recklessly trying to get a message to you, I lost you forever. If I'm guilty of anything, it is of this, of loving you too recklessly and endangering a life which was no longer mine to risk but yours and our child's. Forgive me, my heart. Bernardo

Elvira read and re-read the letter. That closely written sheet of paper was the only thing that kept her from grief-induced insanity. Now that Bernardo was irrevocably lost to her, she clung to these last words of his, seeking in them his voice, his face, his love for her. Without them, she could not have borne the months that followed, Dionisia quietly hating her while violently loving the child, the whole village watching her, curious, commiserating or condemning.

Her main grief was that while Bernardo had courted her, she had taken his love so lightly and that only in the final weeks did she at last abandon herself to the ecstasy of that sea of love with which his captive heart overflowed. If they'd had more time together, this passion for him that now consumed her would have burnt itself down to a warm glow of shared contentment; if they'd had more time together, she could have begun to return his devotion to her, for she had been brazenly selfish with him, offering little reward for his faithfulness.

Dionisia had no pity for her pain, for the unspent passion and remorse that kept her tossing, weeping and sighing for many hours of the night. Hadn't she suffered her own agony alone, and hadn't Elvira been the cause of it? She watched with avaricious eyes as the girl went through the letter again and again, the letter that should have been written to her for her consolation, but Bernardo had forgotten her in his blind devotion to this girl from Quintera.

For a long time, Elvira could get no satisfaction from the words. She read them with violent greed, but they left her always hungering for more and brought her fresh tears. They were all she had, however, and even so tenuous a grasp upon her dead lover was better than nothing at all.

Desperation passed, to be replaced by an interior deadness that was almost worse. Even the scorching sun left her untouched and cold, unable to stir her from death to life. She left the child to its grandmother, and Dionisia, almost ignoring Elvira's existence, devoted herself to Bernardina, spoiling her beyond measure, giving her the affection that Elvira's frozen heart was incapable of supplying. This was her son's child, not Elvira's, and if she tolerated the girl in her house, it was because of the child and also because of the promise she had made to Bernardo.

Dionisia made an idol of her dead son. She was forever recounting to Bernardina tales of his childhood, reliving those years with passionate intensity, and the little girl in her turn would be full of how her father had done this and said that until at times Elvira wanted to scream at them both, 'Yes, but he's dead. Leave him in peace.'

She reached a stage where she wanted to forget him completely, unable to endure suffering for him any longer, and she put away the letter and tried to erase all her memories. The effort both drained and embittered her. Dionisia intuitively realised what she was trying to do, but misunderstanding her motive, she strongly objected.

'While you're under this roof,' she once hissed at her, 'don't ever entertain the thought of another man. You're young, I know, but if my son was capable of sacrificing his life for you, you must do the same for him. And if you do one day go off with another, don't imagine that I'll let you take the child. She's my child, and you'll have to kill me to get her away from me.'

Elvira said nothing. She would have liked to claw out the woman's hating eyes, but did they not share the same pain? She swallowed her pride, her resentment, her daily frustrations and put up with Bernardo's mother because she knew that he would have wanted her to and also because, having no means of her own, there was nothing else to be done. The chance of another, honest relationship was unlikely, and she had food and a home that would one day belong to her daughter because there was little possibility of Arturo ever returning.

Sometimes she thought of Paquita and wondered whether she should have stayed in Madrid, too, where a new life might have been possible one day. But Bernardina loved the old woman, and she grew up idolizing her grandmother's image of her dead father. She would sometimes accompany her to the graveyard, but her mother never did, except for the once when his body was returned and buried in its own soil, and everyone in Los Pinos wept or shook their heads. Elvira died afresh that day and swore she would never go near the place again.

She saw the old woman weep many tears, not just for Bernardo but for Arturo also. No letter ever came from him, but through the newspapers, with their accounts of war trials and lists of wanted men, as well as the periodic intrusive and unsympathetic visits from civil guards and police agents looking for him, they learned something of his activities. Elvira always firmly denied all knowledge of him, fearful of any consequences from the smallest reference she might let slip.

The only comment Dionisia ever made when she was told was, 'I'm glad his father never knew,' but whenever a fresh search was made of the house, with a hostile glare she would spit at the intruders, 'Isn't it enough that you've murdered his brother?' or

'Hasn't his brother paid for his crimes? Why do you want more blood?'

When Bernardina was old enough to start reading her father's books, Dionisia asked her to read out loud, and the two would sit close together, she in her son's favourite place, the child sometimes frowning as she struggled with words she didn't understand but wanting to please. Elvira couldn't bear it when one January day she opened his favourite *Don Quijote*. She wanted to take the book and throw it in the fire, burning inside with anger against them both for unwittingly intruding into a secret place, but she had long since learned to control her wild temper and instead went out into the windswept street, hugging herself against the cold until its very iciness glazed over her feelings and she could return indoors.

Afternoon by afternoon, the two of them slowly travelled the dusty highways with the knight and his squire, laughing and exclaiming together, the old childlike Dionisia her husband had loved returning in those moments. Elvira had never known her in those happier days. Had she known how, she might have tried to draw closer to them both, but neither gave any sign of wanting or needing her company, and her own emotions troubled her.

More and more often, Dionisia sat in the chair while Elvira took over the household and helped in the fields when necessary. The village women tolerated her because she kept herself to herself, but it didn't stop them gossiping about her from time to time. To her own family in Quintera, she was as if dead.

On one occasion, while Bernardina was at school, Dionisia was sitting silently with a bowl of potatoes on her lap, which she had offered to peel while Elvira went off to fetch water. When she returned, she found her with the knife in one hand, and a half-peeled potato in the other, lost in thought. The childlike incomprehension expressed in her eyes as she looked up unexpectedly touched Elvira's heart.

'What are you thinking?' she asked. 'Tell me.'

Her tone, so often brittle, was sympathetic for once, and Dionisia slowly responded, almost as if speaking to herself, wondering, trying to work things out.

'I bore three children,' she said at last, 'one good, one bad, and one who had little chance to prove herself to be one thing or the other. Why, when they were both so ill, did Adriana die and Arturo live? Wouldn't it have been better if he had died? Why did they kill my son? What harm did he ever do? I could have borne it if he'd been killed in a battle. But they murdered him.'

She sighed brokenly. 'So much suffering, all for nothing. So much praying, and there was no one to hear me. Such waste! Such waste!'

EPILOGUE

'Twenty-five years of peace! A slogan of hope, of achievement, of a country slowly progressing, dragging itself from starving isolation to a stability it has never known before.'

They are easy words for Father Montero, who has known neither hunger nor isolation, and he sounds them with fervour from his pulpit. His glance falls on the face of Bernardina Martínez, not beautiful but bright, though there is a certain wistfulness in the depths of her grey eyes. What must she be thinking, still unmarried? And her mother beside her, and the old Dionisia who does not come, all of them blighted by the long shadows of the past?

For their benefit, he suddenly adds, 'They have also been twenty-five years of children without fathers, mothers without sons, wives without husbands, brother without brother. But it's not good to dwell on the past. We must turn our eyes to the future, to a further twenty-five years of peace, so that there may be no more widows and fatherless children. Those men must not have died in vain.'

Well satisfied with his words, the priest approaches the old woman again, begging for this one forgiving gesture. But she rejects him. What are twenty-five years to her, whose agony had lengthened each day into a quarter of a century while she waited in Burgos for her son to be executed?

She takes the priest to the village war memorial, a slab of stone set in the wild surroundings of the graveyard, inscribed with the names of the five young men of Los Pinos, including Gerardo and Cándido, who fought and died for God and country at the Ebro River together, a long way from home.

'My son also fought for his country,' she says, 'but I don't see his name written here. The cross is the only memorial he has, and while I'm alive to protect it, there it stays. You must wait till I'm dead. I don't suppose you'll have to wait for long. No one will stop you then. The young people don't care, and their parents have learned to keep silent.'

And so Father Montero waits, the old woman and the crude cross uncomfortably on his conscience. Perhaps they remind him, too, of a time when God was sleeping.

ABOUT THE AUTHOR
1967

HELEN GRIFFITHS was born in London, England, in 1939, but she grew up in Yorkshire, where she says, "I developed a fascination for and love of animals of all kinds." Her last three school years were devoted to a secretarial education that has stood in her good stead, although her first job on leaving school was on a farm as a dairymaid. At the age of fifteen, she wrote her first successful book for children, *Horse in the Clouds*. Circumstances then compelled her to leave farming for the office, and she worked for an engineering firm, a department store, and a publishing house. In 1959 she married a Spaniard and has since lived a nomadic life between London, Lausanne, Madrid, and Palma. Her husband is now the manager of a hotel in Paguera, Mallorca. She is the mother of two young girls and has written six children's books.

ABOUT THE AUTHOR
2022

Although Helen Griffiths retired from writing junior fiction some 30 years ago, her books are still being read by fans and new readers in various parts of the world, perhaps because the themes are timeless and therefore don't date.

She wrote her first "story" with chalk on a school slate when she was five years old; was awarded the Matthew Arnold Memorial Prize (given only every three years to a London school child) when she was 12 and had her first book published at age 17. This was *Horse in the Clouds*, which immediately became an international success. She was commended by the prestigious Carnegie and Kate Greenaway Medal Awards for *The Wild Horse of Santander*, received the Dutch Silver Pencil Award for *Witch Fear* (voted the best children's book of the year in Holland), and was given the honorary title of Daughter of Mark Twain for her only adult novel, *The Dark Swallows*.

Most of her books have been published throughout Europe and in the United States, as well as in countries as diverse as Argentina, Iceland and Israel, while *Witch Fear* (*The Mysterious Appearance of Agnes* in the United States) still sells in Germany (*Hoxentochter*).

While busily producing a new title every year, Helen also produced three daughters who have since provided her with 13 grandchildren and, more recently, three great-grandchildren.

Born in London, brought up in West Yorkshire, and living some 20 years in Spain before finally settling in Bath, a city totally unknown to her before her arrival there, these very different places forged her writing career as well as her character. She has worked as a cowgirl, a secretary, a teacher of English as a foreign language, among other things, as well as writing books and being a wife and mother. In Spain, she was always rescuing street dogs; in Bath, she somehow managed to acquire as many as five horses (looked after by her daughters). One of her best-loved books, and which received many fan letters from young readers, was *Just a Dog*, a partially true story of how Shadow became a much-loved member of the family and who eventually was brought to Bath because of her astonishing faithfulness and intuition.

Her husband's sudden death in a car crash while the children were still young brought Helen back to England, and it was in Bath that she became a Christian, giving her a totally new life. She has written several books for a Christian publisher under her married name—Helen Santos—which have also been published internationally. But, this apart, for some 15 years, she has had a teaching/preaching ministry, and her sermons, if published, would doubtless fill a dozen books.

Helen was invited to write an autobiographical sketch which appeared in the series *Something About the Author, Vol 5*, published by Gale Research Co., Michigan, where a more detailed biography can be found. She now has the company of two little dogs, as well as regular visits from grandchildren.

She wrote "The Dark Swallows" while she was very young, basing the main plot on a true story told to her by a next-door neighbour about her mother and brothers during and after the Spanish Civil War. Before republishing many years later, she felt some revision was needed. The story is the same, but she trusts that anyone re-reading it might find it enhanced by the revisions, while new readers might be satisfied.